Coming Home

Part 3

of the

'Great War Trilogy'

by

Joan Cupples

2010

First Edition

Published and Printed by

Leiston Press
Masterlord Industrial Estate
Leiston
Suffolk IP16 4XS

Telephone: (01728) 833003
Email: glenn@leistonpress.com

ISBN 978-0-9566012-6-1

Acknowledgements

I have to thank my friends and former colleagues in West Germany for the insights they provided on life in a divided country that also happened to be on the front line between the Soviet bloc and the West, and what life was like growing up in Hitler's Reich and in the starvation years after the war. Wolfgang, Manni, Gabi, Christa, Jürgen and Heidrun all provided the younger perspective. Frau Gutjahr, Frau Domke, Frau Lenz, Frau Schäffer, Herr Schul, and Herr Wolff furnished the memories of the war years and the aftermath.

Above all to my dear colleague, the late Herr Hönig, who entered the Luftwaffe as a Sudetenland Czech in 1933 to train as a fitter and who was eventually released twelve years later only to find that as a defeated enemy, he was unwanted in his own country. Much to the detriment of his health, and regardless of his skills, he was sent down the coal mines in Germany. Through sheer tenacity and hard work buoyed by a lot of residual anger, he was able to carve out a life for himself, his wife and his disabled son. He died, too young, when his overworked and tired heart finally gave out - another casualty of war.

Over the years I have travelled extensively and met many people with interesting stories to tell – not least the Hungarian gentleman I met in Portugal whose own escape from communism provided me with the bones of the story of the heroic Serbs. Thanks to them all for sharing their lives in various campsites around Europe with a young woman with an interest in history, a gift for languages and a taste for wine!

CHAPTER ONE

A joyful day

It was nearly 8 a.m. on December 18th 1946. Outside the day was dull and windy, though not cold. Under the covers, Charlie and Giovanna lay fast asleep, such light as there was kept at bay by the thick wooden shutters. Suddenly Charlie awoke with a start, sat bolt upright and switched on the bedside light. His sleeping brain had told him that this was an important day and he needed to be getting up. Then it came to him. Today was the day that he and his beloved Giovanna were getting married. He turned to his bride-to-be and kissed her softly. 'Wake up my darling,' he said, 'we're due in church at ten.' Giovanna stretched and yawned, then turned to Charlie and put her arms around him. 'Do we have to go?' she murmured, 'can't we skip Mass just for once? They won't miss us will they?' 'They might today,' was Charlie's reply, 'it's our wedding day. They might just notice the absence of the bride and groom. I really think we should be there.'

At that, Giovanna's eyes opened wide. 'Dio Mio', she said, 'we'd better get moving. If I know my father, he'll be early and find us still in our night clothes.' 'And what night clothes would those be, Signora Maldini?' said Charlie with a grin, throwing back the covers to reveal Giovanna's naked body. 'Your perfect skin?' Giovanna squealed with mirth and grabbed the quilt as if to recover her modesty. 'Our birthday suits, then, Signor Weiss.' And running her eyes down Charlie's nude torso, she added, 'Come to think of it your suit looks as if it needs ironing!' 'Well, it's a very old suit,' Charlie replied, 'it's allowed to be a bit rumpled.' 'I'll get the creases out,' Giovanna offered, but Charlie leapt out of the bed. 'Get ye behind me, temptress,' he said, 'you'll be having your wicked way with me next,' and, laughing, he headed down the hall to the bathroom. 'Coward!' Giovanna's voice followed him. 'You're frightened of my father!' But the only reply she got was the sound of a bath being run and Charlie's light baritone singing for joy.

An hour or so later, having breakfasted simply on rich dark coffee, doughy white bread and sweet apricot jam, Charlie and Giovanna were dressed in their best and ready for the day ahead. Giovanna had chosen a fine woollen outfit in a deep crimson colour. It flattered her skin tone and her dark hair, now flecked with silver. 'Look, Charlie,' she said, using the name she reserved for when the two of them were alone, 'no more widow's weeds. No more black.' 'You look beautiful,' he told her. She cast a glance over the man she loved more than any other and conceded, 'You don't scrub up too badly yourself, for an old man.' At that precise moment, there was a ring on the doorbell, the door was opened, and the housekeeper called out 'It's Signor del Piero and Signor Weiss, Madama Giovanna.' Giovanna sighed theatrically. 'I suppose you'd better let'em in Maria,' was her response, and Giovanni and Albert entered the house. They were both dressed in smart formal attire as befits a morning wedding, dark suits, white shirts, black shoes polished to a mirror-like shine and silk ties which exactly matched the colour of Giovanna's dress. 'Clever', Charlie thought, 'Tasteful and clever.' Out of deference to the memory of Arturo Maldini, they had all agreed not to do the white dress and the top hat and tails this time, nor to have a train of bridesmaids and page boys. It seemed a bit overblown for a marriage between people of mature years and a second marriage at that. Albert handed Charlie a tie exactly the same as the one he had on. 'Here, old boy,' he said, 'get this around your neck. We'll all match then. That'll please Sophia.' Suitably clothed, and having doubly ensured that the ring was indeed in Albert's jacket pocket, the two younger men set off for the short walk to the church. Giovanni and his daughter settled themselves at the kitchen table for a final coffee and a quiet chat before the arrival of the hired car that would carry them the few hundred metres down the road to the ceremony.

Giovanni thought he had never seen his girl look so lovely or so happy and he tried to tell her so, but he was by his own admission an emotional old fool, and the words wouldn't come. 'It's all right, Papa,' Giovanna said, 'I know. I know'' and she squeezed his hand and kissed him fondly on the cheek. 'Now don't get me started or my make-up will be ruined!' 'God forbid!' replied her father and the two laughed comfortably. Just then Maria, who had been keeping watch from the living room window, ran in to tell them that the bridal car had arrived. 'It's ever so big and white, Madama Giovanna,' she said excitedly, 'and it's covered in ribbons exactly the same colour as your frock! How did they know what you'd be wearing?' 'I suspect Madama Giovanna and her mother have been in cahoots with the dressmaker, Maria,' said Giovanni, 'there's been a lot of plotting and planning going on the last few weeks. I expect the colour red to feature heavily today, probably in the flowers, possibly in the food, and certainly in the wine!' He turned to his daughter and extended his left arm. 'Shall we go my dear?' and the two of them walked up the corridor and out of the house to the car. A few of Giovanna's neighbours were standing by the gate as they walked down the steps and onto the drive. On seeing the bride, they clapped their hands and called out 'Bellissima! Bellissima!' and wished her good luck. Giovanna thanked them graciously then she and her father got into the back of the waiting car and settled themselves into the plush leather bench seat. The uniformed chauffeur released the handbrake and the car slowly began its short but significant journey to the church.

At the altar rail Charlie and Albert were standing, fidgeting nervously. Behind them the church was filling up with friends and neighbours. One whole long pew was occupied by Caterina and the six Weiss offspring, all dressed in their Sunday best. Near the front, accompanied by Alessandro, sat Sophia, glamorous as ever in dark green, and around her neck the fine lace collar that Charlie had bought for her nearly thirty years earlier. She hadn't forgotten his kindness and chose this way to let him know. Despite his nerves, he noticed, and blew her a kiss. Soon she would be his mother in law and he would officially be a part of the del Piero family he loved so much. In front of him the priest was arranging the things he needed on the altar, above him soft classical music was playing on the organ and all around there was a buzz of anticipation as people awaited the arrival of the bride. From the front door came a signal from the usher that the wedding car was pulling up outside, and the organist, in response to a nod from the priest, loudly struck up the wedding march. The congregation rose and turned as one to greet Giovanna and her father as they entered the church. They made a handsome pair and there were little gasps of admiration from all around. 'È bella,' a child's voice said. It was little Ricardo. 'Tanta Giovanna è bella.' There was a murmur of agreement. She was indeed beautiful. Smiling, and holding tight to her father's arm, she made a stately progress the length of the aisle. At the altar, Giovanni took a step back, leaving her standing next to Charlie. All the participants were in place. The long-awaited wedding could begin.

The next period of time sped by in a blur. Charlie had been determined that he would register and remember every second of this day so that he could relive it again and again, but as it was his emotions were so jumbled that he felt as if he were floating through it all like a runaway raft on a river. Suddenly he was placing the ring on Giovanna's finger and the priest was saying that he and she were man and wife. It was all over bar the signing of the register. Soon even that was done and they turned to face the congregation. Everyone in the little church was smiling and clapping and calling out 'Bravo Carlo! Brava Giovanna!' To the strains of 'Nessun Dorma' sung this time by a fine young tenor from Taranto, Charlie and his wife walked back down the aisle arm in arm and emerged into the weak winter sun. The obligatory photographs were taken, then the assembled company made their way, some on foot and some by car, to the smart nearby restaurant where the wedding feast was to be served.

Giovanni had been right about the use of red. Following Sophia's precise instructions, tasteful little arrangements of red and white flowers adorned every table and above the heads of the bride and groom's seats great garlands were draped, the colour of the flowers and foliage matching not only the flag of Italy but also Giovanna and Sophia's outfits. Charlie clocked it at once. 'She's got a good eye for style, that mother in law of mine,' he thought, and he took his seat next to the woman he loved. 'Hello Signora Weiss,' he whispered in her ear, 'what brings you here?' 'Oh, not much, I thought I'd get married just for a change,' she replied, 'what about you?' 'Me too,' Charlie said, 'having nothing better to do on a Wednesday morning in winter.' 'Seems reasonable,' Giovanna retorted, 'marry anyone nice?' 'Not really,' was Charlie's response, 'just some plain old woman in a red frock, no-one special!' At which remark, Giovanna feigned shock and pretended to slap Charlie's face, before the two of them burst into helpless giggles. On Charlie's other side, Albert, as best man, was taking his duties very seriously. 'All right all right you two!' he admonished, 'don't be falling out before you've even been married five minutes.' Charlie reassured Albert that it was a joke – 'something you don't often get the point of, brother dear' – and that all was well. 'We'll wait to fall out until we've been married for ten minutes shall we?' he asked Giovanna, and the two giggled again like naughty schoolchildren caught out in a playground prank.

The speeches were done and the toasts made with a minimum of fuss. As there were no bridesmaids to thank, Albert was able to confine himself to a short eulogy for his brother, which he managed with great aplomb and to sustained applause. Charlie's wartime exploits had made him a hero amongst those who were glad to see the back of the fascists and their thugs. His work in bringing justice to those evil men closest to Hitler was widely admired. Even now though, there was so much that could not be said that might give a clue as to Charlie's real background. Then Giovanni proposed the toast to the bride and groom, expressing his and Sophia's great happiness that their daughter had found love again, and welcoming Carlo to the family. Charlie accepted the toast on behalf of himself and his wife and declared himself the luckiest and happiest man in all of Italy.

The formalities concluded, it was time for the meal. Again Giovanni's instinct was proved right. All the food was indeed colour-co-ordinated to match the flowers, and thence Giovanna and Sophia's outfits. To start with, green and white gnocchi were served in a puddle of rich tomato sauce. Then came the seafood course of bright red lobsters and crabs just landed in the Gulf of Taranto, simply cooked and served on large white platters with a vivid green fresh herb vinaigrette redolent with basil. The main course was Sophia's own recipe for beef in deep red Barolo wine. It came with some baby peas and French beans which, at his mother's behest, Alessandro had somehow managed to grow in his glasshouse even at this time of the year and had made available to the chef. Finally every guest was handed a little glass bowl of ice cream, each one containing three flavours – strawberry for the red, vanilla for the white and pistachio for the green. It was a feast for the eye and the palate, and everyone congratulated Sophia warmly, for they well knew whose clever hand lay behind both the menu and the décor. Throughout the meal the wine had flowed, red or white depending on each guest's preference rather than on hard and fast rules about what a person may or may not drink with what. The very last offering of the meal, however, was not part of the colour scheme. Even Sophia could not make green, red or white coffee, but what she did do was have every cup topped with a layer of sweet Strega which was then set alight and brought to the tables aflame. It was a grand finale indeed, and provoked an outburst of cheering and whistling that was almost deafening.

It was hard for Charlie to imagine what could follow such a banquet, other than perhaps a nice long sleep, but Alessandro did not lack imagination and had made arrangements for the entertainment to start as soon as the last coffee cup was cleared away. For the rest of the afternoon, there was a series of splendid performances of songs and dances as well as instrumental pieces which kept the family and their guests enthralled until the last of the day's light started to fade. It was with reluctance that they dragged themselves away to their respective houses, pausing only to thank their hosts profusely and to wish them well for the imminent Festive Season. With everyone gone, the del Pieros and the Weisses slowly made their way to Giovanna's house - now officially Charlie's house as well – for a relaxing glass of champagne before the mass exodus back to the farm. It had been a wonderful day. Alone at last, Charlie and Giovanna kicked off their finery, and settled down on the thick sheepskin rug which lay in front of the log fire lit by Maria before she too had gone home. They fell asleep in each other's arms, and did not stir until the soft morning light sneaked in around the edges of the curtains and invaded Charlie's dreams.

Christmas 1946

The dust from the wedding had barely settled when it was time to celebrate Christmas. For the del Pieros, this year was particularly special. For the first time in many years, everyone would be together. Alessandro had leave from his advisory duties and Charlie's return made Giovanna complete again, more complete than she had been when married to Arturo Maldini. All of Albert's offspring would be there, maybe for the last time in the case of Giuseppe, for he was talking of moving away to Milano to further his music studies and make his own life away from the south. At the age of twenty-three, he had gone as far as he could locally. To really develop as a serious singer, he needed to be where the opera and the audiences were, and that, for him, was La Scala. He had inherited his father's rich deep vocal range and intended to put it to good use in making his living. Not for him the light repertoire that had characterised 'I Trovatori' in their day, and certainly not the burlesque favoured by his father's cousin Bert in faraway New Zealand. How the family had laughed when Charlie had told them about him! Even staunch Catholic Sophia had overcome her disapproval of his and Hone's relationship, and was able to see the humour in the contrast between his very feminine appearance and his very, very masculine voice.

Albert's other sons, Carlo and Giorgio, were happy to do the bulk of the work of the farm, under their father's supervision, so there was little that Sophia and Giovanni had to do unless they wanted to. Now in their seventies, they were enjoying their semi-retirement. They had worked hard all their lives and deserved a bit of a rest. Sophia had thrown herself whole-heartedly into the role of grandmother and these days liked nothing more than to spend time with Teresa and Gina when they were not at school. She taught them the skills every woman needs to know, even ones for whom money is not a problem. She taught them how to cook and how to sew, so that they could look after themselves and perhaps a husband some day. For Giovanni, the perfect day was one spent with his youngest grandson Ricardo, pottering in his workshop or the kitchen garden, while Caterina attended to the many tasks of catering for the voracious appetites of her brood.

Over the years, the farm had grown as neighbours had sold up and migrated to America or Australia to join family already there. The wealth made by the success of 'I Trovatori' before the onset of war had brought the concert circuit to a close, had enabled Giovanni and Sophia to buy these neighbouring farms with the result that theirs was now several times the size it had been and had become economically viable again. Big fields coupled with the judicious use of machinery meant good yields, and good yields meant healthy profits. Cannily, they still supported a diverse programme of farming. Pigs and chickens were raised as before, but in considerable numbers now. The larger fields contained the corn which provided the pigs and the hens with their food, while the smaller ones were put to good use producing a wide range of vegetable crops. The pork and chicken meat were sold through local butchers in Matera, while the eggs and the vegetables were taken by the older boys to the twice-weekly market in Taranto where they were soon snapped up by town dwellers ever on the lookout for good fresh produce. Sophia no longer cured her own hams nor made salamis. She had no need to. These days she could allow the butcher to do that chore for her, paying him in kind with a fine suckling pig or two. As a mother of six, Caterina certainly did not have the space in her life that her mother had once had for such time-consuming domestic pursuits. Her days were an endless round of cooking and cleaning, washing and ironing, just to keep her family fed and presentable.

The one agricultural task that Caterina did oversee, though, was the annual olive harvest and the pressing of the oil. The quality of olive oil was far too important to be left to mere men, for a poor product could ruin a whole year's cooking. Every October saw her have the menfolk place the huge hardy canvas cloths beneath the olive trees – and there were now several times as many as there had been when Alberto and Carlo had first helped with the task – in waiting for the first ripe fruits to drop. Once most of the olives were black, the ritual of the harvest could begin. Trees were shaken or set about with stout sticks until all the precious crop had fallen. This was a job everyone in the family loved to do, even little Ricardo, and they really made an occasion of it. It took several days now to get all the olives into barrels ready to go to the local press, but once they were all in, then scrutinised and picked over for quality under Caterina's watchful eye, they would be sent off on the back of Alberto's little truck to the press in Matera where they would be turned into the unctuous dark green extra virgin oil so essential to Italian cooking and eating. Caterina never used anything other. Second and third pressing oil would be sold to local shops and restaurants. When the filled bottles came back, rattling in their wooden crates, the whole family would gather for a celebratory supper prepared by Sophia and Caterina, and the first course was always fresh spaghetti simply tossed in the new oil and sprinkled with black pepper so that the quality of the product could be fully appreciated. It was perfection on a plate!

It was into this much-changed situation that Charlie now moved. He and Giovanna continued to live in Matera in the big house once owned by Arturo Maldini. For the first couple of months after his return Charlie had found he needed to rest a lot. The stress of the work he had been doing, and especially of his involvement in the trials at Nuremberg, had really taken their toll, and he tired easily. The emotional rollercoaster of his reunion with Giovanna and their marriage, too, for all that it was a joyous time, left him drained. It was not until Christmas time, with the wedding behind him, that he started to feel energetic and like working again. Although there was money enough for them both to live and live well, Charlie did not feel comfortable being supported by his wife. His father would have disapproved totally. He could almost hear the old man's voice saying 'you're nowt better than a pimp, lad, living off women's earnings!' He decided to have a chat with Alessandro and see if there was anything he could do to support the reconstruction of the country that had given him so much, not least his adored Giovanna.

Before that, though, there was the matter of Christmas to see to. In the few days between the wedding and Christmas Eve, there was much to do. Presents had to be bought and wrapped, and special foodstuffs located or made. Since it was possibly the last time they would all be together, Sophia was keen to push the boat out in a big way. Having more time on their hands, Charlie and Giovanna launched themselves into the task, and soon Charlie was able to forget his tiredness, and the reason for it, in a flurry of activity that was intended to bring only pleasure. Despite the shortness of time, and thanks to Sophia's skill in planning and organisation, everything that needed to be done was achieved. On December 24th, Charlie and Giovanna made their way to the farm, their car groaning under the weight of food and gifts.

There followed several days of feasting and family fun as Christmas was celebrated. The religious significance of the season was not forgotten, and the whole clan made their way to Mass on numerous occasions, most enjoyably the midnight service on Christmas Eve. Then the splendid voices of the del Pieros and the Weisses were raised in song to praise God and to mark the birth of his son. It was a while since they had sung together, and Charlie found the experience uplifting and deeply moving. Albert and Giovanni could still sing superbly, and now they were joined by Giuseppe the sound was magnificent. Giovanna saw the emotion on her husband's face and took his hand in hers, giving his fingers a gentle squeeze of support. When not sitting around the farmhouse kitchen table eating, the younger members of the family spent their time taking long walks in the countryside, and on occasion, on the beach near Taranto, where Albert, Charlie and the girls had walked so many years before. These days Sophia and Giovanni preferred to remain at home, taking short strolls hand in hand around the farm by way of exercise.

These outings were a joy for Charlie, for there was always someone different to walk with and talk to. Albert and Caterina's older sons and daughters were delightful company, being clever and perceptive as well as affectionate, but the one he liked the most, if he were pressed to admit to having a favourite, was little Ricardo. He was a charming child, now aged six and full of curiosity.

Like his mother, he was good-looking, and like his dad, physically fearless. If there was anything to climb, Ricardo was the first to try. During the olive harvest he had given Caterina nightmares by shinning up the gnarled old trees and shaking the olives out with his bare hands. At the beach, whatever the weather, he ran headlong into the waves before any adult could stop him and emerged dripping and triumphant, laughing with glee at his parents' perturbation. Charlie saw in him the makings, not of an opera singer like Giuseppe, or a farmer like the other boys, but of a sportsman of some kind, maybe a footballer or an athlete. His talent would need to be nurtured and fostered. His good fortune was that his parents could afford to do so. So much talent, as Charlie well knew from his own background, went to waste because of poverty. The mills of Lancashire, and the foundries of Sheffield, were full of lads as gifted at running as the great Jesse Owens or as good at singing as Beniamino Gigli. They just never got the chance to show what they could do and instead spent their lives in humdrum jobs working for just enough money to pay the bills. Thinking of it, Charlie realised that he and Albert had been destined for such a life, indeed it was the life his family still lived. Bizarrely, it was the first war that had broken the chain and set them free. 'Ah well,' he thought, 'they say that what doesn't kill you makes you strong.' It had come bloody close to killing them though.

A beginning and an end

With Christmas out of the way, it was time for Charlie to get down to work. Alessandro agreed to introduce him to a few of his government contacts, certain that there would always be a job of some kind for a man of his skill and experience in the developing foreign office. Since the end of the war, Italy had had to totally rebuild its relationships with both its neighbours in Europe and the rest of the world, for the impression left by Mussolini and Italy's support of Hitler was an overwhelmingly negative one. Former friends and enemies alike looked down on Italy for the way it had conducted its war, especially the capitulation. If the nation was ever to be respected again as a leading power in Europe, some hard work would need to be put in. A man who spoke four of the world's major languages, had lived on three continents and who had acted as a researcher and a witness for the Nuremberg prosecutors would be invaluable to this process. His letter of commendation, signed by the King of England himself, was a powerful reference. As a Swiss national Charlie could not be appointed to an Italian diplomatic post, but he was offered and accepted the post of political attaché, ready to be sent anywhere the minister responsible felt his language and negotiating skills, not to mention his status as a neutral, would be useful to specific pieces of work. It would mean him being away from home for potentially lengthy periods of time, and both he and Giovanna regretted this, but their love was strong and they knew he needed to be active and busy. The alternative, for there was no suitable employment there, was intellectual stagnation in Matera, and he could not face that prospect. Without a challenge, and with no material incentive to do anything in particular, he would soon succumb to inactivity and boredom. He had not turned his back on certain death in Belgium in 1917 only to experience a slow withering away in Italy thirty years later.

In late February Charlie had a letter from his sister Mary in Great Harwood. He opened it as he sat at the table having his breakfast. Looking at the postmark, he saw that it had been underway for some weeks. The letter started prosaically enough, and, as the English always do, talked first about the weather. The winter, it seemed, was terrible, the coldest and the snowiest for years. In the industrial towns icy fog mixed with the smoke from the mill chimneys had made the air very bad. Many people they knew had been ill as a result. It had proved impossible to keep warm and dry, and chest problems were epidemic. Many older people and some infants had died. The disease seemed to seek out those who were already weak. Then, almost as if it was an afterthought, she wrote, 'Our mother was taken into hospital just after Christmas and I am sorry to have to tell you that she did not come home, but died in the Blackburn Infirmary on January the 10th. The funeral was last week. Our father was also ill with the same poorly chest, but he is making a good recovery now. Well, I say a good recovery Charlie, but he is desperately sad and cries all the time. It is all I can do to get him to eat anything. I think he wants to die so that he can be with her. I am at a loss as to what to do other than be there with him if he needs anything, but I fear that it may not be enough in the end. Sorry to be the bearer of bad tidings, especially after all you have been through. All my love to you and Giovanna, your sister, Mary.' And that was it! Nothing about herself, nothing about their brother Joe and his family. Re-reading the letter, Charlie felt as if a knife had pierced his heart. He was alternately grief-stricken and furious. When he had last seen his mother, twenty one years earlier, he had been shocked at how old she seemed for a woman only just in her sixties. He blamed himself for her poor health, sure that the shock of his loss in the war had started her on a downward spiral. Now he was not so sure that he had to bear all the blame. All those years spent working in damp cotton mills and living on inferior food had done for her constitution, so that when a really bad bug came along, she had no resistance. Sophia and Giovanni were only marginally younger than his parents and yet they were as fit as fleas thanks to a decent diet and fresh air It was so bloody unfair! And now it looked like his dad might go the same way because he could not live without her. He was reminded of Wolfgang, who never got over the death of his beloved Liesel, and chose to follow her to God. How he wished he could speak to his sister, but the telephone had not yet reached the Clayton household. It was one of life's many unaffordable luxuries. Charlie folded the letter and wept. Hearing this, Giovanna came running down the stairs to see what was wrong. Charlie translated the letter for her, his voice contorted by sobs. She put her arms around him and comforted him as best she could, but he was inconsolable. He needed to speak to Albert. Albert understood what it was to lose a parent. He would know the right thing to say. So Giovanna drove Charlie out to the farm where he spent the whole morning with his dearest friend and brother going over and over his sister's letter and bewailing the bloody English class system that let some people live in poverty and work themselves into the ground so that others could be rich. Finally, he was all cried out and he and Albert went across to the farmhouse where Sophia and Giovanni were waiting for them. They embraced Charlie and whispered their condolences. They loved him as a son but they knew full well that they could never make up for his loss. Then the wives entered the room, and together they all prayed for the soul of Mary Clayton, now with God, for the health of her husband Jack and for the continuing strength of their daughter Mary. It was one of the bleakest days Charlie could remember.

CHAPTER TWO

Germany revisited

In the months and years after the end of the war, the face of Europe was changing rapidly. The division of Germany into four zones of occupation meant that the Italian government had four sets of military rulers to meet and talk with as they sought to re-establish themselves as a viable nation and to re-establish links with the former enemy. The British, the French and the Americans were relatively easy to deal with, but the Russians, or the Soviets as they had come to be known, were a different proposition altogether. Their leader Stalin was a thug and a bully, cut out of the same cloth as Mussolini, and he clearly had plans for Eastern Europe. Even as early as 1945, after the Yalta conference, and before he was astonishingly given the boot by the British electorate, Churchill had identified the Soviet Union as the next great threat to world peace. Much as they had been needed to complete the defeat of Germany, he feared that their commitment to the spread of communism or 'permanent revolution' and their territorial ambitions would bring them into conflict with the very countries that had been their allies during the war. It seemed unlikely that they would be fostering the development of a democratically-elected government for the German nation.

In this situation, Charlie's first assignment was to assist in setting up Italian diplomatic representation in the more amenable western part of the country. Through the offices of the occupying forces, he was to meet with the emerging political leaders and lay the ground for discussions between them and their Italian counterparts. His job was made easier by the fact that in June of 1946, the Italian monarchy had been abolished and replaced with a republic. Not only did this suit his own mindset, but it made Italy more credible as a modern nation. After all it was the King that had allowed Mussolini to shove his way into power back in the twenties and people had not forgotten it.

Leaving Matera, and more specifically Giovanna, for the first time since the previous October was hard, but in March of 1947 that is what he had to do. In Rome he was issued with a car, and headed for Germany. The further he went the more surprised he was at the weather conditions. His sister had said they were having a harsh winter in England but it looked as if the whole of northern Europe was too. As it was to the British Army that he had to present himself first, his journey was to take him well to the north of anywhere he had ever been in Germany, indeed as far as the once-great city state of Hamburg, and as he progressed the roads became icier and icier, the snow deeper and deeper. The driving was extremely hazardous. In late March it would be reasonable to expect there to have been some signs of coming spring, but this year there were none. Charlie could not remember when he had last been so cold.

And then there was the condition of the country to be taken into account. Germany after the defeat was in a parlous state. There was massive devastation everywhere, the legacy of years of heavy Allied bombardment. Even the riverside medieval square in the centre of Frankfurt, the Römerplatz, where Charlie had once sat in the sun and sipped a beer, and now stood in shocked silence, lay in ruins. The motive for the attack, which had come in the closing weeks of the war when Allied victory was certain, was widely believed to be bitter revenge, for the city had no particular industry to warrant such destruction. Food was scarce and fuel for heating even more so. It had been bad after the Great War, but this time it was far worse. People were cold and starving, such supplies as there were were unaffordable to most. Hotels and guesthouses were feeling the pinch, and Charlie's accommodation was basic at best. It was a desperate time and one the Allies needed to do something about if they were to prevent a re-run of the events of the 1930s. This would be Charlie's personal message to the officer in charge when he got to his destination.

On his eventual arrival in Hamburg, he made his way to British HQ and asked for an appointment to see the senior officer responsible for political liaison. The desk sergeant was clearly impressed by Charlie's papers, not least by the letter signed by the King. 'I am sure General Ross will be happy to see you Mr Weiss,' he said, 'I'll give him a call right away.' Charlie took a seat and waited. Military barracks everywhere look much the same and there was nothing to catch his eye or distract him, just grey walls everywhere. It was just crossing his mind that there was a fortune to be made in grey paint manufacture, when a door opened, the desk sergeant leapt noisily to his feet, saluted extravagantly, saying 'General Ross, Sir!' and the officer entered the room. Good grief! it was young Captain Ross who had given Charlie leave to go to Italy in the summer of 1945, that visit when he had at last been able to tell and show Giovanna how he felt for her. Here he was, less than two years later, a General. He had done well for himself since the war. He recognised Charlie at once, and stepped forward, his hand outstretched, a broad smile on his face. 'Well well!' he said, 'Carlo Weiss as I live and breathe! It's good to see you again. What brings you here?' Charlie's expression told the General that his business was not something to discuss in front of the sergeant, and he was at once ushered into Ross's private office and offered a comfortable chair in front of a roaring log fire. For the first time in days Charlie started to thaw out, and soon he was able to remove his overcoat. Coffee was sent for, and when it came, the General opened the top drawer of his desk and pulled out a small flat bottle of rum. 'Stroh-Inländer,' he said, 'comes from Austria. 80% alcohol. Hard to come by even for a General. Warms the cockles most effectively. Fancy a slug, Weiss?' Weiss intimated that he most certainly did, and a little tot was poured into a schnapps glass and handed to him. The General gave himself a mouthful too, and the two men raised their glasses. 'Prosit!' said Charlie. 'Chin chin,' said Ross and the two men took a sip of the fiery spirit. Charlie had never drunk anything so strong in his life. It was quite literally breathtaking. The General was the first to recover. 'Now, down to business,' he said, 'how can I be of service?'

Over the next hour or so, Charlie explained his mission, and the General gave him pointers as to whom he should be contacting and how, even going so far as to write letters of introduction to the emerging political leaders in the British-occupied zone. Charlie felt as he had when he had encountered Alessandro in Taranto. Bullseye! General Ross could not have been more helpful, and Charlie realised that he was now reaping what he had sown those few years ago. His work had vastly enhanced the Allies' ability to successfully prosecute the Nazis and Ross was grateful. Maybe his rapid promotion owed something to the effectiveness of Charlie's research. Whatever the reason for his support, the General was an important man and what he said held much sway over the local bigwigs. His intervention would give Charlie a lot of credibility, save him a lot of time, and pave the way for his political paymasters in Italy to make useful contacts. He could not expect to have it so easy in the other three zones, unless he got terribly lucky.

Strangely enough, lucky was exactly what he did get, at least to begin with. Back in Frankfurt to meet with General Ross's opposite number in the American forces, he ran into the Major who had led the first soldiers across the Lüdendorff Bridge at Remagen. He remembered Charlie's crucial role in infiltrating the German troops in the village bar, and catching them off guard and blabbermouthed. The intelligence Charlie had acquired whilst pretending to be a drunk old German had been essential to the success of the American advance into Germany. The fact that this man Weiss was a Swiss national who had risked being shot as a spy for the Allies was something not easily forgotten. The Major was thrilled to see him again and to be able to thank him properly for his assistance. He was also able to introduce and commend him to General Green who carried the responsibility for making and maintaining links between the forces and local politicians. Even a hard-nosed American General could be influenced by a story of courage and a letter signed by a King, and soon Charlie was meeting the men who would be forming the first government of post-war Germany. The man who most impressed him was the former Mayor of Cologne, Konrad Adenauer. The two were introduced at a meeting held beside the Rhein in the shadow of the mighty cathedral, mercifully undamaged despite the years of war. Although he was already seventy years old, in Adenauer Charlie could see someone who would be able to move Germany forward towards a brighter future. He was untainted by any links with the Nazis, indeed it was Hitler himself who had had him removed from his mayoral post in 1933 because of his opposition to the party. In the immediate postwar climate, this fact was as useful to Adenauer as Charlie's letter from the King was for him. The two men got on well, and Charlie was able to reassure the German of Italy's positive view of its role as a contributor to a peaceful Europe. In so doing he smoothed the path for eventual negotiations between diplomats of the two states.

Then it was off to the French-occupied zone. Charlie hadn't been in the Black Forest for years, and was thrilled to find it still as beautiful as he remembered it. The war had made relatively little impact here. The tall dark trees were as magnificent, the half-timbered villages still as picture-postcard as ever, and in a country Gasthaus, Charlie found the juicy wild pork schnitzels to be just as huge as he recalled them to be. For the first time since leaving the generosity of the Americans in Frankfurt, he felt full after a meal. He wondered if the French had chosen to take on the stewardship of this zone for aesthetic and culinary reasons rather than military ones. The poor old British had the icy north, the Americans the boring middle and stodgy conservative Bavaria, and the French the beautiful south and west. Typical! He made his way to the ancient and exquisite university city of Tübingen where he hoped to find the French officer who could put him in touch with the local equivalent of the men he had met in the other two zones. This time his task was much more difficult. He had reckoned without the degree of loathing that the French felt for the Germans after more than four years of occupation. They were not anxious to give status or credibility of any kind to anyone German, even ones who had opposed Hitler. As far as these French soldiers were concerned, all Germans were Nazis and all were responsible for what had happened to their country, even if, as they said so often they 'were only obeying orders'. In a way he could hardly blame them. France had suffered terribly, he had seen it for himself in the months after D-Day, and the tales which had emerged later of rape, forced labour, summary executions and reprisal killings were horrific. Perhaps the French would never be able to forgive what had happened. They would certainly never forget.

Occupation leaves deep scars, ones which an Englishman or even a Swiss could not truly understand. Charlie had talked to Giovanna and the others about what life in Italy was like when the Germans were there, but it had been nothing like the French experience of being forcibly taken over and oppressed by an enemy. By the time the Germans became the enemy, they were on the point of being kicked out by the Allies anyway. The French officers he met were not in the mood to be facilitating political discussions between the despised Germans and their one-time cowardly handmaidens, the Italians, so in the end Charlie left the French zone empty-handed and returned gratefully to the warmer climes of Rome. His first assignment, whilst scarcely an unmitigated triumph, had been successful enough and he hoped he had done something to foster a civilised relationship in the future between his adopted homeland and at least some of the people who would be responsible for the rehabilitation of Germany. His report filed, he spent no longer in Rome than necessary. He did not even pause to take Mass at St Peters, but made his way back to Matera and Giovanna as quickly as he could. He had been away from her for a mere six weeks but it felt like months.

News from the north

Spring had already started when he got back to the south, and on the farm things were buzzing. There was more work than Albert and the two older boys could handle now that Giuseppe had left for Milano, so Charlie took to going there most days, with Giovanna, to lend a hand. It was better than sitting around in Matera waiting for the telephone to ring with another assignment, and it enabled him to spend time with Ricardo. The lad showed an aptitude for languages and was keen to learn English, so as well as helping with the planting of the crops and the inevitable weeding, Charlie set aside an hour each day for the tuition of his young charge. The boy had a good ear and learned quickly and soon he was forming basic sentences.

One day in May, a letter with a Milano postmark came to the farm, clearly some news from Giuseppe. Bizarrely it was addressed to Sr. Carlo Weiss, so the others had to wait until Charlie and Giovanna turned up before they could open it. They were fairly champing at the bit when Giovanna's car at last pulled up outside the house. Caterina could not contain her impatience, and rushed out to greet her brother in law, the unopened envelope in her hand. 'What does it say, what does it say?' she cried, shoving the letter into Charlie's hand. 'Just a moment, woman,' Charlie replied, 'give me chance to draw breath!' So saying, he took the letter from her, carefully folded it, put it in his jacket pocket, took Caterina in his arms and kissed her on each cheek. 'Good morning Caterina,' he said, 'how are you today?' 'Open it! open it!,' was her reply, 'open it now! tell me what it says at once!!' Charlie laughed softly, and hugged her again. 'I will, I will, as soon as we're inside where everyone can hear.' He and Giovanna followed Caterina into the kitchen where Sophia, Giovanni and Alberto were sitting expectantly. Charlie first greeted everyone, slowly and deliberately, kisses for Sophia, handshakes for the men, then he took a seat at the table and asked nonchalantly if there was any coffee. By this time the steam was fairly coming out of Caterina's ears, but she crossed the room to the range, and poured a small espresso for Charlie. 'Now open it!' she commanded, but Charlie first had to put some sugar in his coffee then give it a good, slow, stir before taking a sip. 'Delicioso,' he said, 'Grazie Caterina.' And he took another tiny sip. Albert could take no more of it. In English, for emphasis as much as for the protection of the ladies, he blurted out, 'Charlie Clayton you are an infuriating bugger. Now open that bloody letter and tell us what's in it right now or…' 'Or what?' Charlie's tone was sanguine, though he knew he was really pushing it by now. 'Or I'll bloody do it for you, you daft ha'porth!' At that Charlie held up his hands. 'Guilty as charged, Albert,' he said, 'I am indeed a daft ha'porth,' and took the letter from his pocket. He picked up a knife from the table and slit open the fine white envelope. Inside was just one sheet of notepaper, covered in Giuseppe's tidy handwriting.

Charlie read aloud. 'Dear Uncle Carlo, I have had the most amazing stroke of luck, and I have you to thank for it. I don't know if you remember passing through Milano on your way to Nuremberg a couple of years ago. You had a car which you gave away to a busker singing outside La Scala. You told him he had a beautiful voice and might sing inside one day. Well, that busker is now the principal tenor here. His name is Marco Bocelli, you may have heard of him. He says your kind remarks gave him the courage to audition for the chorus of Aida. He got the job and from there he was soon getting bigger and bigger solo roles. Now he is terribly famous and the toast of Milano, not to mention Paris, London and New York. I met him at a party given by a rich Milanese woman I have got to know, and when he heard my surname he asked if I was related to a Swiss man called Carlo Weiss who worked for the British Army at the end of the war. When I said that it was my uncle, he fairly fell on my neck and begged me to write and tell you how grateful he was and is for what you did that day. He says he was on the point of giving up and going back to his village in Tuscany when you met him. He says he hopes you don't mind that he sold the car to pay his rent and buy food which enabled him to stay in Milano long enough to go for the audition. He describes you as his life saver, and has offered me, as your nephew, all the help and support I need to do well in my career. As you can imagine, he has a lot of influence in the world of opera. I have already been taken on in the chorus for a brand new production of Aida, and who knows? one day I might be treading the boards as a lead, the same as Marco. He sends you his very best wishes and his everlasting thanks. Please send my love to my mother and father, and my grandparents, oh, and to you and aunt Giovanna of course. Your nephew, Giuseppe. p.s. did I remember to say thank you to you? If I did, thanks again. G.'

When Charlie finished reading there was a momentary silence in the room, then Albert said 'You never told us about that. That was a good thing you did back then, and now it's come back to benefit our boy. Why didn't you tell us?' 'Didn't seem important, though I am glad to have been of use. I seem to have spent a lot of my life being helped rather than helping,' Charlie said, his tone matter-of-fact. 'What?' was Albert's response. 'Is that how you see it? Well I'm darned sure I wouldn't be here if it wasn't for you.' Charlie was touched by Albert's words, but explained that he was thinking more of all the people who had given him a helping hand on his travels, most of them members of Albert's own family, like Dick and his sons. 'I always felt I took more than I gave to those people,' he told Albert, 'so I'm glad to have done something for one of you, even if it was by accident.'

'Read it again, Carlo,' Caterina begged, 'especially the last bit. I want to hear it again.' Charlie obliged and read the whole letter over, pausing from time to time when discussion broke out around the table. Sophia knew of Marco Bocelli, having heard him sing on the radio, and confirmed that he was indeed a most gifted tenor. His rendition of 'Nessun Dorma' was said to be the best ever. 'Yes, better even than yours, my darling,' she said to her husband, 'hard as that may be to believe!' Charlie suspected he had heard the best ever performance of that aria in Canada but said nothing. For her part, Giovanna was most curious about the 'rich Milanese woman' that Giuseppe referred to so casually. Who could she be? Was she old or young? Was she beautiful? Even more intriguingly, what was her relationship with Giuseppe? Patroness? Something more? Giovanna was about to engage is some slightly lurid speculation when she caught Charlie's eye and though better of it. Across the table Caterina was looking daggers at her. 'I tell you what,' said Charlie, skilfully defusing the tension between the two sisters, 'when it comes on we'll all go and see a performance. I'll write and ask Giuseppe to get us tickets. Signor Bocelli is bound to oblige. Then we'll see for ourselves.'

Signor Bocelli was indeed happy to oblige and got them six front row seats for the night of the tenth of June. By a happy coincidence that day was Albert's fiftieth birthday so there was plenty to celebrate. A flurry of shopping ensued, for the women did not want to look like country bumpkins amongst the stylish Milanese, and the men could not be allowed to show them up by being less than up to the minute in their attire. Clothes for the daytime and full evening dress for the opera would be required. Giovanna got on the telephone to Giuseppe to make sure that there was an after-show table at the best restaurant for the big night, and that three comfortable rooms were reserved in one of Milano's smartest hotels. 'When the del Pieros do things,' she told Charlie, 'they do them properly!' Charlie found the cost staggering, but shrugged his shoulders and went along with it all. Maybe this would be the last time that all six of them would have such an experience together.

A glorious journey

A few days before the 10th, Albert's second son Carlo drove his parents, his grandparents and his aunt and uncle to the railway station in Taranto and saw them all off on the train to Milano. The plan was to take some time to look at the country as well as to go to the opera at La Scala. It was the first time Albert and Caterina had ever left their children to look after themselves, and, despite her excitement at the prospect of seeing Giuseppe on the stage, Caterina was a little nervous as to how they would cope. It was Sophia who reassured her that her sons and daughters would be fine. 'The boys can do anything that needs doing on the farm, and the girls know how to cook so they won't go hungry, and if they have a problem they can always telephone Alessandro in Taranto,' she said. 'But what about little Ricardo? He's only a baby.' Caterina was still concerned. Albert stepped in. 'If I know my kids at all, he'll be spoilt rotten,' he said, 'we won't be able to do a thing with him when we get back! Now stop worrying and let's enjoy our holiday. We certainly deserve it.'

For the rest of the trip, Caterina put her worries behind her and did as her husband suggested. Having never travelled anywhere except locally before, she was fascinated by what she saw from the window and begged Charlie for a running commentary on what they were passing through. For Sophia too it was all new and she was as excited as her daughter to see places they had only ever heard the others talk about when they came back from 'I Trovatori' tours. The hot dry farmland of the south gave way to mountains crossed by magnificent bridges and cut through by tunnels, then these in turn yielded to the beautiful Amalfi coast which elicited squeaks of pleasure from the women. The train line ran alongside the spectacular Bay of Naples, its many islands like green jewels in the scintillating blue sea. In the distance to their right, Vesuvius rose up stark and forbidding. There was no time to visit Pompeii and in any case, the women declared they could live without ever seeing such a sad scene. With lunch out of the way, and a very delicious one at that, the train pulled into the massive station at Naples. There was a furry of activity as passengers got off and on. With no time to disembark before the train set off again, Charlie explained to the others how it had been when he and Albert first arrived in the city the day after the end of the Great War. He described the euphoria people had felt and the celebrations that had taken place that night. Little did the Neapolitans know that they would be doing it all again in a few years' time.

From Naples the train followed the coastal plain north, arriving in the evening in Rome. This was as far as the family wanted to travel in one go. They had decided to spend the night in the capital city and take in some of the famous sites there the next day. For Charlie this was at last the chance he had been waiting for since 1918 – nearly thirty years. One way or another, events, politics, the pressure of time or just the call of love had got in the way of him doing this place justice. Deposited at their hotel by taxi, the six took no time at all to freshen up and set off on foot in search of a restaurant. They walked about looking at menus in doorways, and peering in through steamy windows to find a convivial place, and everywhere they looked was some beauty spot or famous landmark. At the Trevi Fountain, Albert did what he had done all those years before, he threw in a coin and made a wish. Not for an end to war this time, but for a lasting peace so that his sons should never have to go through what he and Charlie, Giovanni and Alessandro and millions of men since had done. 'Pace in Italia' he whispered as the coin joined the hundreds of others on the tiled floor of the fountain.

That night Rome did them proud. At the top of the Spanish Steps they found a splendid ristorante serving everything that is good in Italian cuisine. No rough peasant dishes here – this was refined urban cooking at its best. The salmon ravioli were served in a light lemony sauce sprinkled with fresh herbs, the pasta paper thin yet slightly firm to the bite. After that came delicious spring lamb, slowly-cooked so that it fell off the bone, accompanied by little spears of tender young asparagus and sweet early peas. A fine selection of desserts and cheeses rounded off the meal. Chilled white wines helped the first two courses down – the Frascati and the Orvieto were especially appreciated – but it was a heavy honey-tasting Montepulciano that perfectly complimented the richness of the desserts and a deep red port the cheeses. Used as they all were to eating well, nevertheless each of them found the experience exceptionally pleasurable and via their extremely obliging waiter, conveyed their highest admiration to the chef. Touched, he emerged from the kitchen to acknowledge the applause and thanks, bowing and removing his toque as he did so. 'Bravo!' called Sophia, and they all took up the cry. The man was a maestro in the kitchen and they would not be forgetting his show-stopping performance for a long time to come.

The next day they spent the morning wandering about the ancient sites of the eternal city. Luckily they are all fairly close together, for, fit as they were, both Sophia and Giovanni found the pavements hard and unforgiving on their ageing knees. They marvelled at the Coliseum and were impressed by its sheer scale and size, not that they much liked what had gone on there of course. On the other hand, they found the Forum a bit disappointing despite its role in history. It wasn't as grand as they had imagined. Saving the best 'till last, it was late morning before Charlie led them to the Vatican and onto St Peters Square. The place was positively buzzing with visitors, and Charlie could pick out any number of languages being spoken. There were priests and nuns from all over the world, rubbing shoulders with the local faithful. Mass had just ended and people stood about in small groups chatting in the late morning sun. Albert reminded Charlie, as if he needed reminding, of the first time they had been there. 'In those days we had to make ourselves look old,' he said, 'now it just comes naturally!' Laughing, they all made their way to the Sistine Chapel, which had impressed even Albert all those years ago, despite the rampant trappings of Popery of which he had then so strongly disapproved. To be fair, he wasn't entirely sure that he approved of all the ornamentation now, he just noticed it less these days. On entering the chapel, their eyes drawn upwards, the group fell silent. It was astoundingly beautiful. There was so much to look at you could hardly take it in. Awestruck, they all crossed themselves with holy water and genuflected before taking a seat in a vacant pew near the back of the church. From a position of comfort and unhindered by the presence of worshippers, they were able to survey Michaelangelo's masterpiece. Prosaic Albert was the first to comment. 'Must've taken a while to do,' he said, voicing the very thought he had had on first seeing the place in 1918. 'Ages,' Giovanna said, 'a lot of time and a lot of painters lying on their backs high up on rickety medieval scaffolding. It must have been exhausting.' 'Worth the effort though,' was Albert's comment. 'Aha, so you approve now eh, chapel boy? Or have you become an art critic all of a sudden?' Charlie said with a grin. But Albert was not to be drawn. The intervening years had given him confidence and composure. He was no longer so easy to lure into one of Charlie's pranks. 'Neither,' he replied, 'but I know something beautiful when I see it, and I'm looking at it right now.' 'Well said, Alberto,' Caterina chimed in in support of her husband. 'Oh look!,' Albert went on, 'there's something else beautiful here,' and he took his wife's hand and gave it a little kiss. Charlie felt suitably chastised and said so. In English he whispered to Albert 'sorry mate, taking the mickey is a bad habit of mine. I won't do it again.' This time Albert turned the tables. 'There you go,' he said, 'typical Catholic. Think you can just say sorry and all will be forgiven.' Charlie was quite shocked, until he caught the glint in Albert's eye. He could hardly contain his mirth. 'Damn!' said Charlie. 'Touché!' said Albert and the two laughed companionably. 'Ssssh!' said Sophia, and her sons in law obediently stopped talking and admired the ceiling. An hour or so later they boarded the train that would take them all the way to Milano. Almost as soon as the train left the station, the serving of lunch was announced, and they made their way to the restaurant car. All that walking around Rome had worked up an appetite and a nice leisurely meal was just the ticket.

It was late in the evening before they finally arrived at their destination. The journey through Tuscany to Firenze had particularly pleased Sophia, for she was at last able to see the landscape where her precious son had been found all those years earlier. The rolling gentle greenness of the countryside had impressed her too, and she could see how it was that Alessandro had so liked to garden there. Soon they were passing through the outskirts of Milano and heading into the big city. Giuseppe was waiting to greet them at the station and was able to show off his knowledge of local customs by expertly hailing two taxis to take them to their hotel. Despite the lateness of the hour it was still possible to use the bar and to get a light snack. As Giuseppe pointed out, this was Milano and not Matera. People did things differently here, as they would assuredly see in the morning.

As promised, in the morning they did see just how different this place was from the part of Italy they were used to. It was still exactly as Charlie had noticed on his first visit – wealthy, sophisticated and leisured. Glamorous women sat at café tables in the sun sipping an espresso, be-ribboned lapdogs on their knees, a cigarette in a long holder held between their impeccably manicured fingers. Immaculately-dressed young men, their hair slicked back with pomade, danced attendance on these beauties, leaping up to light their cigarettes or to order more coffee. No-one seemed to be rushing to get to work or indeed rushing to get anywhere. They were content just to sit and be seen as they whiled away their days. Sophia, Giovanna and Caterina were especially curious about these people. 'What do they live on?' Sophia asked her grandson. 'Their family inheritance,' he replied, 'and gifts from rich lovers. They don't work, well not in any way that you understand it grandmother.' Sophia was taken aback. 'Are you telling me these women are' and here she lowered her voice to a shocked whisper, 'whores? They look so respectable.' 'This isn't Naples,' was Giuseppe's reply. 'These ones aren't back at the bordello cooking up a pot of penne alla puttanesca. There's a lot of money around here despite the war. A lot of posh people got very rich thanks to Mussolini, and they didn't all lose it when he was kicked out. These women are reaping the benefit of their fathers' hard work as well as taking advantage of their class and their attractiveness to men. You won't find them in the glass factories or selling haute couture in the arcades. Their job is to make rich old men look good at the opera or the racetrack. I see them night after night, being squeezed and pawed and pretending to like it. It's only in the daytime when their sugar daddies are at the bank or the factory that they can spend time as they want, and that is why they surround themselves with these pretty young gigolos and sip coffee or go shopping. They can afford to. As long as they conduct themselves discreetly in public, no-one minds.'

'Well, well, my boy,' Caterina interjected, 'you've become very knowledgeable all of a sudden. Not from personal experience I hope?' 'Well I haven't become a gigolo, if that's what you mean mother,' her son replied, his tone sanguine, 'but I have met one or two of these girls, one in particular who has become a friend. A friend, I said, Giovanna,' he reiterated forcibly in response to his aunt's raised eyebrow. 'She's the one who introduced me to Marco Bocelli. Maybe you'd like to meet her while you're here.' Sophia's face was a picture of disapproval. Her grandson making friends with a, well, with a posh puttanesca! 'I don't think so,' she said, overriding anything her daughters might have said, 'there won't be time.' And that was that. Sophia had spoken! Charlie and Albert exchanged amused glances. Sophia could be so Catholic at times. They'd have to find a way around her. For themselves, the men most certainly wanted to meet Giuseppe's friend and hear her story. It was potentially more interesting even than the opera. Charlie was pretty sure that Giovanna and probably Caterina would be keen as well. A bit of parent-deceiving was called for!

The day was spent taking an unhurried look at the sights of Milano. The women gasped at the array of goods on sale in the couturiers in the glass-covered arcades, and could not resist making the odd purchase or two. Well, you couldn't find stuff like this in Matera or even Taranto, could you? The men wondered at the magnificence of the architecture, especially the cathedral and the opera house and were astounded by the traffic and the hectic way people drove about. Lunch filled a pleasant hour or two, then came a trip to a gallery, and soon it was time to be heading back to the hotel to prepare for the opera. At this point Giuseppe had to leave them for it took a good while to get into his heavy costume and thick greasepaint. He gave Charlie their tickets and six passes so that they could come backstage afterwards, where he promised to introduce them to their host, Signor Bocelli. With their cries of 'break a leg!' ringing in his ears, he leapt into a taxi and sped away. The others made their way to their rooms to bathe and dress themselves in their finest array. This was to be a night to remember.

And so it turned out to be. The seats were the very best in the house – front row and centre. The orchestra was superb under the expert baton of none other than Maestro Bartoli, whom Charlie had seen conducting this very opera years before in Vancouver with the Opera Veronese, now apparently plying his trade with the prestigious Milano Opera. The huge chorus was packed with singers all of whom were good enough to play lead parts, and the leads, well! they were astounding. The mezzo's voice in her rendition of 'Ritornà Vincitor' was electrifying, the best Charlie had ever heard, but the tenor brought the house down. Marco Bocelli could certainly sing and his 'Celeste Aida' provoked an outburst of applause that forced him to perform the aria again. Charlie looked about him at his family. They were transfixed. None of them, not even Giovanna, had ever witnessed a spectacle like this. The size and scale of the production, the quality of the performances, the sheer volume of the music, all made for an overwhelming impact. The women were weeping openly, the men were pretending not to but every now and then Charlie saw Albert and Giovanni surreptitiously dab at their eyes with a handkerchief. It was sensational! In one of the intervals between acts, Albert leaned over to Charlie and said 'well, I can see why you like this opera business so much, matey. It's bloomin' marvellous isn't it? That's my boy up there! I'm so proud of him I could burst.' 'Me too,' said Charlie, 'he's part of something really special.'

At last the fourth act drew to a close and the audience as one rose to their feet to applaud the company. The men of the chorus stepped forward to take their bow to much acclaim, not least a shrill ear-piercing whistle from the man sitting two seats away from Charlie. Yes, Albert, forgetting he was at La Scala and not some country fair or village hall, was signalling his approval in the time-honoured rural manner. If he had noticed it, he would have been felled by the look he got from Sophia, but he was too busy letting his precious boy know how he felt. The ladies of the chorus took their bow, then came the principals. When Bocelli as Ramades and the soprano playing Aida stepped up, the audience clapped and stamped their feet in a frenzy of appreciation. 'Bis! Bis!' they cried 'More! More!' 'You have to hand it to the Eyeties,' Charlie thought, 'they love their opera and certainly know how to show it.' These Milanese made the Canadians seem tame, dour even. The company duly obliged with a series of encores - solos, ensemble pieces, all the arias – which protracted the show until nearly midnight. Even then the audience would have kept them on the stage but finally Maestro Bartoli begged for them to be let go. Eventually the weary performers left the stage and the clapping subsided. The house lights came up and people started readying themselves to depart. Sophia declared that she was too tired to stay any longer and that she wished to return to the hotel. It was agreed that she and Giovanni would take a taxi at once, and leave it to the younger ones to go backstage and congratulate Giuseppe. Charlie saw

the older couple into their transport, then rejoined his wife and her sister waiting impatiently by the stage door. Albert, it seemed could not contain himself but had gone in ahead of them, so keen was he to see his son and tell him how proud he was.

They found him holding forth in the men's dressing room, surrounded by chorus members in various states of undress and makeup removal as he heaped praise upon them for what they had just done. Giuseppe was looking only slightly embarrassed, being actually rather thrilled that his dad had enjoyed the show so much. He was glad though to see his mother walk in and at once went over and embraced her. Then he turned and introduced Caterina, Giovanna and his uncle Carlo to his colleagues. At that point there was a sharp rat tat tat! on the door and a voice called out 'Are you decent boys? Cover up, we're coming in!' with which Marco Bocelli walked into the room, followed by a strikingly beautiful young woman in a splendid purple evening dress. The gentlemen of the chorus rose to their feet and applauded the tenor. 'Bravo Maestro!' they cried, 'Bravo!' 'Grazie, ragazzi!,' Bocelli replied, 'Grazie!' His eyes scanned the room and alighted on Charlie. He recognised his former benefactor at once. 'Signor Weiss,' he said, 'I have been longing to meet you again so that I could thank you personally for your kindness,' and he shook Charlie by the hand most warmly. He turned back to the chorus members and explained. 'Boys,' he said, 'this gentleman saved my career and possibly my life in a simple act of generosity a few years ago. I have him to thank for the fact that I am still in Milano and still singing. I could have been growing grapes in Tuscany by now if it were not for this man.'

Charlie was somewhat embarrassed to be so singled out for praise and, blushing, muttered 'Well, the Chianti's loss is La Scala's gain,' which drew laughter and applause from the assembled company. 'You are too modest, Signor Weiss,' Bocelli went on, 'It is an honour to meet you and I would like to invite you to join me for a little late supper to show my appreciation. But first allow me to introduce my dear friend, who will be joining us.' He turned to the woman who had come in with him, and said, 'This is Giuseppe's uncle, Signor Weiss, the one I told you about, and the other gentleman is most assuredly Giuseppe's father. The family likeness is striking. The lovely ladies are, I presume, his mother and his aunt?' Giuseppe stepped in and made the introductions. He clearly knew the young woman well, for he embraced her and kissed her on both cheeks before presenting his family. Her name, it seemed, was the Contessa Francesca da Mosto. On hearing this, Caterina and Giovanna exchanged knowing looks. This must be the rich woman Giuseppe had spoken of in his letter! She didn't look as old as they had imagined she would be. This girl was scarcely a year or two older than Giuseppe himself. Yet she clearly had influence. Maybe having money, a title, and stunning looks was enough. Then Giovanna remembered what it was that Giuseppe had said about these girls. They lived off wealthy old men and were really just high class tarts. They may seem to have everything but they still had to do what women had been doing for money for centuries. How shocking! How exciting! Just as well their mother wasn't still here! Hands were shaken, heads bowed and curtseys made, and soon they were formally known to one another. Now they could go and dine.

It was some hours later that the Weiss couples made their way back to their hotel. The after-show supper had turned into a long drawn-out affair, with animated conversation flowing back and forth like the wine, and a lot of laughter. Marco Bocelli had turned out to be absolutely charming, and his lady friend the Contessa equally so. Sophisticated as they were, they managed not to make Caterina and Albert feel like simple country folk, rather they expressed their admiration for the way they had enabled and encouraged Giuseppe to take his chances in the competitive world of opera. Marco Bocelli, especially, knew how hard it could be to get a foot in the door, no matter how great your talent. This was why he had so appreciated Carlo's generosity, and why he wanted to help Giuseppe as much as he could. His influence was as great and as widespread as his fame and he could do a lot to make a young singer's life a lot easier. He was already grooming Giuseppe for minor roles in the coming season. This information caused a great deal of excitement. Albert felt he would burst with pride. A Donkin was going to make it as a serious singer after all! No-one would know he was a Donkin, to the world he would be a Weiss, but Albert would. He resolved to write to his uncle Dick and tell him the news. He did not wish to belittle his cousin Bert's glittering career in faraway New Zealand, but he felt sure that Dick would be thrilled to have a relative treading the boards at La Scala. And all of it due to Charlie's moment of generosity. At that moment Albert realised again just how much he loved Charlie and how much he owed him.

Sleep came hard after such an eventful and exciting day, but it came at last and it was a late breakfast for the younger couples the next morning. Sophia and Giovanni were already fed and watered and raring to get going by the time the others emerged, blinking in the bright light of the summer morning. It didn't take long to despatch a swift espresso and some bread and jam though and by ten they were on their way to meet Giuseppe, Marco and the Contessa for the guided tour of La Scala. Charlie well remembered his first visit, and told the tale of how he had crept in, lured by the sound of the soprano practising 'Un Bel Di'. He had been on his way north to Switzerland and poor sad Wolfgang, and the music had beckoned to him. It still did. Looking around La Scala's magnificent auditorium was a wonderful experience for them all, and, feeling for all the world like naughty schoolchildren, they could not resist the urge to go to the piano and take to the stage as 'I Trovatori' once again, just as Charlie had fantasised years earlier. This time, however, Giovanni took a back seat. His voice was not what it was, and besides, who would dare sing a tenor part when Marco Bocelli was at hand? Charlie could still play the old tunes, and Albert could certainly belt out a song. Giovanna's mezzo too was holding up well, so the three of them entertained their hosts with a selection from their repertoire, much to the delight of all present. 'Bravo! bravo!' they cried. 'We weren't bad were we?' said Albert cheekily, 'not bad at all!' For the final number, the rousing Toreador's song from Carmen, Albert took the lead and Marco and Giuseppe joined in with the chorus. Even the Contessa added her light soprano to the mix. The French words 'Toreador, en garde! Toreador! Toreador!' tripped off their tongues. It was a joy. Sophia, Caterina and Giovanni listened attentively as the six voices rang out in sweet harmony around one of the world's greatest opera houses. When the song was done, there was nothing left to do or say, but just to go. First some lunch, then to the station to get the train back to the south. The whole trip had been fabulous, but now it was over. Time to get back down to earth.

CHAPTER THREE

London and an extraordinary encounter

In the September of 1947, Charlie was again summoned to his duties. This time he was to travel to England for meetings with civil servants working in the Foreign Office. The task was to pave the way for discussions between Italian and British politicians. Charlie was quite excited at the prospect as he had not been in England since the beginning of 1943, over four years previously . He expected to find it much changed, especially as the returning troops and their newly-enfranchised wives had kicked out Churchill's toffs and replaced them with the new men and women of the Labour Party. Charlie wondered if it would feel like New Zealand had ten years earlier, when the politicians there had brought in the Welfare State to ease the burden of the Great Depression. He knew that there had already been some moves along that line since the end of the war, and was interested to see if democratic socialism could operate well in a country riddled with the legacy of the class system.

This time it was no smoky little fishing trawler that carried Charlie across the North Sea but a BOAC aeroplane that delivered him swiftly to London's newly re-opened civilian airport at Croydon in Surrey. As he landed he recalled some famous aviators who had also arrived at this place – Charles Lindbergh and Amy Johnson to name but two, but perhaps the most remarkable was Charles Kingsford Smith who had flown all the way from Australia. What a feat! Charlie's comfortable commercial flight from Rome paled into insignificance and for that he was glad. Flying was convenient but he didn't enjoy it and was always glad when the wheels touched down and the aircraft came to a halt. He preferred to make his way on land or by sea wherever possible, only resorting to the skies when time was an issue.

In this instance, it was, for he had people in London to meet and deals to broker between their employers and his. Her rather hoped that he might even get to meet a politician or two, so that he could work out for himself what their plans for Britain were. It was not supposed to be his brief he knew, as a neutral Swiss in the pay of the Italians, but he couldn't help being interested in what the future might hold for his and Albert's families. He made his way to London by train, arriving at Victoria in the early evening. His hotel room had been reserved in advance by a most helpful secretary in Rome, so all he had to do was check in and look for somewhere to eat. That was when the effect of the war became really apparent. On his way through Surrey and south London Charlie had obviously noticed the massive devastation of buildings caused by years of air raids. He had expected that, for he had been in England at a time when the bombs were dropping. What he had not been ready for was the continuing state of austerity, as Britain struggled to pay for saving the world from the Nazis. Food was still scarce and what there was was severely rationed. As a visiting diplomatic attaché from a foreign land, Charlie could have demanded concessions, but he chose not to. He wanted to see what ordinary people were eating in post-war London. Not a lot as it turned out, and that rather bland and uninspiring. The oxtail soup was thin, with extremely little evidence of the tail of an ox – perhaps just a swish as it passed the pot, Charlie thought. The steak and kidney pie was more pastry than filling, and the accompanying vegetables overcooked and watery. Only the pud was up to anything. Somehow the cook (for the word chef did not really apply in this case) had got hold of enough sugar and powdered egg to make a creditable steamed sponge which was served with a blob of tinned condensed milk in lieu of cream or custard. Maybe it was because it was such a long time since he had eaten a steamed pudding, or maybe it was because his mother's efforts had always been a bit hit and miss, for whatever reason Charlie really rather enjoyed his dessert. The whole meal offered less real food than he was used to back in Matera where the farm provided whatever he and Giovanna needed, but it was enough. He could see himself losing weight if he stayed in England for too long though.

Thinking of his mother, he felt a pang of sorrow, and resolved to write to his father and sister as soon as possible. Perhaps, just perhaps, he could manage to see them while he was here. He had no fear that anyone in Great Harwood would recognise him these days – the passage of time had ensured that he no longer resembled the light-haired blue eyed boy who had marched off to war in 1915. He was still slim and tall, but infinitely fitter now than he had been then, and his stride was markedly more energetic. The outdoor life he now enjoyed was so much healthier than the one he had lived in the years spent bent over a loom. Back at his hotel he put pen to paper – no time like the present – and suggested to Mary that he should perhaps find time to visit her and their father while he was in the country. After all, he was bound to get some time off as part of the assignment, and he didn't fancy spending it in dirty, devastated, dreary London.

The next day Charlie made his way for a pre-arranged preliminary meeting with a senior civil servant at the Foreign Office. He had rather hoped to be able to meet with the Minister, or better still the new Prime Minister, Clement Attlee, but this was only so that he could personally get an idea of what sort of men these British Labour chaps were. He knew his own lowly status as a mere attaché would not qualify him to meet with politicians, this would be left to his elected paymasters at some future date. He was not surprised therefore when it was made clear that this was indeed the case. His discussions with the Minister's secretary were cordial enough though and he felt sure that progress could be made, once British disapproval of Italy's conduct during the war was reduced. He could see that task taking some time. Many British and Allied lives had been lost liberating Italy from the Germans, and memories were still fresh of the horrors of Anzio and Monte Cassino. Simply switching sides and deposing the dictator had not been enough to rehabilitate the image of the whole Italian nation. Quite the opposite. The capitulation was looked on as something to be ashamed of. The British would need persuading that Italy's new leaders were not cut from the same cloth as the old ones. It would take a lot of work for the civil servants to lay the foundations for future Ministerial contacts. In the meantime Charlie did what he could in London, always being available when summoned for talks and keeping in constant communication with Rome so that he could pass on the very latest information.

When he was not so engaged, he liked to spend time at the Houses of Parliament, sitting in the Strangers' Gallery and listening to the debates as the new Government worked on the continuing development of the Welfare State. The rhetoric was much as Charlie hade heard over ten years earlier in New Zealand. It was the rhetoric of social justice and a fair deal for all regardless of social status, and as such Charlie had absolutely no quibble with it. He only wished the proposed National Health Service had been in place before his own mother's health had been broken by her life in the mill. Maybe she would be alive today if so. At least his siblings and their offspring would benefit, though from what his sister Mary had had to say in her reply to his letter, it was probably too late for his dad. The old man was still grieving for his wife, and seemed to have lost the will to live. With no work to go to since retirement, he rarely left the house. He had no interest in food, and had even given up going to the pub with Joe of a Sunday. Mass had long been abandoned, as he could not find it in himself to forgive God for taking his beloved Mary. He was wasting away, and it was Mary's suggestion that Charlie should get up to Great Harwood sooner rather than later if he wanted to see his father again.

One day in October, Charlie was walking through the lobby of the House of Commons, when he saw none other than Winston Churchill himself, holding court before a few of his constituents. The great man had aged considerably since the war, probably due to the disappointment, nay the insult as he saw it, of having been rejected by the ungrateful electorate. He had won the war for them and they had thrown him out. Charlie could easily understand how it had come to pass. The returning troops were not the same sort of people as those who had come back from the Great War. They were not as humble and dutiful as your average Tommy Atkins. They were no longer prepared to be unquestioningly subservient to the officer classes. Many ordinary men had been made up to officers in the field and were all too aware of the weaknesses of some members of the traditional officer class. The time to take a share of the power had come, and the way to do that was to get rid of the toffs and the Tories and bring in the working man's party, Labour. It was a shame that 'Winnie' as they fondly called him, had also had to be sacrificed, for he was well-respected in the land, but there was a mood abroad that his time had passed and a new broom was called for to deal with post-war concerns.

Charlie tended to agree with that viewpoint but nevertheless, he was thrilled to see the former leader and went up to where he sat in the hope of having a few words. Churchill had commanded an active fighting unit in the trenches during the Great War, and his courage was not in doubt. He had seen what Charlie had seen, not that it could ever be discussed. He was also closely linked in some people's minds with the Gallipoli debacle. which meant that in New Zealand and Australia his name was not always as revered as it was elsewhere. Too many lambs had been led to the slaughter that April day in 1915. All the same, there was no getting away from the fact that he had been the right man for the job in the fight against Hitler and the Nazis. Charlie's experience at Nuremberg had convinced him that it was a great evil that had been snuffed out, and for that he gave Churchill every credit.

At last the constituents were shown out by a House of Commons usher and for a moment or two, Winston Churchill sat alone, lost in thought. This was Charlie's chance. It was now or never. He went over to the settee where the ex Prime Minister was gathering his papers together. 'Mr Churchill, sir,' he said, 'may I introduce myself to you?' Churchill looked up, adjusted the specs on the end of his nose and stared quizzically at the stranger. 'And who might you be, young man?' he said, in his unmistakable gravelly voice. It was a while since Charlie had been seen as a young man, and it came as a pleasant surprise. Then he recalled that Churchill was a good twenty or so years older than he was himself. He had already been reporting from the Boer War when Charlie was a mere toddler in Great Harwood. Perhaps a chap of fifty seemed young to him. Charlie asked if he could sit down and was waved brusquely into an armchair. He introduced himself as Carlo Weiss, a Swiss national acting as a diplomatic attaché for the Italian government. 'Swiss, eh?' the old man growled, his voice almost hostile. 'You'll have had an easy war then did you?' 'Not especially,'

Charlie countered, and sketched the bare bones of what he had done with the New Zealanders, the Americans and then the British culminating with his activities in bringing the top Nazis to justice. Churchill was impressed. 'Good for you lad,' he said, 'a man of principle obviously.' He summoned an usher with a flick of his fingers. 'Let's have some tea,' he said, 'I'd like to hear more.'

For the next couple of hours Charlie sat with probably the most famous Briton ever to draw breath and discussed the history of the past twenty years from Mussolini to Franco and onto Hitler. Poor stupid mad Hitler, who had underestimated the British, the Empire, the Americans and above all, the Russians. Churchill's voice became dark. He had sat next to Stalin at Yalta, and saw him as an even greater threat than any of the others, diabolical as they were. 'He is a brute, Mr Weiss,' he said to Charlie, 'he is made of the same material as Mussolini but he is infinitely more evil and ruthless. He cares for no-one but himself and his own evil ambitions. He will stop at nothing to spread communism across the world and would kill his own mother if she stood in the way. Mark my words, young man, what happens in Russia will affect what happens the whole world over in the next twenty years. We should have pushed them back to Moscow from Berlin, but we didn't. I believe we will live to regret that.' The old man's voice was steely. He knew what he was talking about and it filled Charlie with dread. Just like before, it seemed the seeds of the next war had been sown at the end of the last one. Would mankind never learn? He was about to say as much when he noticed that Churchill was slumped back on the sofa and was fast asleep. The hovering usher caught his eye. 'The former Prime Minister gets very tired, sir,' he explained, 'he needs to rest now. Perhaps it is time you left him.' Charlie rose to his feet and made to leave. 'Please thank Mr Churchill for me when he wakes,' he said, 'it has been a most interesting afternoon.' So saying, he pressed a business card into the usher's hand. On the back of it he had written 'best regards, and thank you for your insights.' 'Please see that he gets this,' he said, and Charlie turned and walked out of the House of Commons and into the early evening sun. As he made his way to the Underground, Big Ben was striking six. Time to find somewhere to get a meal before the food ran out and the cafés closed.

A family crisis

A couple of days after that meeting, Charlie boarded a train at Euston for the journey up to Great Harwood. He had the weekend to himself and had decided to act on his sister Mary's ominous suggestion that he visit sooner rather than later. The train made slow progress in a northwesterly direction, stopping frequently at places Charlie had hardly even heard of. Watford, Hemel Hempstead, Leighton Buzzard – they all meant little to him. It was only when they got to Bletchley that he had some idea of where he was. This was the place where the fiendish Enigma code had been broken by men and women of genius and dedication, and where the end of the war had been hastened considerably by the availability of German military secrets. Without them it might still be going on, which was unthinkable. Even this austere, rationed, penny-pinching peace was better than war. The train passed through bruised and battered Coventry, where the ancient cathedral had been flattened by German bombers in a night of terror for no other reason than that they could do it. They then came to Birmingham, once one of the industrial powerhouses of the world, now a city picking itself up again after six years of damaging bombardment and turning its attention once more to the manufacture of benign products rather than the weapons of war. Ploughshares, not swords.

North it went through rural Shropshire and prosperous Cheshire, with a stop at Crewe, then at last the train came to the scruffy southern side of the city of Manchester. Here Charlie would have to change to a bus for the final part of his journey to Great Harwood. It was getting late in the day and he had no idea if there would still be any way of getting there, but he was in luck. The last bus was due to leave the station in a little over fifteen minutes, and would get him to his father's house by nine o'clock, after taking in every little town and village on the way. It would be a journey of rediscovery if nothing else. There was just time to pick up what passed for a sandwich to eat on the bus, and he was off. Some time later, he arrived at the front door of the house where he had spent his childhood, and from which he had marched, as a man, albeit a very young one, to war thirty years earlier. It looked no different, but why would it? It was Charlie that had changed.

He tapped quietly on the front door, to avoid drawing attention to himself at this late hour, and immediately heard footsteps from inside the house. The door was opened by his sister Mary, who took his hand and pulled him into the hallway, quickly shutting the door behind him. Then she put her arms around him and squeezed him hard. 'Thank goodness you've come Charlie,' she said, 'our dad'll be chuffed to bits to see you. I told him this morning you were coming and he's been talking about nothing else ever since. He's got precious little to be happy about these days, I certainly don't seem to be able to cheer him up any more. Oh, thank goodness you've come,' she said again. She pushed open the door to the back kitchen to reveal their father sitting in an armchair by the range. He seemed to be asleep as far as Charlie could tell. Mary's voice was unusually shrill and clear as she said 'Look who's here, dad, it's our Charlie come back from Italy,' at which the old man's eyes opened and he turned towards his son. 'Charlie?' he said, his voice frail and old. 'Is that you? Your mother and I thought you were dead, didn't we mother?' The latter part of his sentence he addressed to Mary. Mary quickly caught Charlie's eye. Her look was sad and resigned and said it all. There was nothing to be gained by correcting their father. It probably comforted him to think his wife was still alive. Charlie went over to his dad and placed a hand on his shoulder. 'No, Dad,' he said, 'I'm not dead by any means, I've just been away, but I'm here now.' 'You look different,' the old man said, 'you look old. Not like my boy at all.' 'Well, I am nearly fifty, Charlie replied, ' and I've fought in two wars, maybe I'm entitled to look a bit older.' The old man's eyes narrowed, and focused on his son. His memory clearly returned to him suddenly. 'You know your mam died? They took her to the hospital and never sent her back to me.' His voice broke and he started to sob. Charlie put his arms around his father's shoulders and said in a soft voice, 'Yes dad, I know. Mary told me. It was the winter that killed her. She couldn't take the cold.' The old man sat up straight. His voice emerged clear and strong, full of anger. 'It wasn't the winter Charlie, it was the bloody mill as killed her. It was the bloody looms and the cotton dust and the bloody damp as killed her. It was the poverty and the hard work and the bad food that did for your mother. Not the bloody winter!' And he started to cry uncontrollably again. 'And she left me here to get on without her. Well, I can't Charlie, I bloody can't!' From his mouth he let out a groan of agony which came from his broken heart. Charlie looked over at his sister. She was in tears too. Charlie had never heard his father swear so much, not in front of a lady anyway, and he had certainly never seen him cry.

25

It was shocking to behold. Mary turned away, unable to watch any more. Charlie held his father in his arms, something else he had never done in his life, and whispered comforting words until the sobs subsided. From the other side of the room came the sounds of Mary making tea. 'Aye, that'd be right,' Charlie thought, 'A nice cup of tea. And perhaps a sandwich before bed, if there's any butter left what with the rationing and everything. Maybe even get some sleep eh?' Charlie doubted that he would, but it was worth a try. It had been a long day. Long and very tiring indeed.

The next morning Charlie's father seemed a little more cheerful. Having company was a rare event now that his beloved Mary was gone. Others of his generation had also succumbed to the winter. Their old lungs, clogged with fine cotton fibre and dust breathed in over decades in the mill, had not been strong enough to ward off the evil bug that went around in that long icy winter. In damp houses they could not afford to light the gas fire that would keep them warm and dry. One after another they had gone until at last it had got to the point where he did not even ask after them for fear of hearing the worst. Laid low by his own grief, he could not offer comfort to others in the same position, and so he had withdrawn into his shell, seeing only his daughter Mary and sometimes his son Joe and Joe's wife Annie. It being Saturday, Joe and Annie did not have to work after lunchtime, so in the early afternoon they came to the house, bringing with them precious rationed food as their contribution to a meal. Charlie felt guilty that he was unable to chip in. Without a ration book, he could not buy anything of use to his family. They waved away his apologies. 'You don't look like you eat a lot, our Charlie,' Joe said, to which Charlie replied that in the past couple of weeks in England he had indeed eaten much less than usual and was becoming used to it. He told them about the food that he and Giovanna got from the farm, and expressed the wish that he could send some to them, but they all knew it was impossible. On hearing of the Italian abundance, Joe looked rather cross. 'We're supposed to have won this bloody war you know, Charlie,' he said, 'yet here we are bloody starving while the Eyeties can scoff all they want. Even the bloody Germans are getting help from America now. It's a bloody scandal!' Annie glared sharply at her husband. All this swearing was a disgrace, no matter how provoked he might be. Charlie was taken aback by the strength of his brother's feelings which were no doubt widely shared. Once again the victorious nation was paying the price of fighting a virtuous war. It seemed unfair in the extreme. The Americans were giving money to Germany, while poor, hungry, ravaged Britain was struggling to pay back every last cent it had received. Where was the justice in that? Two years after the war, people were still queuing for basic foodstuffs, bomb sites were everywhere, and new clothes were a fantasy. No wonder people were pouring out of Britain and going to places like Canada and Australia. There was just so much deprivation and hardship a person could take, and the ones with an ounce of spirit left were saying 'enough is enough.'

It seemed foolish for Charlie to go outside the house, just in case. It was a long shot but you never knew, some sharp-eyed person might see and recognise him or at least put two and two together. There would be no walk around the town this time. The men spent the next hour chatting of this and that, Charlie deliberately keeping the conversation light, while the women prepared a simple dinner of Lancashire hotpot, virtually meat-free and full of vegetables from Joe and Annie's allotment. Luckily it was the right time of year and, despite the harshness of the winter just gone, there were plenty of onions, carrots, potatoes and big fat marrows to bulk out the meagre ration of mutton in the stew. The meat was finely diced so that everyone got at least a few bits on their plate. Runner beans completed the meal. Once it was eaten, Jack Clayton fell asleep for his customary afternoon doze, and the younger ones migrated to the front room – the almost never-used 'parlour' as it was called – for an emergency council of war out of their father's earshot.

His health was of great concern to them. The old man was getting into his eighties. He was not as fit as he had once been, and the loss of his wife, so suddenly and unexpectedly, had come as a body blow. Sometimes he was confused and forgot that his wife had died, mistaking Mary for her and at other times he was downright low. Charlie understood something of these matters, through talks he had had with Alessandro, and knew that their father needed help. Otherwise he might just do what Wolfgang had done, and decide to die. Mary too, needed some support, for she not only feared for her father's safety when she went out to work, she found his changes of mood very upsetting. Their father, Charlie explained, was suffering from what the doctors called melancholia, most probably brought on by their mother's death. He had seen people with this illness after the Great War, both in Italy and in Yorkshire. As far as he knew there was no medicine for it other than herbal tonics. He told them about the asylum where Alessandro had been found and how good food, useful work and gentle exercise were used to help people. Since none of these was an option for Jack at his age and in austere post-war England, the family had a problem. The only thing to do was to enlist the aid of the doctor. Jack hated doctors and would never normally go and see one, but this aversion was a good deal to do with the fact that you had to pay through the nose to see one. With Charlie promising to pay, he would perhaps be persuaded to seek help. It was agreed that Charlie would talk to his dad, as the eldest son. With any luck he would listen to what Charlie had to say and agree. The alternative, to continue with the status quo and do nothing, was unthinkable, both for Mary and for the old man himself. When the old man awoke, Charlie went in to speak to him alone. Jack's initial reaction was one of anger. How dare his children talk about him as if he was an imbecile? How dare they presume to know what was good for him? But Charlie was patient, and once the old man had vented his initial anger, he had to concede that he was feeling very poorly and that something needed to be done if it could. 'I know I'm not always nice to Mary,' he said, 'I get fed up and snap at her. I sometimes hear her crying. We need to do something for her sake if nothing else.' Of course, there was no guarantee that the doctor would have a cure – there was no magic wand after all – but at least it was a start. Charlie knew from experience that even just by recognising that you have a problem, you take a step towards fixing it. He knew too how much it had taken his father to go along with him. Jack was a proud man, a strong man. Of late he felt he had been weak and a burden on his family and he hated to admit it. Charlie took the old man's hand in his and squeezed it gently. 'There we are father,' he said, his tone soothing, 'no need to say any more. It's not your fault. Let's just try and get it sorted shall we?' At that point the others came into the room. 'Dad'll see the doctor on Monday,' Charlie told them. 'We'll ask him to come here so no-one else knows anything about it. Let's hope he can make our Dad feel better, eh?'

In the afternoon of the next day Charlie returned to London by bus and train. He felt as if he had been a catalyst for an important change in the life of his family, as he had all those years earlier with dear old Wolfgang and his estranged sons and daughters. Maybe now Mary and Joe would have the courage to tackle problems head on rather than let them drift and get worse. Before he left his father had drawn him aside and thanked him for coming. 'I know our Mary and our Joe love me, and want the best for me,' he had said, 'but they're not very good at making decisions. Mother and I did all that for them you see. Now she's gone and I can't be bothered, they're floundering a bit. Make sure to keep an eye on 'em when I'm not here any more, won't you son?' Charlie had promised to do his best, as much as he could from a distance. 'That's all a man can ask,'was his father's reply, and suddenly put his arms around his son and gave him a hug. A week later, on his breakfast table in London, Charlie found a letter from Mary. Their dad had seen the doctor. It was, as Charlie had said, melancholia, for which the best treatment known was good food and gentle exercise. The former was out of the question, but Jack had agreed to start taking daily walks to Joe's allotment, to do a bit of gardening and get some air. The doctor, it seemed, understood what Jack was going through, having lost a son in the desert war. Once Jack had realised that what he was feeling was normal, that everyone who loses a loved one feels grief, and that it doesn't go away quickly, he began to feel less helpless and sorry for himself. The tone of Mary's letter was optimistic, almost cheerful. She ended it with 'thank you for coming, Charlie, thank you thank you THANK YOU.' Three days later, his preparatory work in London complete for the time being, Charlie made his way back to Croydon Airport where he boarded an aeroplane bound for Rome, from where he could make his way to his home, his darling Giovanna and, so he hoped, some decent food. He felt he had at last redressed a little of the pain he had caused his family by deserting, and, accepting a nerve-steadying brandy from the uniformed BOAC hostess, settled himself for the flight.

Alarm bells

In Rome at the seat of government, Charlie's employers were extremely pleased with what he had achieved on his visit to London. He had definitely paved the way for the resumption of good relations between the two former enemies. The Whitehall mandarins he had met had let it be known that they were impressed by his knowledge and understanding of the political situation in Europe and his willingness to work hard to achieve his adopted nation's aim of becoming a major player on the post-war continent. Like them, he had no desire to see another war and like them felt the way forward was for Europe to be more united rather than remaining a group of disparate nation states at loggerheads with one another. Living in the past was not going to achieve anything. Not that history should be forgotten, and what had happened in Germany especially should never be forgotten. But it was time to break the mould, to stop leaning on old feuds and enmities as an excuse for inactivity. In Italy the politicians broadly agreed with that point of view. It remained to be seen whether Mr Attlee's men did too. They had rather more to forgive than their Italian counterparts.

In particular, the insights that Charlie had gleaned from his meeting with Churchill were of great interest to the Italian government. The official view was that Stalin was an ally and therefore one of what the Americans would call 'the good guys'. Churchill's opinion of Stalin and the threat he posed contradicted that view, yet if anyone was in a position to know what the Russian leader was like, it was certainly Churchill. The two had met frequently, at Teheran and Yalta most famously. The only other man who might have an opinion was the former American President Franklin D. Roosevelt, and he, sadly, had died just before the end of the war in Europe. His replacement, Vice-President Truman, was not as perspicacious as his predecessor, and much easier for the bluff outgoing Stalin to hoodwink. The Italians were particularly interested in Stalin's plans for Europe, because of their own geographical location. The always-volatile Balkans lay across the Adriatic to the east, and the Russian sphere of influence began just over their northern border with Slovenia and Czechoslovakia. It was all rather too close for comfort if Stalin's ambitions were indeed territorial and hostile as Churchill suggested. Neutral Switzerland and defeated Austria would be unlikely to stem a Russian tide should it come to that. The Italians realised that they were going to need the help of the powers of Western Europe even more than they had thought. His report on the assignment filed, and his gratifyingly huge pay cheque handed over, Charlie made his way back to Matera.

Family affairs

The London assignment had kept him away for several weeks, much longer than the last one, and Giovanna greeted him with more than her usual show of devotion. For a couple of days she wouldn't let him out of her sight. She had missed him terribly and was completely at a loose end when he was away. Of late she had taken to spending a great deal of time at the farm helping her mother. Sophia was finding her role as keeper of the household rather arduous and Caterina had enough on her plate caring for her own family to be able to give much by way of a hand. So Giovanna had gone over there to help her out, and in order to get some company as well. But now that Charlie was back she wanted to spend her days as well as her nights with him, and it was obvious to her that something would have to be done about the Sophia situation.

To Charlie it seemed that the needs of ageing parents were something that every son and daughter would have to face sooner or later. His recent experience in Great Harwood had shown him that. There appeared to come a time when roles were reversed, and once-powerful mothers and fathers began to rely on their offspring as his own father had made it clear he did on him. Giovanni no longer took a major part in the work of the farm, even of the planning or the business side of things, having handed it over to Albert and the boys. If he did any work, it was because he wanted to. The same could not be said for Sophia. She still ran the house as she always had, as well as supervising the domestic education of her grand-daughters. One day, when Charlie was still away in London, she had confessed to Giovanna that she no longer had the energy for it all. She did not want Caterina to think less of her, but she was finding the girls hard going. They were lovely girls, unfailingly polite and helpful, but limited in their skills like so many modern young women. They were less interested in learning to cook and clean for a man and to sew their own clothes than they were in having a career and some fun. The war had changed everything. As well as the significant loss of male life, which meant there were fewer potential husbands about, there was no longer the respect that there had once been for tradition and the established ways of doing things. The American GIs had shown young Italians a different way of being. Apart from that these girls were well off and did not need to make do and mend. Once out of school and working, they would easily be able to afford to buy what they wanted without relying on a man to provide for them. Sophia felt she was trying to train them for a role they did not wish to take on. Perhaps she should be preparing them for life in a man's world, but she did not know about that. All in all, Sophia concluded, she was pretty much no use to anyone any more. Giovanna tried to reassure her mother that she was still a valuable member of the family with a lot to contribute, but on her dark days, when the knees were sore and her energy low, Sophia could not be convinced. A solution was required, and quickly.

As had happened in Great Harwood, it fell to the next generation to come up with an answer. Giovanna and Caterina, and Charlie and Albert realised that they needed to find a way to relieve the pressure on Sophia without making her feel useless. Charlie also remembered how angry his father had been at first when he became aware that his children had been discussing him. Tact and consideration were called for if feathers were not to be ruffled. Discussions were held and brains wracked for an answer to the dilemma. It seemed impossible to change anything without hurting Sophia.

In the event, as is so often the case, the solution presented itself naturally, giving the lie to all the soul-searching. The girls themselves came up with it. Jointly, and without consulting their parents, they had decided that next year they wanted to go off to a technical college to get secretarial training The idea was to be able to get jobs and be independent. Teresa and Gina were now eighteen and seventeen respectively, and were ready to move out of the confines of the family and rural life and into something more exciting. The fact that Giuseppe had left and was making a success of his life in Milano had acted as a spur to the young women. They both found country life with its emphasis on domesticity stultifying and they craved some of what their brother had. They did not want for themselves what their grandmother wanted for them, or so they thought. They were modern girls.

Much as Caterina hated to admit it, she had to let them go and make their own way in the world. There was nothing for them locally, no work, and certainly no prospect of finding a suitable husband with enough education and, well, enough 'oomph', for her daughters. It pained her but she knew the time had come for them to fly the nest. The question was, to where?

The answer to that question was fairly obvious, even if the girls hadn't made their wishes known explicitly. Milano of course. There they would get the further education they needed and there they had family in the form of Giuseppe. Ah, but wait, the doubts crept in, Giuseppe was a young man and could not reasonably be expected to act as chaperone for his sisters. Not even in this day and age. Who then? It was Giovanna who proposed that the Contessa da Mosto be asked to take on this role. She was young enough to understand the girls yet old and wise enough to see that they were safe in the city. The Contessa? Nice as she was, as far as they knew she was a glorified 'puttanesca'. Her relationship with Marco Bocelli, maybe even with Giuseppe, was ambiguous to say the least. But she was charming, well-connected and intelligent. She would be able to help the girls and protect them without clipping their wings. Caterina resolved to write to her at once. There would be the small matter of persuading Sophia of the Contessa's suitability – for who could forget her look of disapproval back in Milano in the summer? – but Caterina was certain she could bring her mother around in due course. In fact, Sophia was so relieved to be losing the task she now found too much, that she quite forgot to object to the choice of chaperone and gave the plan her blessing. The girls were thrilled. It was everything they wanted. They could scarcely wait to get going. Of course, there were anxieties and some tears were shed, but all in all it felt like a grand adventure. The next few months would drag by for them as they champed at the bit to start their new lives. For Caterina and Albert the next few months would be tinged with sadness as they prepared to let their precious daughters go.

Before that, however, there was the matter of Charlie and Giovanna's first wedding anniversary needing to be marked, this to be hotly followed by the Christmas celebrations. The anniversary was a low-key affair. Charlie took his wife for a few days in Palermo, where they stayed in a far grander hotel than the one he, Albert and Giovanni had used over twenty years before. The place was still teeming with life and mystery though, and, poignantly for Charlie, there were still the same desperate groups of poor young men and women and their children queuing up to board boats for America to escape the poverty of post-war Italy. It was as if the years between the wars had made no difference. These people were just as anxious to get away as their predecessors had been. For Giovanna, Palermo was a real eye-opener. She had never encountered such a cosmopolitan mix of human beings in her life, and she loved it. There was a real air of foreignness about the place. The African influence was palpable. 'Look, Charlie,' she cried, 'from here you can get a boat to Algeria or Libya, even Egypt. We could see the Pyramids! It's terribly exciting!' 'Exciting indeed, my love,' Charlie replied, 'but I think your parents are expecting us back at the farm for Christmas. Somehow I don't think a postcard from Cairo saying 'wish you were here' will satisfy them.'

Giovanna was forced to agree, but with reluctance. Having been the dutiful daughter, then the good wife, all her life she was now, at nearly fifty, feeling like having the adventures she had missed out on because of the wars. Charlie, being a man, had been able to travel all over the world on his own, something a woman could never do. By the time she had married Arturo Maldini, he was already too old to want to gad about, preferring to stay at home in his magnificent villa in Matera, sipping wine, eating just a bit too much and smoking the cigarettes that would eventually kill him. His hectic working life as an impresario had given him all the adventure he wanted. Giovanna had to compromise. She had knowingly traded excitement and the thrill of the unknown for a life of comfort, even luxury, with a man old enough to be her father. Now she was married to a much younger, more active man, and peace was abroad in the land at last, she wanted to recapture her youth and have some enjoyment. So, in Palermo, looking out to sea, she made Charlie promise to take her with him, wherever his work took him, so that she could at last see his world. He was delighted to concur. He missed her a great deal when he was away. If she came on his trips, they would not only be productive, they would be pleasurable, no matter where they ended up. In the end it didn't take long to find out. The Christmas decorations were scarcely put away in their boxes and Giuseppe, weighed down with home made food, loaded onto the Milano train when Charlie was summoned to Rome to be given his next mission.

CHAPTER FOUR

Growing concerns

As the war receded a new era dawned. It was an era the new Italian government hoped would be a peaceful one in which Italy would play a major role. However, there were signs of developments to the north and east which threatened that hope. The post-war division and occupation of Germany had been designed to prevent the rise of another Hitler at the head of a powerful well-armed nation. The four victorious allies each had control of a large chunk of the country as well as a quarter of the nation's capital, Berlin, but their presence there was never seen as a permanent state of affairs. There was always the underlying assumption that the Germans would at some future date again take control of their own destiny in a modern democratic state.

Early in 1948, however, it became apparent that the Russian dictator Stalin has other plans for the Soviet-controlled east of the country. He began to make it known that he had no intention of pulling his troops out. Instead, he planned to use eastern Germany and all the countries which bordered it as a buffer zone to protect the Soviet Union from what he, in his paranoia, saw as the hostile intentions of his former comrades in arms, especially the United States. The actions of the Allies in crushing the communist parties of West Germany, France and Italy only served to reinforce that belief and also had deprived him of any possible powerbase inside those countries. A strong eastern bloc of communist nations would provide a viable competitor for the hated capitalists, the Americans, and their spineless European handmaidens. The 'iron curtain' to which Churchill had so presciently referred as early as 1946, was indeed being drawn. Seething at the amount of aid being poured into western Europe under the Marshall Plan, Stalin resolved that this 'dollar imperialism' would stop where his influence began. Since the end of the war the government of the Soviet Union had systematically and brutally snuffed out any potential democratic government in Hungary, Poland, Czechoslovakia and the many other countries which surrounded her western borders. These were replaced by communist puppet regimes, Stalin's lapdogs. Germany was the final frontier – the place where east and west met head-on. And nowhere did they come closer than in Berlin. The ancient city may have been theoretically under the control of the Allies as well as the Soviets, but it lay deep in eastern Germany and was completely surrounded by lands earmarked for Stalin's communist cushion. The Soviet leader was infuriated by what he saw as American financial colonisation in Germany, and at loggerheads with the Allies' view that the German economy should be allowed to regain its former power and status as a capitalist nation under a democratically-elected government. In February of 1948, at the same time as finally snuffing out any hope for the anti-communist citizens of Czechoslovakia, the Soviet Union took things a stage further and stated its claim to the whole of Berlin as a city within its sphere of occupation.

It was in this context that Charlie was recalled to Rome. Stalin was rapidly emerging as a figure almost as evil and dangerous as Hitler, and Charlie's paymasters were gravely concerned about what would happen in Berlin. They were also alarmed to contemplate what further territorial ambitions the dictator might have which could have an impact upon the integrity of Italy's borders. Charlie had insights into and understandings of Stalin's character gleaned from his lengthy conversation with Winston Churchill. He also knew Germany and the

Germans and could speak to them fluently and productively. Thanks to his work at Nuremberg, he was respected by the Allied Command. It was time to put that respect to the test. An observer was needed on the ground, someone who could interpret events as they affected not the all-powerful United States, not even poor battered Britain and France, but little war-torn Italy. Occupied once, the politicians had no desire for the experience again. They had lost the stomach for brutal leadership, having suffered under both Mussolini and Hitler's henchmen. The Italians may have been relegated to the sidelines when postwar Europe was being carved up, but they sat at the heart of the continent and wanted their voice heard. Charlie was the obvious man for the job. In March of 1948, despite his employer's serious misgivings. but true to his promise to his wife, he and Giovanna boarded a flight from Rome to Templehof in west Berlin.

As they flew over the mountains of Italy then Austria, Charlie and Giovanna were able to look down on the terrain that Giovanni and Alessandro had fought over with their comrades in the Great War. No wonder so many Italians had been lost. The landscape was full of high ridges, treacherous ravines and deep gorges with swift-flowing rivers. Anyone falling into one of these, even if not badly wounded, would have no chance of getting out. There were probably thousands of bodies there that would never be found and brought back to their grieving families. Giovanna realised how lucky they had been to have got both their father and their brother home. The Dolomites and the Alps had become the final resting place for so many, just as the muddy fields of Paschendale and the Somme had for thousands of Charlie and Albert's compatriots.

Flying east, it became clear just what a huge country Germany was. Charlie had no experience of the rural eastern side of the country and was staggered by the size and the productivity of the fields below. The east was supposed to be producing food for the west in return for products from the industrial Ruhr, but the fact of the matter was that Stalin was beginning to stop the transportation of supplies to the perceived enemy and only massive aid from America was stopping the people of western Germany from starving to death.

Over Czechoslovakia, the plane crossed into Soviet airspace and at once began to be accompanied by fighter jets bearing the hammer and sickle and the familiar 'CCCP' insignia of the Soviet air force. Undeterred, the pilot continued his course north towards Berlin. From their window Charlie and Giovanna looked down in shock on the still devastated ruins of Dresden, bombed into near oblivion by the British and the Americans on Saint Valentine's day 1945, just weeks before the end of the war in Europe. Charlie had long suspected that the city was destroyed simply out of revenge for some of the British towns damaged by the Luftwaffe in what had been dubbed the 'Baedeker' raids. These were carried out over beautiful and historic places like Bath and York, towns and cities that had no military significance at all. But what had happened in Dresden was worse than all of those raids put together. So fierce had been the bombardment that the very air had caught fire and thousands of innocent women and children had been consumed by the fireball. It was an inexcusable act of barbarism, and, as he cast his eyes over the results of that night, Charlie felt ashamed to be British. Occasionally, and this was one such occasion, he wanted to apologise to the German people. Then he remembered what he had heard in Nuremberg, and reason once again prevailed.

The airport at Templehof was bristling with military aircraft, tanks and armed service personnel. There was clearly a very high state of tension. Stalin's declaration that he wanted all of Berlin was something that the Allies could not and would not countenance. But his plan to cut off the supply routes through his sector put the citizens of Berlin in grave danger.

As it was, small amounts of essential food and equipment were still getting through but it became daily more difficult. On arrival, Charlie and Giovanna were taken to their hotel by a young British officer working under the command of General Ross. This was the same General Ross who, as a mere Captain, had been Charlie's boss in Nuremberg and who had later been so helpful to him in Hamburg in the icy March of 1947. It looked as if all that arduous and heartbreaking work put in in the summer of 1945 was about to bear fruit once more. As they say, sometimes it's not what you know, but who. Charlie was certainly glad to have such a good contact already in place. General Ross was one of the most senior British officers in Berlin, and if anyone was likely to know what was going on, Charlie thought, it would be him.

As soon as the two men met, however, it became clear to Charlie that the job before him was not to be an easy one. General Ross still largely adhered to the official British line that Stalin was an ally. He didn't think Stalin had any plans that would endanger Italy or any other country of western Europe. He saw the Americans' view of him as a left wing aggressor as one born of anti- communist hysteria fanned by the ramblings of an old man, an old man embittered by having been rejected by the electorate and searching for a new place in history. Charlie was shocked to hear Churchill described in these terms, Until recently, he had been a hero, one who could do no wrong. Suddenly he was not to be believed. Well, Charlie believed him. He had seen and heard enough of dictators to agree with his perception of Stalin as an amoral murderous brute. He had after all ordered the assassination of his own second in command to ensure his personal supremacy in the Party. Poor, clever Trotsky hadn't seen it coming, hadn't protected himself, and he had paid the price. It was easy to blame a rogue killer, a madman, especially in somewhere as volatile as Mexico. Only the fact that the war had started had prevented the finger from being pointed at Stalin. It was not until much later that the connection was made. How many more murders had he got away with? Charlie wondered. Lots, if Hitler and Mussolini were anything to go by. There was clearly nothing to be gained by talking to General Ross. In the French sector of the city he found much the same attitude. The commanders of the French forces were blinded by their hatred of Hitler, and could not see that Stalin was cut from the same cloth. The Americans shared Charlie's view of the dictator and his troops, but they were stretched very thinly and could not offer any practical assistance. Mr Weiss was on his own.

Charlie needed to find people closer to Stalin and the administration of the Soviet Union if he was to learn anything which would help him in his mission. He clearly needed to be in East Berlin talking to people on the ground, not in this or that High Command hobnobbing with soldiers. The plan was fraught with danger. As a diplomat, Charlie could hope to be treated well wherever he went. He had, however, no reason to trust the Russians. Their record on decency was not a good one. They had entered Berlin in 1945 like a ravening horde from the east, looting and pillaging, raping and killing, destroying property and people with total disregard for anything or anyone but themselves. They might just get the impression that an Italian diplomat with a Swiss passport was a spy for the Americans, in which case they could make life for Charlie very difficult at best, very short at worst. There was also the question of getting about. It was easy enough to get into the eastern side of the city, but getting out could be a bit tougher. Relations between Stalin and the western powers were deteriorating by the day. A week after their arrival in the German capital, Charlie reluctantly came to the conclusion that this mission was not one on which Giovanna could safely accompany him. He would need to have all his wits about him just to survive. Having to watch out for his wife would only be a distraction. It rankled to admit it, but his paymasters in Rome had been right. He needed to get Giovanna on a plane and out of there while it was still possible to travel. This time General Ross was able to be helpful, and a day or so after the decision had been reached, Charlie was kissing Giovanna goodbye at Templehof. A British military aircraft would take her to London where she could catch a commercial flight for Rome. Over the years she had picked up enough English to manage arranging the journey. It was the long route, but by far the safest one. As they embraced in the departure lounge, Charlie wondered when he would see her again. Her face showed her feelings and tears started to fall. Charlie claimed one last lingering kiss and then, for fear of changing his mind and begging her to stay, turned sharply and walked briskly away from her and out of the airport.

The onset of conflict

By staying on in Berlin, Charlie found himself witnessing another of the most extraordinary events of the twentieth century. The Somme and Ypres, the desert war, the Normandy landings and the trials in Nuremberg – he had been there for them all. The only big one he had missed, luckily, was the bloodbath of Paschendale, and that by a whisker. Now he was to stand by and watch as the world teetered on the brink of yet another conflict and drifted into what came to be called 'the cold war'.

As spring turned to summer, relations between the Soviet Union and the western powers chilled dramatically. Stalin was reported to be livid when a new German currency was introduced to replace the old mark which was rapidly spiralling into worthlessness as a result of rampant inflation. He declared that there would be no future access to West Berlin through Soviet-controlled territory, thus denying the citizens of that city food and essential supplies. What followed was, from Charlie's, or indeed anyone's point of view, a miracle.

Despite pressure from some American sources for a military assault on Stalin, for his actions were widely viewed as naked communist aggression, the western powers decided against the use of force. Instead they organised the most extraordinary act of humanitarian aid ever seen. For months on end they sent every available aircraft stuffed to the gunwales with provisions and materials of every kind for the poor beleaguered people of West Berlin. They had to show Stalin that they did not intend to give in to his territorial demands and abandon the historic city to his barbarism. Day after day the skies above Charlie were full of the low drone of transport planes circling on their approach. There was scarcely any let up in the night either, but missed sleep was not begrudged. The alternative was unthinkable. Stalin was clearly serious in his plan to starve the city into submission and the Allies equally serious that this should not happen. From what Charlie was hearing, the people of Berlin had already suffered enough in the closing stages of the war. They had lost just about everything but their spirit to the incoming Russians, and they were not about to lose their freedom now.

Charlie sat in pavement cafés, only open as long as there was any coffee to sell and people with cash to pay for it, and talked to ordinary Germans about their fears for their country. They were worried that Germany would never be reunited, that somehow Stalin would make the post-war division permanent, although it was never intended to be so. They grieved for relatives and friends trapped in the communist east on the other side of what Churchill had so perceptively called 'the iron curtain'. As Berliners they sensed that they were the lucky ones, while they still had the support and help of the Allies in the west. God forbid that it should ever be withdrawn! The Red Army would move in like lightning, just as they had in 1945. The price of defeat was indeed high. Those who remembered the end of the Great War did not recall ever feeling in so much danger. Germany, and especially Berlin, was the buffer zone between the free world and the forces of communism. It seemed that at any time something could happen which would ignite a spark and the world would again be plunged into war. This time, however, the stakes were higher, because both sides now had nuclear weapons. If Stalin chose to, he could obliterate not only Germany but probably the whole of Europe. It was a terrifying time to be alive and living in Germany. Charlie listened and groaned inwardly. Did no-one ever learn from history? The days when wars could be won were over. The existence of the nuclear bomb was bad enough, but to have it in the hands of a paranoid brute was a recipe for disaster.

From his position in besieged Berlin, Charlie could see only too well what Stalin's ambitions were. He wanted to turn the whole of Europe into a satellite state of the Soviet Union. From his secret forays into the eastern zone Charlie could see what life would be like if that were allowed to happen. People's lives were already severely restricted and their opportunities few. So far from it being an ideology which made people free, communism as interpreted by Stalin seemed hell-bent on imposing ever more controls. These people had more by way of chains to lose now than ever before. It was no wonder that the brave amongst them were risking life and limb to escape to the west. It was from these escapees that Charlie got the most chilling information. What was going on in eastern Germany and the other countries of the Soviet bloc was just as bad as what had happened in Nazi Germany or Mussolini's Italy. Secret police kept watch and anyone they suspected of opposing the government simply disappeared. In Russia, millions of dissidents had been killed or shipped off to prison camps where they were forced to do hard labour until they renounced their beliefs or died. In what way Stalin differed from Hitler, Charlie was at a loss to understand.

The summer melded into autumn then winter and still the airlift continued. Charlie was beginning to think he had probably found out all he could and should be reporting back to Rome. But how? Getting into the east to gather information was relatively easy but getting back into the west had become much harder as border controls and passport checks were intensified. Troops were now beginning to fire on those trying to get out of the east, and there had apparently been a number of deaths, not that the communist authorities admitted them. His problem now was getting safely out of east Germany altogether. Charlie had no official status that would entitle him to anything. His job had been basically to spy on Stalin and try and understand his agenda. As such he could not expect the allies to help him. General Ross had returned to London and Charlie no longer had anyone in Berlin he could ask for a favour. There was no reliable means of getting to the west other than by flying, as all the road and rail links had been cut. He felt very alone and isolated. Contact with his paymasters was by now sporadic at best, and with Giovanna non-existent. He needed to get to somewhere where the postal and telephone systems worked so that he could re-establish a proper link with his old life. Money was also becoming a problem, as he had been away far longer than anyone had envisaged. All right, he could live more cheaply that he could have if Giovanna had stayed, but it still cost something. He had long since moved out of the hotel and into a small cold apartment on the fifth floor of a tenement block, and there he could make his own food from what little there was available to buy. He lived as a German now, with all the suffering and the hunger that that entailed. It was wearing, frankly. Post-war austerity in London had been bad but this was infinitely worse for there was no guarantee that supplies would get through. There was no sign that Stalin was planning to lift the blockade, so little chance that things would get any better. It looked like time to take to the road once more. The realisation made Charlie sigh. He was getting too old for this adventuring malarkey. He was nearly fifty-two for pity's sake! Still, he couldn't stay where he was. This could go on until he was ninety. He packed up the few things he needed and sold what he couldn't carry for a few Pfennigs on a flea market in the shadow of the Brandenburg Gate. On the appointed day in January 1949, while it was still pitch dark, he quietly pulled the door of his apartment shut and tiptoed down the stairs. He slipped the keys silently under the landlady's door, and stepped out into the icy Berlin morning.

He had no funds to pay for transport, even had there been any running, so once he left the city he would have to throw himself on the mercy of passing farmers and businessmen for lifts. Hopefully they wouldn't also be doubling as members of the burgeoning secret police that spied on everyone and everything these days. The Russians had spent most of the past few years taking what they liked from Germany to feed and clothe themselves, but now and then they liked to give something back. In this case it was rule by fear. The developing Ministerium für Staatssicherheit was modelled on and would carry out the functions of the dreaded MGB which was already terrorising Russian citizens and keeping them in line. Being German, they would probably make a better job of it than the Russians. Charlie's heart bled for the people he was leaving behind. Even Germans deserved better than this. They were human beings after all. Their future looked bleak indeed.

A lucky break

By the time it got light, Charlie was already out of Berlin and heading south west on a road still littered with the detritus of war. Shell craters and bits of blown up military vehicles were all about, evidence of how fierce the fighting had been in the last days as the German Wehrmacht tried to return to the safety of Berlin. With the Americans and the British in hot pursuit, they can scarcely have imagined what horrors awaited them in the form of the Red Army. Many of them must have wished they had given themselves up whilst they could. At least they would still be alive. As it was, the Russians treated returning soldiers with contempt bordering on barbarity. Some of the few who had escaped their attentions had been only too willing to share their experiences with Charlie in return for a cup of hot coffee. It was a salutary lesson, and one that Charlie needed to pass on to his employers.

Not long after leaving the city, Charlie managed to get a lift in a battered old farm lorry being driven by a stout grey haired woman. The woman was accompanied by a young man of about twenty five. She wound down the window and called out in a strong country voice. 'Können Sie fahren?' Charlie confirmed that he could indeed drive, and the woman motioned to him that he should step up to the vehicle. As Charlie hauled himself up to the cab of the truck, the woman extended her hand and gave her name as Frau Schmidt. 'Carlo Weiss', Charlie replied, and the two shook hands firmly. Frau Schmidt nodded her head in the direction of the young man and said 'Mein Sohn, Johann.' The younger man said nothing but smiled at Charlie. 'Mein Sohn kann nicht mehr sprechen,' the woman explained, 'er hat in dem Krieg zu viel gesehen.' Charlie was shocked but tried not to show it. This lad had lost the ability to speak because of what he had seen during the war? Whatever it was, it must have been atrocious. Charlie was at once put in mind of Alessandro and his fellow-patients at the asylum. Even they, for all they had gone through, could still speak, well most of them. Charlie reached in and shook the young man's hand. 'Freut mich, Johann,' he said – pleased to meet you. He threw his bag into the back of the truck on top of the stinking heap of whatever it was that Frau Schmidt was transporting, jumped into the cab and settled down. Frau Schmidt, it seemed, was going all the way to Magdeburg and had only picked Charlie up because she needed someone to share the driving, now that Johann had become too nervous to be of use behind the wheel. Charlie, of course, was only too happy to oblige. Frau Schmidt drove like a woman possessed. As far as the road would allow it she went at top speed at all times. She certainly seemed to be in a hurry. Every now and then she pulled off the road and dragged a metal can of fuel out of the back of the lorry. This she poured through a funnel into the petrol tank. She had clearly prepared herself well for the journey and had no intention of risking running out and not being able to fill up. In fact she must have been stockpiling the precious petrol for months.

The mission was clearly important. When she was not driving like a maniac Frau Schmidt fired questions at Charlie, seemingly determined to establish who he was and what he was doing walking through her country. She could tell from his accent that he was not a German, and on hearing that he was a Swiss, visibly relaxed. Even the secret police were not recruiting the Swiss. They were turning Germans against each other and encouraging sons to inform on their fathers, but at least they were keeping it in the family so to speak. Having already decided that she was an unlikely government agent, Charlie reassured her that he was not in the pay of Stalin's henchmen, and that he hated what was happening in eastern Germany almost as much as she did. After what felt to Charlie like a strenuous interrogation, she seemed satisfied.

The kilometres passed. Around midday, not far from Potsdam, Frau Schmidt drove the truck into a quiet forest and stopped the engine. It was lunchtime. From under her seat, she pulled out some bread and some cheese, rather a lot of bread and cheese. She then went around to the side of the truck and unscrewed a muddy board which was fixed just above the wheels. The board appeared to disguise a narrow storage compartment, and to Charlie's absolute amazement, out of this cramped space crawled three young adults. They stood stretching and blinking as their muscles and their eyes became accustomed to their environment. Frau Schmidt looked hard at Charlie. This was the moment of truth. If he was not who he said he was, the jig would be up. But of course, he was, and no stranger to secrecy either though she did not know that. 'Wer sind sie?' he asked Frau Schmidt. The older woman told him that these young ones were her other three children and introduced them as Rainer, Werner, and Gisela. Hands were shaken and pleasantries exchanged. 'Angenehm, Herr Weiss,' the three spoke almost in unison, polite and respectful. The bread and cheese were brought out and for a while silence reigned.

Then Frau Schmidt turned to Charlie and told him about the purpose of her journey. Her husband had apparently been arrested by the authorities for saying in public that the Soviet blockade of west Berlin was a crime against humanity. Leaving her to run their tiny smallholding near the border with Poland, he had set off for his work in Frankfurt an der Oder one day last August and had never returned. She feared the worst, suspecting that he was either already dead or rotting in some Russian prison or labour camp. The authorities were now turning their attention to her and her younger children. Johann they had written off as an idiot, good for nothing and no threat at all. Rainer, Werner and Gisela, though, were intelligent and could pose a threat if they could gather others like themselves together. Frau Schmidt knew it was only a matter of time before they too faced some trumped up charge and quietly disappeared. So she had decided to take matters into her own hands and get them out of the country. She had a cousin in a small town called Eschwege on the river Werra, just inside the west zone. As a girl she had spent many of her holidays there and it was a charming place. If they could get there, their future at least would have purpose. There was work and education there. They could make something of themselves. It was too late for her and for Johann. Anyway she couldn't leave just in case her beloved husband did come back, unlikely as that seemed. Her job was to get the young ones away, and she was determined to succeed. The thing was, would Herr Weiss help? He could go with them into the west and see them settled. Maybe he could even get a message to her in some way to let her know they had got there. A letter from the west zone would be intercepted, but a birthday card posted in Switzerland or Italy would be perfect and would tell her that her babies were safe. Deeply moved, Charlie agreed. He was surprised to find himself helping someone who, until a few short months earlier, he had seen as the enemy.

Lunch over, the young ones returned to their uncomfortable hiding place. Charlie could see now why Frau Schmidt was driving like the proverbial clappers. The longer her children were in there the harder it got for them to keep still and avoid detection. Charlie now also understood the reason for the pile of stinking dung and straw in the back of the lorry. Even the most zealous of policemen would hesitate to dig too deeply into that disgusting midden, so her precious petrol would remain undiscovered. Frau Schmidt explained that she had an older sister in a village just south of Magdeburg, and it was her house which was their target for today. The next day it would be the border and the crossing into the west zone. There was talk that a formal border fence would soon be built, but for now it was a piece of barren land apparently bristling with soldiers. The authorities were becoming alarmed at the number of people choosing to migrate to the west and were clamping down. The wave of emigration was depriving the east of too many of its most talented and courageous citizens, much to the benefit of the hated capitalists in the west. People had already been shot trying to leave the Soviet-controlled sector. It would be a dangerous mission for them all.

A few bone-shaking hours later, as darkness began to fall, the unlikely travelling companions reached the city of Magdeburg. The scene of devastation that confronted them was as terrible as anything Charlie had so far seen, including Dresden. In many ways it was worse. He had been prepared for Dresden for he had read about the Saint Valentine's Day raids, but he had no idea that this ancient town had been subjected to the same ferocious bombardment. Frau Schmidt was visibly shaken. She had not been to Magdeburg since before the war, and to see it lying in ruins shocked her to the core. She could not hold back her tears. 'Scheise Krieg!' she muttered. Then her voice became loud and strong as her anger rose. 'Warum denn hier?' – why here? And indeed it was hard to understand why such a place should be the target for the full aerial might of the Allies. Unless, the thought crossed Charlie's mind, it was done in retaliation for Bath or York. Tit for tat! How petty could you get? And at what cost to the women and children cowering terrified inside their houses and apartments? War, Charlie decided, was a very blunt instrument indeed. Frau Schmidt took over the driving duties for the last few kilometres to the village where her sister lived. Just after six o'clock, the lorry turned into a farmyard and came to a halt outside a small half-timbered cottage. They had arrived at last. This time it was Johann who unfastened the plank and released his siblings into the evening air. The three tumbled out and took faltering steps in the yard until feeling returned to their cramped and aching limbs. A woman built in the same sturdy mould as Frau Schmidt emerged from the house and hurried her visitors inside. Acting on the woman's instructions, Charlie drove the lorry into a wooden barn and he and Johann covered it with a tarpaulin. The barn door was then pulled to and locked with a huge iron bolt secured by a very stout padlock. Their job done, Charlie and Johann made their way across the pitch black farmyard and entered the house. Only then was a light switched on inside the building, where, Charlie noticed, all the shutters had already been wound down. There would be nothing for prying eyes to alight on here tonight.

Frau Schmidt made the introductions. 'Meine Schwester, Frau Lenz,' she said, 'und mein Schwager, Herr Lenz.' Hands were shaken. Frau Schmidt went on to explain, ' Herr Weiss kommt aus der Schweiz und hilft mir beim Fahren.' Thus Charlie's credentials both as a driver and as a person you could trust not to be a secret policeman were established. As usual, first names were not offered. There would be no relaxation of the rules even under these circumstances.

Herr Lenz went over to a small wooden cabinet from which he took out a bottle of clear liquid and eight tiny glasses. 'Pflaumen-Schnapps,' he said, 'Hausgemacht.' 'Home made plum brandy eh?' Charlie thought, 'what a treat!' Herr Lenz poured a measure of the schnapps into each glass and handed them around. Once each person had a drink, he raised his hand and called out 'Prosit!' to which the assembled company replied 'Zum Wohl!' The fiery liquid hit the back of Charlie's throat with a whoosh and made his eyes water. It was a while since he'd drunk anything stronger than a cold beer. He coughed, and the others laughed, but in a kindly way. These Swiss were not as good at drinking as Germans, everyone knew that. 'Lekker!' Charlie managed to splutter – delicious! - and this caused another wave of laughter to erupt. Brilliantly, and without even trying, Charlie had shown his vulnerability and endeared himself to the Lenzes. He was one of them. What followed was an evening of robust country food and earnest conversation. No-one wanted to talk politics, they had had enough of all that. It had been rammed down their throats during the war and even more since the communists took over. Instead they talked of family news, and of their hopes and fears for each other. Who knew when they would all be together again, if ever? Charlie sat and listened.

These people were being punished twice for having lost the war. What Frau Schmidt was doing was an act so brave yet so desperate. She was prepared to risk her own life to safeguard her children's future, and, even as a mother, to give them up so that they could be free. It was humbling, and Charlie said so. 'Danke schön, Herr Weiss,' she replied, her voice matter of fact, 'Wir machen was wir müssen.' We do what we have to do! How many tears had this woman cried, how many sleepless nights had she gone through to get to this point? Charlie would never know, for the strong, practical Frau Schmidt was not about to let down her defences and tell him. A man who hadn't been to war couldn't possibly understand.

Ten o'clock came and it was time for bed. They needed to be on the road again at six in the morning, so that they could get away before the cows needed milking and the neighbours stirred. Only Frau Schmidt and Gisela were offered a room and a bed. The rest, the men, made themselves as comfortable as they could on armchairs and rugs. The combination of the journey, the splendid food and the schnapps had worn them all out. They were asleep before their heads had even touched their makeshift pillows.

Early the next morning, they were awakened by the sounds of Frau Lenz as she brewed coffee and prepared the breakfast. Because it was a farm, there were fresh boiled eggs to go with the heavy black bread, and real butter to spread on it. There was thinly sliced white cheese and home-made Leberkäse too. It was luxury on a level that Charlie had almost forgotten in drab, cold and hungry Berlin. There you were lucky if you got a single roll and a smear of unidentifiable jam. Frau Lenz's jams were packed with fruit from her own orchard – plums principally, the ones that didn't get turned into the heartwarming schnapps they had enjoyed the night before. Only the coffee left something to be desired, for decent stuff, Frau Lenz explained, was hard to come by at any price. The travellers didn't care. They fell upon the food with gusto and declared that Frau Lenz's 'fettes, dickes Frühstück' – her big fat breakfast – was the best in the known world.

By six, they were ready to go. Frau Lenz had packed them a hearty lunch of dark sourdough bread, cheese and cold meats, along with some pickles from her larder. This was wrapped in thick paper and stashed in the back of the lorry under a hessian sack to protect it from Frau Schmidt's fetid cargo. The farewell between the sisters was brief and formal, for neither dared risk showing too much emotion. They knew it was possible they would never see each other again. A brief hug and Frau Schmidt turned and stepped up into the cab of the truck. It was left to Charlie to thank their hosts while the young ones clambered into their secret compartment for the last part of their journey. For the first two hours, they rumbled along in the dark, the weak lights of the lorry only just illuminating the bumpy road ahead. By daylight they were near the town of Halle and at once noticed a huge increase in the amount of military and police traffic. From here they would need to stick to the country roads even if it meant much slower progress, for the likelihood of there being a police checkpoint on the main roads was high. And so they headed south and west through Sachsen-Anhalt, getting ever closer to their destination, the river Werra and the border with the west. In a quiet wood, they stopped to eat the lunch made for them by Frau Lenz. She had done them proud, but the food weighed heavily in their mouths. It was the last meal the family would ever have together, and its significance was not lost on the younger ones. They did not break down though, instead they took their cue from their mother and kept a brave face.

The weather was cold and they did not linger. There was so much to say, and so little point in saying any of it.

From a hill in western Thüringia they looked out across at the land the young ones would soon, God willing, call home. All there was to do was to wait for darkness so that their approach to the border would be less conspicuous. The last few kilometres would be covered on foot without the benefit of headlights or even torches. Nothing, but nothing, must draw attention to their presence. It took Charlie right back to 1917 and the night travelling he and Albert had done. How they hadn't fallen off slippery mountainsides or into rivers in the dark was a miracle. Someone up there must have been watching out for them then. He hoped the selfsame someone would be watching out for these young people tonight. Like him and Albert, they deserved their chance.

As soon as the last little glimmer of wintry light faded, they set off. The young ones had small haversacks on their backs containing a few items of clothing, and a precious memento of home, but nothing that would give the authorities any information as to where they had come from. They had effectively jettisoned their identities, just as Charlie and Albert had thrown theirs into a shell-hole that night near Ypres. Once safely in the west zone, they could reveal who they were, but for now they were nameless. They emerged from the woods and made their way down towards the low-lying land which would take them to the river. At this point the Werra is near its source, so not wide, but in the middle of winter, unless frozen, it is fast flowing and treacherous. First, however, they had to get across the fields to the river bank undetected, then see what the river was doing and plan how to cross it. Charlie had that sinking feeling that considerable coldness and wetness was about to be involved. Crossing the Werra would not be as easy as it had been bestriding the little trickle that was the Seine. In the still night they could hear the sound of men talking, but it was impossible to tell where they were or how far away. They had to be border guards of some kind. Who else would be abroad on such a cold evening? There was nothing for it but to go with all possible speed. It was decided that Frau Schmidt would come no further, for fear that she might slow the younger ones down. Johann would go with them and wait until they were safely across then return to his mother.

It was time. One by one she took her children in her arms and gave them a swift but very firm hug. 'Auf Wiedersehen,' she whispered to each of her sons, but Charlie knew, and so did they that it was really 'Goodbye.' The last was Gisela who gave out a little sob as she embraced her mother, but quickly stifled it on catching Frau Schmidt's stern glance. 'Du müsst jetzt mutig sein, Schatzi,' the older woman said, exhorting her daughter to have courage. Then she kissed her precious girl full on the lips, and released her from her arms. Her last act was to shake Charlie's hand. 'Auf Wiedersehen, Herr Weiss,' she said, 'bitte meine Kinder in Sicherhait halten.' - keep my children safe. Charlie promised to do his best, and Frau Schmidt turned sharply on her heel and made her way back to the woods and the comparative safety of her battered old truck.

Keeping low and moving as swiftly as they could the Schmidt children and Charlie scuttled across the few hundred metres of open ground that stood between them and the river. The earth had been freshly cleared of any bushes or small trees that might offer cover to potential escapees – a clear sign that something much more formal and forbidding was planned for this place. Luckily there was only a slip of a moon peeping out from behind the clouds as the five crossed what to Charlie felt like No Man's Land. In the cold night air, they could clearly hear the men they had heard before, only this time their voices were louder, nearer. There was no doubt that they were police, and that they were patrolling the river bank.

'Scheise, noch mal!' one said to the other, 'Mir ist's kalt.' – 'Shit! it's cold!' 'Mir auch,' the other agreed. 'Great,' thought Charlie, 'a bloody weather report given by two German guard dogs is all we need!' Just then the five arrived at the edge of the river. It was only a few metres wide, but it was indeed very full after the winter rains. They were certainly going to get wet at the very least. Half frozen too by the look of it. Gisela's pale face showed how frightened she was. The river was too much for her. Charlie could tell that she was going to need help to stand up against the current. The others were strong enough to manage unaided. He bade Rainer and Werner to get across as quickly and as quietly as they could, and wait for him and Gisela on the other side. He went to take Gisela's hand to help her into the water, but Johann pushed him aside. He stared at Charlie, his eyes full of pain and determination. 'Ich mach's,' he croaked the words out through lips unused to speech, 'sie ist <u>meine</u> Schwester.' Gisela gasped. Her beloved Johann could speak again and wanted to be the one to help her across the river. She took his arm and together they walked into the raging water. Charlie dropped in behind them and the three started the treacherous crossing together. Up ahead Charlie could see that the Rainer and Werner were already on the other side and were making their way to the shelter of a small wooden cowherd's hut. Behind them he sensed that the border guards were getting ever nearer. He could smell the smoke from their cigarettes wafting on the night air. 'Schnell! schnell!' he whispered to Gisela and Johann. At that precise moment Gisela's foot slipped on a rock and she plunged into the icy water up to her shoulders. As she did so, she involuntarily let out a high pitched scream. The sound must have reached the patrolling guards almost at once, for the noise of booted feet running towards the river could be heard immediately and powerful torchlight illuminated the water. Capture seemed imminent. 'Wer ist da?' Charlie heard one of the guards call, but he was scarcely about to answer. Johann shoved Gisela's hand into Charlie's and motioned that he should get her the rest of the way. Then he called out loudly in reply 'Ich bin's. Johann. Ich bin's!' – it's me, Johann, it's me! And he turned and, waving his arms frantically, splashed his way noisily out of the river and into the beam of light on the eastern bank where the two guards were standing, by now pointing their rifles towards him. 'Was machst du?' one of the guards growled. From where he and Gisela stood, frozen with cold, yet motionless for fear of drawing attention to themselves, Charlie could hear Johann, adopting the mannerisms and tone of a simpleton, explain to the guards that he was escaping from the west. He wanted to be a communist, he said. He couldn't stand the Americans any more with their negro jazz and their disgusting Coca Cola. It was a masterful performance. The guards were completely taken aback and started to laugh. This was a story to tell the lads back at barracks! Some idiot from the west zone actually trying to break <u>in</u> to the east! What a turn up for the books! Let him come! The more the merrier. 'Geh' doch, Johann,' one said – off you go. And he pointed poor foolish Johann towards the trees, and gave him a little push. 'Da sind die Kommunisten!' he said. 'Im Wald.' The two guards left the idiot Johann to search for the communists in the wood, and as they walked away, still guffawing, but mercifully taking the light with them, Charlie thought he heard one say, 'was ein Arschloch!' Little did the guard know what the 'arsehole' had just achieved. Johann had saved their lives. He dragged Gisela the last few metres out of the river and over the field to the hut where Rainer and Werner were standing, dumb with amazement at what they had just seen and heard their brother do. He had set them free. The four crowded into the rough little shelter where Charlie, thanks to lessons taught him years ago by Albert, soon had a small fire going. They were, at least for now, safe and soon they would be warm and dry. From way over the other side of the river they heard an old engine start up, and a heavy vehicle begin to move, and they knew that Johann had made it too.

CHAPTER FIVE

A new start

The next day, having breakfasted meagrely on the remains of Frau Lenz's lunch, the four of them walked downstream until they came to the charming medieval town of Eschwege, where they presented themselves at the office of the Polizei. There the three Schmidt children told their story and claimed asylum. In keeping with West German policy, they were made most welcome, and the formal process of issuing them with citizenship papers was begun at once. It was simply a matter of finding them a place to stay until their claim could be processed, and, with typical German efficiency, not to mention thorough record-keeping, it took the desk sergeant no time at all to locate the whereabouts of their mother's cousin, Frau Heidrun Domke. Frau Domke lived in an apartment house near the centre of the town. She had no telephone, so there was nothing for it but to go there and hope to find her at home. To Charlie's surprise the sergeant offered to take them there in his police car rather than expect them to find their own way in a strange town. From Charlie's experience, the police in Italy were far less helpful, more likely to say 'non posso far niente' – I can't do anything – than to actively assist. Maybe it was something to do with the West's regret at the loss of the East to the Soviets. Whatever the reason, it was only a matter of a few minutes before they were pulling up outside a splendid half-timbered building just off the market square. The house was five stories high, and from the number of door bells and letter boxes, seemed to be divided into five apartments. It was painted white, with the timber frame picked out in deep crimson. Each window was decorated with plant pots and troughs, and even in deepest winter there was something to see growing in them – generally hardy ivies and dwarf evergreen shrubs. It reminded Charlie of Troyes which he and Albert had passed through not long after leaving Ypres. Even in the most difficult circumstances, and like Troyes in 1917, post war Germany was definitely experiencing difficult circumstances, people thought it was important to prettify their surroundings however they could. The contrast with drab and scruffy Great Harwood could not have been greater.

The policeman accompanied them, to the door of the house, and rang the bell marked 'Domke, Frau H'. It looked like the young ones' cousin lived on the ground floor in 'Wohnung Nummer 1'. That pleased Charlie. He'd had enough of rickety cold stairs in the flat he had rented in Berlin. The peel of the bell ringing about inside the building was immediately followed by the sound of feet scuttling across a tiled floor. Then the net curtain over the front window was pulled to one side, and a woman could be seen peering out into the street. The expression on her face was one of surprise, which immediately turned to alarm as she spotted the policeman at her door. 'Ich komme, ich komme!' she cried, her voice full of anxiety. A policeman was rarely the bringer of good news these days. There was a rattle of keys being turned and bolts being drawn and almost at once the great wooden front door of the house was opened. It revealed a stocky grey-haired woman of about sixty or so wearing a white apron over a smart black woollen dress. She was cast from the same mould as Frau Schmidt and Frau Lenz, but her clothing showed that she was rather better off than either of her country cousins. 'Guten Tag,' she said, rather nervously, 'Ist was los?' – is something the matter? The policeman took charge. First he introduced himself as police sergeant Hoffman, then he quickly reassured the older woman that nothing was wrong, indeed that he had a pleasant surprise for her. He went on to introduce the young ones to their cousin explaining how they had bravely escaped from the East Zone with the help of Herr Weiss and that they needed somewhere to stay until their citizenship papers were ready. Charlie noticed that the officer was not presenting this to Frau Domke as a matter of choice, rather as a duty she was expected to fulfil. There was seemingly no formal provision for the numerous refugees making their way to the West, and the authorities expected those who had family, however distantly related they may be, to be put up by them at least until they found their feet. In the face of what amounted to an official command, Frau Domke invited them in.

The apartment was immaculate, much as Charlie had expected. The traditional German Hausfrau, and Frau Domke was obviously such a one, takes great pride in her surroundings and woe betide a speck of dust that dares to settle on her polished furniture and her sparkling glassware. For the Schmidt children, used to the relative chaos of farm life, this was all new and somewhat intimidating. Apart from anything, their own clothes were grubby after the truck, the river and the night in the hut. Their embarrassment was clear for all to see and they all insisted on removing their shoes before stepping onto the gleaming tiled floor. Their cousin ushered them in and showed them to fat leather seats, onto which they gingerly lowered themselves, apologising for the state they were in. Frau Domke waved their words away with a polite 'Es macht nichts' but Charlie could see from her eyes that she was already rehearsing the clean up job that would be needed to get her precious furniture back to an acceptable state. However, there was nothing to be done, for the sergeant had information to convey and instructions to deliver, and this he did with admirable brevity and precision over the next few minutes. His job done, he rose to his feet and made to depart. In keeping with the local custom, he twice rapped the table at which he was sitting and said 'Klopf klopf!' – knock knock! – which substituted for the otherwise obligatory handshake of everyone present. Then, after actually clicking his heels together, much to Charlie's amusement, he turned sharply and left the group to get on with it.

By this time Frau Domke had got over her shock at being visited by the police and at having family she had never met billeted upon her, scruffy young family at that. She remembered her duties as a hostess and offered to make coffee for everyone. To accompany the coffee, she suggested 'das zweite Fruehstueck' – the second breakfast, generally taken in the mid morning by workers who have only had white rolls and jam before an early start to the day. The visitors accepted the offer gratefully, for they were starving after the night's exertions. It was a long time since Frau Lenz's lunch had been polished off. Frau Domke busied herself in the kitchen while the Schmidt children and Charlie held a whispered conversation in the living room. They had arrived safely and looked like being able to remain in the West Zone without much difficulty. Whether they could stay with this cousin for long was another matter. She was terribly proper, unlike their own dear mother who was a good deal more relaxed. She was also a lot older than their dear Mutti. They feared they might find it hard to fit into her well-ordered life. There would inevitably be a clash of some kind, probably when one of them forgot to hang up their clothes, or left a dirty cup in the living room. Obviously they needed to be here for a little while until the paperwork could be done, but after that they would have to make their own way. For that they would need help from someone who understood more about the ways of the world. Someone like Herr Weiss, for example. But could he stay around to help them? They had been told only very little about him, just that he was Swiss and usually lived in Italy. Did he have a family to go back to? Was someone waiting anxiously to hear from him, believing him to be stuck in besieged Berlin? Charlie was touched by the young ones' concern for him. They were showing a maturity beyond their years, and were a credit to their parents. Of course he wanted to get back to Giovanna as soon as he could, but he could also see that he had a duty here. Frau Schmidt had entrusted her precious children to him, and he owed it to her to see them safely settled. In a hectic few minutes of verbal exchanges, he agreed to stay in Germany and help them, just as long as he could get to an international telephone to let his wife know he was all right. The sense of relief amongst the Schmidt children was palpable. At that moment Frau Domke returned, bearing trays of dark bread and sliced sausage, cheese and pickles, along with a pot of aromatic coffee, the like of which Charlie had not smelled for months. The westerners may have been getting help from the Americans, but it looked and smelled like very welcome help indeed. With cries of 'Mahlzeit!' and 'Guten Appetit!' the young ones fell upon the food, groaning with pleasure at every mouthful. Charlie was content to sit back and watch them tucking in, taking the time to savour the delicious rich cream-topped coffee poured by his hostess. Only when the first cup had disappeared did he too help himself to some bread and cheese. Then suddenly, when the heat was off, the enormity of what he and the Schmidts had risked and achieved hit him. He thought of brave Frau Schmidt quietly stockpiling petrol, and preparing her battered old lorry to conceal her darling children. He thought of the young ones lying in fear of discovery in their cramped and stinking hideaway as they jolted and rattled their way westwards, and most of all, he thought of poor brave damaged Johann risking being shot to enable his siblings to escape. To everyone's consternation and amazement, not least his own, he started to sob. Frau Domke looked away, embarrassed, after all real men don't cry, well, not real German ones anyway. Gisela stood up and went over to Charlie. She placed an arm gently about his heaving shoulders and said softly, 'Sie können jetzt ruhig weinen, Herr Weiss, die Gefahr ist vorbei' – 'you can weep now, the danger is past', thus giving him permission to let out all the suppressed emotions of the last few days. In that instant, the built up tensions and anxieties ebbed away and, for the first time since arriving in Berlin, Charlie felt like a free man.

Where the past meets the present

After breakfast, there was business to attend to. For Charlie the most pressing item was to make contact with Giovanna. Few people in rural Germany had telephones. Much of the infrastructure of society had been destroyed in the last weeks of the war as the Wehrmacht had made its frenzied retreat to Berlin, slashing, burning and laying waste to everything in their wake in a feeble and doomed attempt to prevent the Americans and the British from catching them up. The hardship and poverty of the years immediately after the fighting ceased meant that even basic supplies were hard to come by. Luxuries like domestic telephones were out of the question. National and local government offices had them though. By now Frau Domke was warming to this stranger who had saved her cousins from the communists, even if he did blub like a baby. She told Charlie about her sister's boy, Günther, who was something important in the Arbeitsamt – the Labour Exchange as Charlie knew it. He had a telephone in his office for his own use only. Maybe Herr Weiss could make a call to his wife from there. The young ones, glad of a chance to be useful, cleared away the breakfast and washed up, while Charlie and Frau Domke set off into town to track down the nephew and his precious 'Apparat'.

On the way Frau Domke took the opportunity to pump Charlie for details of life in the East Zone, and to get a report on the health of her two cousins Frau Schmidt and Frau Lenz, who, Charlie heard for the first time, had the Christian names of Christina and Gabrielle. She was shocked to hear of the disappearance of Christina's husband. Those communists were clearly just as evil as she had read in the pages of the Eschweger Tägliche Zeitung. Although she had never married, she said, she could imagine how dreadful it must be to lose your soulmate and the father of your children. Then the old woman started to say something else, 'Ich selbst...' but checked herself. A tear came into her eye. Charlie looked at her with concern. What could be upsetting her so? 'Frau Domke,' he said gently, taking her arm, 'was ist's?'

The woman thought for a bit, sat herself down on a park bench, then slowly she replied that, like Herr Weiss, she too had tears to shed. Hers were for the fiancé she had last seen as he marched proudly off to war in the summer of 1914, full of hope and enthusiasm. He had been a hero at Mons in the opening skirmishes. He and his pals had seen those English soldiers off right smartly, nearly ending the war before it had properly begun. For a while after Mons, his letters got through regularly. Then came 1916 and the battle of the Somme and after that the mail pretty much dried up. She feared the worst, but no telegram came, so she remained optimistic that he would one day march back into her life and that they would pick up where they had left off. They would get married, have some children and lead a nice quiet decent life – 'ein anständiges Leben' - together. For a year she heard nothing, then, in the summer of 1917 there were reports of fierce fighting in Belgium in a place called Paschendale near a town called Ypres. The loss of life was said to be catastrophic, not just for the hated Allies but among the German boys too. At the end of the year the news she had been dreading finally came. She was at her work as a seamstress one afternoon, when her fiancé's mother unexpectedly came into the shop, a thing she rarely, if ever, did. She looked terrible, as if she had aged twenty years overnight. Her hair had turned white and eyes were red and swollen from crying. Heidrun took one look at her and she knew. Her darling was dead. The English had spent three years trying to kill him and now they had. The two women fell into each other's arms and sobbed. A few days later, the older woman was also dead. Quite unable to live with the loss of her only son, she had thrown herself from a bridge into the fast-flowing Werra. From that day on Heidrun determined never to love anyone again. True to her resolve, she had remained single and lived alone for the past thirty two years, always wearing black, only taking the title 'Frau' when her age dictated that the term 'Fraülein' was no longer appropriate. She was a victim of the Great War, just as so many German women her age were. So were the generation that followed them, thanks to Hitler. Now it looked like Stalin was making widows of her dear cousin and the women of the East. Would it never end? Would Germany never be at peace? So saying, Frau Domke put her head in her hands and cried quietly.

Sitting beside her, Charlie was dumbstruck. This was the other side of the coin, described in graphic detail. He knew only too well what Frau Domke's fiancé had gone through, but he could never tell her that. Had he and Albert stayed in the trenches, it might well have been either one of them that had killed the German, assuming they had survived long enough to do so. They would assuredly have tried. Like many of the women in Britain, Frau Domke and others like her in Germany had been condemned to live single lonely lives because their toffs and the generals had just had to give their British counterparts a bloody nose. Now her cousins were suffering because Stalin had to show the Americans who was boss. Charlie wondered if anyone actually ever won a war. It didn't seem like it. Poor battered so-called victorious England was on its knees physically and financially, nearly four years after the end of the fighting. Rationing was certainly still very much in force. His own family had less meat on their table most days than Frau Domke had offered him and the Schmidt youngsters for breakfast. Fairness didn't enter into it. Yet this woman sitting beside him had lost her love, her happiness and her future, and was herself a casualty of war along with the murdered millions lying in France and Belgium. Theirs had been a death sentence. Frau Domke had got life, and had been punished every day since. Hearing her story Charlie felt he would never be able to put the war behind him. There were reminders everywhere, thirty years on, and they kept on popping up when you least expected them, to.

The woman gradually recovered her composure and the two of them made their way into the business centre of Eschwege and the Arbeitsamt. From her chair behind a thick glass screen, the stern-faced receptionist was at first reluctant to allow them to see Frau Domke's nephew, her boss, because they did not have an appointment, and no-one, but no-one, saw Herr Schwarz without an appointment. She eventually agreed to telephone through to his office, and was clearly surprised that he was prepared not only to see them, but actually to come downstairs to collect them, personally, himself. Almost immediately, the sound of metal heel and toe plates bouncing on marble stairs heralded Herr Schwarz's arrival in the lobby. He was a tall, fit-looking man in his early forties, and he bounded athletically across to the desk where his aunt was standing. In keeping with German custom, he shook her hand – no sloppy face-kissing like the French for these people! – and acknowledged her quite formally. 'Guten Tag, Tante Heidrun,' he said, clicking his highly-polished heels together, and slightly nodding his head. She responded in an equally formal manner. It all seemed very cold to Charlie, and was nothing like the way he would ever have greeted an aunt of his own. He formed an instant dislike for this fellow with his pseudo-military mannerisms. But then he thought to himself that this chap was not from an army background, surely. He was, from what his aunt had said, one of the lucky ones. Way too young for the Great War and just too old for the second one, he had managed to avoid being sent into combat and instead had been able to live a nice quiet life as a 'Beamter' – a civil servant – with all the status and perks involved with that highly respected, even privileged, position. He was the very picture of success. His clothing was immaculate, and his every hair was in place. He doubtless had a spacious and well-appointed apartment, a lovely wife who stayed home and cared for it, and two children, one of each, both doing well at school. To Charlie's eye, he looked a bit self-satisfied, a bit smug. He seemed like a man used to having people to boss around, probably mostly women as one by one his younger male colleagues were forced to enlist. The women would be only too ready to do his bidding, whether in the office or at home, since two of the virtues most valued in a member of the female sex were devotion to duty and obedience. Much as he was predisposed to hate him, Charlie knew he must not let these completely unfounded first impressions get in the way. He needed this man if he were to be able to telephone Giovanna, so, on Frau Domke's signal, he stepped forward and shook the man's hand, even managing a smile as she introduced them. 'Herr Schwarz, Herr Weiss,' she said, and the irony of their two names was not lost upon Charlie. She might as well have said 'Herr Chalk and Herr Cheese!'

The nephew turned to the woman behind the desk and issued a gruff command. 'Frau Schäffer - Kaffee für drei im Büro' Not a 'bitte' or a 'danke' to be heard! The rude swine! The receptionist leapt to her feet at once, saying 'Jawohl, Herr Direktor, sofort,' and hurried off to make the coffee. Herr Schwarz pointed his visitors in the direction of the staircase, and led them up the stone steps to his office. It was a grand staircase and it led to a grand room, wood-panelled and thickly carpeted. Charlie was beginning to think he was right about this fellow. He was the Director of a small town Labour Exchange and he had an office that could have belonged to the chairman of the Board of some big London company or other. Being a German civil servant obviously meant something rather special. There was no comparison with the experiences men just a few years younger than him had recently gone through, not least poor damaged Johann.

The three crossed the room and sat on either side of Herr Schwarz's great mahogany desk. The desk had a dark green leather inset upon which was laid a thick block of soft white blotting paper. Fountain pens, pencils and three colours of ink were arranged meticulously along the top end of the block, all just waiting to be called into signing duty or whatever it was Herr Schwarz did. To the right of the desk stood a big black telephone. There was, Charlie noticed, no evidence that Herr Schwarz was actually working on anything. There was no paperwork in progress, no ledgers open, nothing. Their arrival must have given him something to do. No wonder he had come down to collect them. Perhaps he needed the exercise! A chap could seize up sitting at a desk all day! 'You have to stop, this Herr Cheese,' Charlie thought to himself, 'he'll pick up on it and get nasty.' At that moment there was a gentle cough to be heard from the landing outside. 'Herein!' — enter! - called their host, peremptorily, and the heavy wooden door was pushed open to reveal Frau Schäffer struggling to carry three coffees, cream and sugar and get into the Director's office at the same time. Charlie leapt to his feet and went to help her. Herr Schwarz, he noticed, stayed right where he was, in his seat of power, ensconced in his mahogany fortress. 'Darf Ich?' Charlie asked the woman — May I? — and her grateful smile spoke volumes. Charlie carried the tray to the desk and placed it next to the telephone. Then he turned to the flustered receptionist and said 'Danke Schön, Frau Schäffer.' 'Bitte Schön' came the customary reply and the woman turned quickly and slipped silently out of the office, shutting the massive door behind her.

Herr Schwarz settled into host mode, graciously offering his visitors cream and sugar to accompany the delicious-smelling coffee. 'You'd think he'd made it himself!' thought Charlie, but what he said was 'Danke, Herr Schwarz, sehr nett von Ihnen.' — very kind of you. No point in ruffling feathers when you need a favour. Even the feathers of a goose like this man.

The coffee taken, Herr Schwarz leaned back in his chair and asked what he could do for his guests. Frau Domke explained how it was that Herr Weiss had helped their young cousins make their dangerous escape from the east zone, and him a Swiss with no need to get involved except for the goodness of his heart and his desire to be of service. Now it was Herr Weiss who needed some help, and that was to have the use of a telephone to make a call to his wife in Italy, telling her he was safe and well. Günther was the only person she knew who had access to a machine on which international calls could be made. So they had come to throw themselves upon his generosity and ask the favour. Herr Schwarz listened attentively. It was an excellent story, and one on which he expected to dine out for some time to come. He especially liked the bit about cousin Johann pretending to be escaping <u>into</u> the East Zone. Those communist border guards must be even more stupid than people said they were! There was a bit of a problem though. It was rather frowned on to use the office telephone for personal calls, although of course a chap did from time to time and the finance people turned a blind eye, seeing as they were all at it themselves. An international call, however, had to be connected through the international operator and would show up on the bill as a much higher amount than usual. The accountants were bound to notice and have questions to ask. It would not be possible to cover up a call to Italy. Herr Schwarz was troubled and thought hard. He was just about to say no when the solution came to him. Herr Weiss was a hero! He had helped three young Germans to get away from the Stalinists and become free! He could hardly stand in the way of a hero now could he? In fact, once it became known that he, Günther Schwarz, had helped this brave Swiss, he would be something of a hero himself in his own little way. Let the finance boys criticise him then! They wouldn't dare! He hadn't been able to show the world his manly qualities in the war, but he could now.

News from home and abroad

Nodding and smiling, he picked up the receiver and turned the calling handle briskly. Frau Schäffer came on the line at once. 'Ja, Herr Direktor?' Herr Schwarz's voice was decisive and strong as he instructed her to connect him at once to the International Exchange in Frankfurt. 'Herr Weiss will seine Frau in Italien telefonieren,' he explained. 'Jawohl, Herr Direktor,' the woman replied, excitement in her voice. A few moments later, the big black telephone shrilled and it was indeed Frankfurt calling. Herr Schwarz handed the receiver to Charlie and he and Frau Domke tactfully left the room. Charlie was sure they were hovering on the landing but he didn't care. In what seemed like no time at all the operator had taken the number in faraway Matera and had made the connection. Charlie's heart was pounding as he heard the sound of the telephone in his own house ringing. He could imagine Giovanna hearing it, looking up from her book or her sewing and thinking to herself 'who rings at this hour of the day? Civilised people are having lunch.' She would now be getting to her feet, and making her way down the tiled hall to the panelled entrance foyer which contained the telephone. She might even be slightly annoyed, and mutter 'Si! si! lo veno' - 'Yes, yes I'm coming!' Charlie pictured her arriving in front of the big old wooden telephone which was mounted on the wall, and picking up the receiver. 'Pronto!' he heard Giovanna say, 'chi parla?' The sound of his wife's voice knocked all the breath from his body. My God! he had missed her these past few months. He could scarcely speak. 'Chi parla?' Giovanna said again, slightly crossly. 'E Charlie,' was all her husband could say before bursting into tears. Giovanna let out a high squeak of shock. 'Charlie! Caro mio!' and she too cried for happiness.
There was not much time for small talk, for international telephone calls not only cost a fortune, the lines were erratic and could be cut at any time so they both recovered their composure as quickly as they could. Charlie told her where he was and gave her a brief resume of recent events. Most of all, he reassured her,

he was safe and well, just not quite able to come home immediately until he saw the Schmidt youngsters settled. He owed that much to their mother who had, after all, got him out of the east zone while getting out was still possible. Giovanna knew from the newspapers how bad things were becoming in Germany and understood that he must do his duty as he saw it. Much as it pained her, she agreed that he must stay. Then she went on to say that she also had news for Charlie, and this was not of the happy variety. There had been some events in the family and Charlie needed to know about them. One concerned Alberto's uncle Dick with whom Charlie had lived and worked all those years ago. Before Christmas, a letter had come to Matera from Scarborough. It was addressed to Charlie, but she, Giovanna, had opened it as she had no idea how long it would be before he came back. As it was in English, she had asked Alberto to read it. As he did, he gasped with shock and sadness. It was from his cousin Jeannie, now quite grown up and with a husband and children of her own. Her news was bad. It seemed her father was in the habit of striding around the hilly town at all hours and in all weathers. Since his beloved Eliza had died of cancer towards the end of the war, he could not sit in the house but needed to get out to breathe the fresh sea air and think his thoughts. Despite his age – eighty six - he was still fit and strong and his legs carried him about at a brisk pace. Early one morning, before the sun was quite up over the icy sea, he had stepped out onto the promenade, not expecting there to be any traffic, and he had been knocked down by a taxi speeding a woman to the maternity unit of Scarborough Hospital. He had died almost instantly at the scene. Jeannie assured Charlie that her father had not suffered, that his death was nothing like as protracted and painful as her mother's had been. He had had, as the English say 'a good innings'. In recent years, he had missed his wife terribly, but still had many friends in the town and was often to be seen sitting on a bench and chatting to folk. He looked set to live for a good few years more. His loss was sudden and unexpected and had hit Jeannie hard, for she was used to caring for him, as she had for her mother, along with her children. She felt there was nothing for her in Scarborough any more, and as soon as her husband was demobbed and came home, they planned to sell up and move to New Zealand, where her sister Alice was prepared to help them get on their feet. Charlie was flabbergasted to hear all this. He hadn't even known about Eliza's death, the wartime postal service being what it was, and now this tragedy involving Dick. Poor Jeannie! His heart went out to her. A young woman alone looking after little ones with her husband on military duty, and caring for ailing and ageing parents. It could not have been easy. But was New Zealand the answer? Charlie had not forgotten the time he had spent on the farm with Alice and her ghastly menfolk. All he could hope was that time or the influence of women had mellowed them. Or better still, that they had all dropped dead!

Anyway, this was not the moment for that conversation. Giovanna had said that 'events' had taken place. 'What else?' he asked her, 'not more doom and gloom I hope?' Giovanna's second piece of news was quite the opposite of doom and gloom, at least as she saw it, although some of the family thought differently. It concerned Giuseppe, by now well established as a solo performer at La Scala. It seemed he had indeed been having an affair with the Contessa da Mosto and that she was expecting his baby in the spring! Hundreds of kilometres to the south, and a couple of decades back in time, the news had caused shockwaves to reverberate around the del Piero family farm. Alberto and Caterina were to be grandparents and were naturally excited, but their son was not married to the mother of his child and the pair was showing no sign of planning a wedding. Apparently, the Contessa's family wanted her to marry more appropriately to her social standing, and an opera singer from the sticks did not fit the bill. Without her father's blessing, marriage was out of the question. This state of affairs did not go down well in Catholic Italy, certainly not in the rural south. Sophia, predictably enough, was horrified that her grandson had tied himself up with a 'posh puttanesca', and was bringing disgrace on the del Piero name. She had known from the outset that woman, that Contessa, was trouble, and here was the proof! Her beloved Giuseppe had been led astray by an upper class tart and was now bringing a, well, a bastard, into the world! Oh the shame! And to think the woman had been chaperoning her precious granddaughters! What the neighbours would make of it all, she dreaded to contemplate. And, so saying, Sophia took to her bed and there she had stayed for several days until Giovanni had persuaded her to come out. 'It's done, Sophia,' he said, 'no amount of crying and wringing your hands will undo it. Now come out and support your daughter and son-in-law. This should be a happy time. This baby will be our great grandchild, no matter whether his or her parents are married or not. We've had enough death and destruction these past few years, let's just be glad that there is new life and a future to live for!' Giovanna confessed she had never heard her father be quite so forthright with her mother before, and it had done the trick. The old woman got up, tidied her hair, smoothed her apron, and emerged defiantly to face the world. Let the neighbours gossip! She was going to be a great grandmother! And her great grandchild would be the handsomest, the most talented and the cleverest child in all of Italy, so there!

As she told the story, Giovanna could hardly keep the mirth out of her voice and Charlie could just see Sophia re-writing history for public consumption. She had always admired the Contessa and was delighted that she and Giuseppe were to have a child together. Of course it would be better if they were married but these were modern times. It was nearly half way through the twentieth century, and she, Sophia was a modern woman. That was too much for Charlie and he burst out laughing. In faraway Matera, Giovanna was chortling too. How she missed having her darling Charlie by her side to share these moments. Suddenly she went quiet and serious. They had been talking for twenty minutes. It was time to end the call. Even Herr Schwarz's finance boys might have something to say about such an expense. Charlie used the final few seconds to tell his wife how much he loved and missed her. Squeezing back the tears she said 'Ti amo Charlie', then in English 'Come home soon.' A final 'ciao' and it was time to hang up.

Charlie slumped back in his chair, drained by the torrent of emotion he was feeling. He covered his face with his hands and wept, tears of –what? surely joy at having spoken to Giovanna after so long, relief at hearing her say how much she loved him, and maybe too some sorrow for Jeannie Donkin and the splendid man that had been her father. All in all, he felt quite empty. This time it was Frau Domke's turn to be the comforter. She crept into the office and handed Charlie a glass of icy mineral water, and a soft silk handkerchief for his eyes. 'Na na, Herr Weiss,' she said, 'es ist schon gut,' and she patted his hand in a kindly manner. Charlie was touched. He hardly knew this woman, and was once, although she did not know it, her hated foe. But here she was, responding as women always do when care is needed, with sympathy and concern. Herr

Schwarz at least had the decency to stay out of his office until Charlie was quite recovered. Maybe he wasn't so bad after all. Or maybe he just couldn't bear to see a grown man cry like a girl. A few minutes later Charlie and Frau Domke went down the marble stairs and bade him farewell. Charlie was grateful for the use of the telephone, and said so as he shook the Direktor's hand. 'Auf Wiedersehen, Herr Schwarz,' he said but secretly he hoped it was 'goodbye'.

Retracing steps

For the next few days and weeks, there was not a lot to be done. The wheels of bureaucracy took their time to turn, and until they had come to the end of their rotation, the Schmidt youngsters had to stay where they were. Luckily, their cousin turned out to be less starchy than they had feared, so with a bit of give and take it was possible for the generations to get along. The winter was a delight. Every day dawned bright and sunny but icy cold, and the young ones and Charlie soon got into the habit of leaving the apartment after breakfast and going for long walks in the countryside. They would take some bread and cheese or sausage with them and not return until the light was fading. This gave Frau Domke some needed breathing space, for her small and immaculate apartment was at full stretch to accommodate four extra people. Luckily the authorities had the means to make some funds available for refugees from the east, otherwise she would have struggled to feed her guests. There was no way of the young ones earning a living, as all they knew was farm work, and in mid winter there is precious little that can be done. The livestock were all in barns and nothing was growing. Luckily for Charlie, not eligible for any assistance and long since out of money from his erstwhile employers in Rome, there was a US airbase nearby and once again his translation skills came to his rescue. The job was procured for him by Herr Schwarz, and meant he could work a day or two a week and earn some much-needed cash. It also reunited him with the Americans, and re-established some personal connections made years earlier with members of the occupying forces. Two years on, General Green was still the man in charge in these parts, and he had not forgotten the part Herr Weiss had played in helping the US to cross the bridge at Remagen in the closing days of the war. In fact, he still told the tale every now and then when he wanted his troops to go above and beyond the call of duty. From his desk in Frankfurt, he was glad to approve the appointment of a civilian translator, knowing full well that there was no-one better equipped for the job than this brave Swiss. In fact, he went a stage further than that, for when he was told what it was that had brought Herr Weiss to Eschwege, he offered his services in helping the Schmidt youngsters to settle in the West. Frankfurt, he told Charlie, had much more going on than Eschwege by way of education and employment, and, by pulling strings and calling in a few favours General Green could get them jobs and places on college courses. He could even arrange housing. If the young ones were prepared to knuckle down and work hard, they could certainly carve out a good life for themselves in the emerging German economy.

And so it was a few weeks later, their new West German identity papers in their pockets, that Rainer, Werner and Gisela, along with Charlie, boarded a train In Eschwege to take them the couple of hundred kilometres south and west to the state capital of Hessen. Frau Domke had accompanied them to the station and there was genuine sorrow at the parting. The older woman had turned out to be warm and loving beneath her fastidious, even slightly forbidding, exterior and the young ones felt real affection for her. With promises to come back ringing in the air, they leapt excitedly into their carriage. Charlie took a moment or two longer to say his farewells. Frau Domke and he had become quite close, each having exposed their vulnerability to the other. For once, as the habitual 'auf Wiedersehens' were said, it was not her hand that Frau Domke offered but her cheek. Honoured, Charlie bent and kissed her lightly on both sides of her face. 'Wie die Franzosen,' – like the French – he said. 'Ja!' she said, and laughed, 'wie mann's in Frankreich macht. Es ist viel freundlicher.' Like they do it in France – much more friendly. With one last 'auf Wiedersehen' Charlie turned away and joined the young ones on the train. They had been watching the interaction between their mother's cousin and their new friend, and were stunned. The old girl was a softie at heart! Up in the hot cabin of the locomotive, the driver and his fireman built up a head of steam, and suddenly, with a mighty 'choof!' the wheels started to turn and the train began to move forward. The Schmidt youngsters crowded to the platform side of the carriage to wave goodbye to their cousin. She returned their salute, but much more restrainedly, indeed she could be seen to be dabbing her eyes with a square of fine silk. Charlie caught her glance. She mouthed some words at him. 'Bitte auf die Kinder gut aufpassen Herr Weiss.' – please look after the children well. Charlie mouthed back that he would , and then she was out of sight as the train pulled out of the station. Charlie wondered if he or the Schmidt children would ever see Frau Domke again. He hoped the young ones would, for the old lady had been kind to them, but for himself, he doubted it. His future lay elsewhere, and once he had the youngsters settled, he would not be lingering in Germany.

A few short hours later they arrived at the imposing structure that is the central station in Frankfurt. Built at the height of the age of the train, the Hauptbahnhof had all the hallmarks of nineteenth century confidence. Large, lavishly decorated and with grand glass arcades, it reminded Charlie of other stations he had seen in England at places like York and Manchester. It struck him how alike the British and the Germans had been at one time, both major industrial economies and doing very well. How had it all turned so sour? The commonly-accepted version was that the Germans were jealous of the British Empire, their own colonial ambitions having been dwarfed by the success of the Victorians. But Charlie had read some theories that it was in fact bitter industrial competition that had originally drawn the two states into the first war as each tried to outdo the other. 'My ship is bigger than yours!' 'My navy's faster than yours!' He could just hear the King and the Kaiser taunting each other like playground rivals. Or rather the super-rich powerful industrialists who professed to put king and country first, but who were really devoted to the making of money, and lots of it. Behind them were the upper class lackeys, the half witted younger sons of the aristocracy who had found their way into the army for lack of anything better to do. Yes, it was the toffs and the generals on both sides that had allowed the greatest ever human catastrophe to happen. Charlie shook his head as if to dispel his thoughts. Funny how they just crept in when you least expected them. He got to his feet and collected up his few belongings. 'Auf Kinder!' he said, 'Jetzt geht's los!!' – come on kids, we're off!

In Frankfurt it was already spring, for the city was a few degrees warmer than the countryside, and everywhere lime green shoots were appearing in municipal gardens and sticky buds were on the trees. When Charlie had passed through this city exactly two years earlier, in the spring of 1947, the signs of wartime destruction were to be seen everywhere. Now there was evidence of rebuilding on a massive scale as the scars of war were covered over. Charlie guessed the same might be happening all over Germany, or at least in the west, where American money was pouring in. People made homeless by bombardment would be being re-housed in the brand spanking new, if deeply ugly, apartment blocks that Charlie could see springing up all around the city. It was ironic that the same wasn't happening even yet in London and the other ravaged English cities. Winning the war had used up all the money. Winning the peace was harder to do, and it looked as if Germany might have the edge there.

The four of them walked into town from the station and headed for the river. Charlie wanted to see what the Römerplatz looked like these days, and as they entered the old square he was pleasantly surprised. The ancient market place had been partially rebuilt, but not in the horrible modern grey concrete that was being used for housing. Instead skilled builders and craftsmen had re-created some of the medieval merchants' houses that had stood on that spot for hundreds of years until being obliterated in a fit of pique one night in 1945. The facades were half-timbered and painted in bright traditional colours. At every window there was a trough of winter pansies and primulas in full bloom, the yellows and the purples jostling for attention with the reds and the pinks. It was stunning. After the dull, damaged east zone it was a sight for sore eyes, and the youngsters let out a gasp of pleasure. 'Das ist also schön !' Gisela put into words what she and her brothers were thinking. 'That's what money can do!' Charlie was thinking, 'You won't find this in Coventry!' They walked across the square to the river and the old iron bridge – the Eiserner Steg – that crosses the Main and joins central Frankfurt to its southern suburbs. In the spring sunshine, the water glistened and dazzled them. On the bank they sat at one of the many cafés that were doing a good trade and ordered a restorative Kaffee und Kuchen. The coffee was served with cream and was rich and flavoursome. Charlie ordered a little tot of fiery Kirsch schnapps to go with his. The selection of cakes was astounding. The youngsters could hardly choose between them. Creamy sweet Schokoladentorte or slightly sour Zwetschgenkuchen with its topping of stewed plums? Safe and familiar Apfelkuchen or something more mysterious with spices from faraway places? Eventually they did decide and their choices were carried to the table by a waitress in a smart black dress with a crisply starched white apron and a lacy cap, a creature from a bygone era. You wouldn't know there had even been a war, the way people were sitting so relaxed and chatting in the sun, enjoying the afternoon and the fruits of the baker's art. It reminded Charlie of other places, like Portofino where people had gone to have fun even though the Great War was raging, or Milano the first time he had visited that city in 1925. Where it didn't remind him of was anywhere in postwar England. These Germans knew how to switch off and enjoy themselves. They expected to work hard but also to have time for pleasure. In many ways Charlie was envious and wondered if Britain would ever really get closer to the way of life people took for granted on the continent.

The coffee drunk and every last crumb of the cake devoured, it was time to find out where they would be living. They headed for the Strassenbahn, the tram, that would take them to the American military headquarters which lay a few kilometres to the north of the city centre. There General Green's aide would be expecting them and would show them to their quarters. They passed through heavily guarded gates, where a sentry made a phone call to make certain that these Germans were in fact bona fide visitors, and made their way to the General's office. A smartly- uniformed young American woman was waiting for them there and she stepped forward to greet them as they arrived. She introduced herself as Lieutenant – which, in the American way she pronounced Lootenant – Jenny Jones. 'Welcome, Mr Weiss, welcome Schmidt family!' she said smiling cheerily, 'come in!' and she ushered them into a drab khaki-painted waiting area. 'Do take a seat,' she went on. The Schmidts looked at each other with some alarm. It had just hit them forcibly that they would have to conduct some of their life in English in the future, and they hardly had a word between them. Charlie thanked the Lieutenant, and intimated to the youngsters that they should sit down on one of the comfortable couches that lined the walls. The aide explained that the General was not there at present, but that he hoped to meet up with Mr Weiss and the Schmidt family within the next day or two. In the meanwhile, they should settle themselves in and find their way around their new home. She then led the party, who by now had fallen into a nervous silence, out towards a waiting Jeep and gestured that they should get in. Throwing their few things into the back, Charlie and the Schmidts boarded the vehicle. It was a far cry from the conditions they had endured in their mothers' ropy old truck. It wasn't luxurious by any stretch of the imagination, but they had the wind in their hair and the sun in their eyes, as they were driven west up the Mainzer Landstrasse to where their apartment building was located. As they drove, the Lieutenant explained the situation to Charlie. It seemed the General had a useful contact who owned some flats, and was prepared to let refugees from the east have one for a minimal rent until they could find something of their own. Many people in the West Zone felt sorry for those trapped in the Soviet bloc and were pleased to do whatever they could to help them. Many had family still caught behind what Churchill had so perceptively dubbed the Iron Curtain. Herr Raab was such a man. He could have let the apartment several times over since the war, could have named his price, but instead he chose to keep one flat spare for the most needy. This humanitarian attitude of his would now benefit the Schmidts. Charlie expressed their gratitude, and the hope that they would be able to meet and thank Herr Raab themselves. Lieutenant Jones was a fast driver, though not a dangerous one, and they soon found themselves outside a large old house that had somehow miraculously escaped the bombing which had destroyed so much of the city. The apartment set aside for Mr Weiss and the Schmidts, she explained, was on the fourth floor, and there was no elevator. 'Good for staying fit!' she joked. 'Blimmin' marvellous!' thought Charlie, 'at nearly fifty-two I need this, as the Americans say, like a hole in the head!' The group made their way up to their new abode. It was hard to say who found the climb worse, Charlie or the Schmidts, none of them being used to stairs after the weeks at Frau Domke's ground floor flat in Eschwege. Certainly Lieutenant Jones took it in her stride, and bounded up the hard stone steps as if they were an assault course created for a child. Charlie at least had the consolation that it was one floor lower than his tatty little place in Berlin hade been. It would still concentrate the mind when planning a trip to the shops though. You don't pop out on impulse for a crusty little white brötchen or a bottle of wine when you live four flights up!

The Lieutenant showed them into the flat, and gave Charlie all the information he needed to operate the appliances and the heating. It seemed to him that all they had to do was to get some food and settle in. General Green had already thought of this though, and when Lieutenant Jones opened the cupboards, they were full of tins and packets of American food of all kinds. In addition to that, there was a small refrigerator which contained milk and butter, some square white bread, ready-cut, sliced cheese and ham and fresh vegetables for a day or two. The Schmidt children were impressed. Herr Weiss was clearly a man of some importance to the Americans. How lucky that they had him to help them start their new life. Mutti would be thrilled if she saw all this! Leaving them to explore the rest of the apartment and decide who would sleep where, the Lieutenant turned smartly on her heels, saluted Charlie in the typically languid US Army manner, said ''Bye for now, Mr Weiss, 'bye kids!' and made her way rapidly downstairs to the Jeep. From four floors below Charlie heard the great door of the apartment house slam shut. An engine revved up noisily, and the Lieutenant was gone.

Big changes

Over the next few days, the Schmidts and Charlie explored the city and tried to get their bearings. The General had allowed a breathing space between their arrival and the start of their work and education, so they were able to become familiar with the layout of the town, and to get used to the abundance of supplies and facilities available in the west zone. There were not only provisions in the shops, there were great paintings in the Kunsthaus, films at the cinema and books in the public library. Food for the body and the soul indeed. The Schmidts also used the time to get going on their crash course in English. Charlie agreed to be their first teacher, but made it clear that they would need to find another tutor to take over when he left for Italy. This he would do, he told them, as soon as he felt they could manage to put the components of their new lives together. They needed to achieve a balance between work and education, care for themselves properly and allow some time just for fun. This day, he advised them, needed to come sooner rather than later. He was dying to get back to Italy and his beloved Giovanna.

Much in Frankfurt had changed since the end of the war. The bombing which had rained down in the closing days of the conflict had been disproportionate to the city's strategic importance, and much of what had been the old town had simply disappeared. Charlie had not visited Dresden since flying over it with Giovanna, but he suspected that, without the huge influx of American money enjoyed by the West Zone and with Stalin's continued emphasis on funding military activity, the rebuilding in the East would be nowhere near as advanced as here. As it stood, life in Frankfurt was starting to return to relative normality. There was much to be done and money to be earned. Charlie was intrigued to note how many of the workers on the building sites and the roads were clearly not Germans but foreigners, many of them of a Mediterranean appearance. Some enterprising souls from further south and east, anxious to avoid being drawn into Stalin's ever expanding web, had obviously realised early on that post-war western Germany was desperately short of manpower and had made their way there to see what scraps of work they might pick up. Short on education, but long on physical strength and willing to work hard, these men that Charlie watched as they went about their daily tasks were impressive. Some of them had a smattering of basic German, and he was able to talk to them about their lives as he walked along the city streets. Most of them were living in cramped and dreary conditions, often sleeping six or more to a room and eating very poorly, but they did not care, for their priority was to earn money to send back to the families they had left behind, especially those whose families were in countries rapidly being turned into satellites of the Soviet Union. Many of them harboured the hope that they may one day get their wives and children, mothers, fathers, sisters and brothers out to join them, though inside themselves they knew that the communists' grip was tightening by the day and that escape was becoming less and less likely. Charlie admired their courage and dogged determination. Some of them had faced great hardship to get away. One man told Charlie how he and five other men, all relatives, had managed to wriggle out of Tito's iron grip in Yugoslavia. Posing as rather unlikely holidaymakers, they had travelled on foot down from the mountains of their native Serbia through Bosnia-Herzegovina to the Croatian coast. He described how they had ducked and darted through the tiny lanes of ancient Sarajevo with its mosques and veiled women, hardly speaking and being careful to avoid drawing any attention to themselves. Then they had picked their way alongside the steep-sided gorge where the dark green river Neretva runs through to the sea, and crossed at Mostar by the single exquisite arch of the medieval bridge. Their poor scruffy clothes and meagre luggage did not fit well with their cover story and they knew it would not be long before some eagle-eyed military policeman demanded to know what they were doing so far from their homes. They had to act quickly if they were to avoid suspicion, so almost as soon as they got to the coast they dispersed, arranging to meet again only under cover of darkness. Charlie's informant, whose name, it transpired, was Goran, then told how he had scouted around amongst the deserted holiday homes formerly owned by rich Italians until he had found a small wooden boat. This he managed to row up the coast to the port of Split where he met up once again with his companions. The beautiful coastline of Croatia is dotted with innumerable small islands which offer excellent cover and the group were able to head north pretty much unseen except by fishermen and others lucky enough to be able to afford a holiday by the sea. No-one was curious as to why six men should be crowded into one small dinghy. In Tito's Yugoslavia they could be illegal emigrants or they could be members of the secret police. It paid not to ask. What you don't know, you can't be forced to tell.

Taking it in turns to row, the men hugged the rocky coast as far as Pula, hoping to be able to go overland from there to Trieste in Italy where they would claim asylum. However, the countryside leading to the border was bristling with Tito's troops and military police, well prepared for just such an eventuality, and a new plan had to be devised. Although it seemed the height of folly, they decided to try and get to freedom in Italy by sea. This meant rowing west from just north of Pula to Venice, a journey across deep waters and one fraught with danger. The little boat which had doubtless suited its former owners as a pleasure craft pottering about in the shallows off Split would now be severely tested by the waves of the open Adriatic. They would have to leave Croatia by night to avoid detection, and cover the distance to Venice in the shortest possible time, which would put a severe strain on them all. For Goran, though, the worst danger came from the fact that only he of the six travelling companions could swim. If someone was swept overboard by a wave he might not be able to save them. But what choice did they have other than to go on? Give themselves up as defectors and face imprisonment or worse? They wouldn't be able to help their wives and children from a prison cell or the gallows.

Listening to Goran, Charlie was reminded of the perils he and Albert had faced as deserters . Everyone they had met on their long journey was a potential informer or policeman. Like Goran and his comrades, the price he and Albert would have had to pay for capture would also have been high, except that in their case there was no doubt as to whether the punishment would have been prison or execution.

Goran went on, eating his simple midday bread and cheese as he spoke. The men had spent the appointed day of departure resting in the shade and taking on as much food and drink as they could lay their hands on, which, frankly, wasn't much. As darkness fell, they made their way to the little cove where their boat was hidden. They had agreed that the noise of the oars in the still night air would attract too much attention from people who might be on the shore, so the first part of the journey would need to be accomplished by Goran swimming and towing the boat using a sturdy rope tied around his strong upper torso. Once out of earshot of the land, one of the others would take over with the oars, then it would be every man rowing flat out in rotation to get into Italian national waters as quickly as they could. To begin with, this had worked well. They had slid stealthily, almost silently, away from the Yugoslav coast and had gone mercifully unseen. A kilometre or so out to sea, Goran had untied the rope from his bruised shoulders and had clambered back into the boat, exhausted from the effort of towing both the craft and its five occupants. One of the others had taken up the oars and begun rowing with all his might. After half an hour, another of the comrades had taken over, and so it went on. It was a dark night with little moonlight, so they felt safe from observation as long as they remained quiet. However, about half way across, or so Goran reckoned for they had no compass and no way of measuring their speed of travel, they had run into one of those sudden storms that can build up in the Adriatic when the weather is hot, and soon lightning and thunder were all around them. Huge waves began to toss their inadequate little boat about most alarmingly. Goran's companions were simple country men with no experience of the sea. Unable to swim and fearful of drowning, they began to cry out with fear. Goran tried to soothe them. 'Stay still and hold on to the boat!' he commanded them but order was giving way to panic. One of the men, Goran's brother in law in fact, his sister Jelena's husband, had started to make frantic efforts to empty the boat of the sea water that was crashing in over the sides, using only his bare hands, causing the boat to rock wildly. Another, Goran's cousin Ivo, tried to restrain him and a struggle ensued. All at once a great wave hit the boat hard from the side, nearly turning it over, and in a split second both men were swept overboard into the dark boiling sea. Goran jumped in after them to try and haul them back, but the force of the waves and his damned weakness and tiredness from the swimming earlier stopped him from making any progress. All he could do was watch his kinsmen being dragged under to their deaths. His remaining companions, aghast, pulled Goran back into the relative safety of the dinghy, where he lay for a few moments on the planks sobbing and gasping for air while they continued on their way.

Charlie listened, appalled. He and Albert had come close to being detected on their travels, especially that idiotic night on the town in Florence, but they had never faced even the threat, let alone the reality, of death. He realised how lucky they had been. He also realised how desperately Goran and his kinsmen must have wanted to get away from the communist regime in their homeland to take the risks they had. The rest of the story Goran kept short. He and his remaining three companions at last arrived at the Lido di Jesolo where they made landfall on Italian soil. They had at once made their way to the little police station in the town and declared themselves as refugees from Communism. The Italian authorities had been marvellous, Goran told Charlie. Despite their smart uniforms and swaggering appearance, the policemen they met could not have been more helpful. Charlie was pleased that his erstwhile colleagues had treated with humanity the four bedraggled men who stood before them and who had been through so much. Lodgings were found, clothes and supplies provided, and the men rapidly issued with identity papers which meant they could travel on. Charlie was reminded of how well the West Germans had treated the young Schmidts as they fled the east, and was touched that even after years of barbarism, the spirit of human kindness was still alive and well in postwar Europe. Thus Goran and his kinsmen had made their way to Germany, on a train paid for by the Italian government. With no idea about their new homeland, they had simply stuck a pin in the map, and had pitched up at the Hauptbahnhof in Frankfurt. Their grasp of German was minimal but Goran knew that 'Arbeit' meant 'work', for he had seen pictures that had been taken at the liberation of the death camps in 1945 in the Serbian newspapers, and the words 'Arbeit Macht Frei' were emblazoned on his memory. In his own case, he said, he hoped that the chilling slogan would prove to be true. He had gone up to complete strangers in the street uttering the single word 'Arbeit?' and eventually people had directed him to a large concrete building in the centre of town on which was hung the sign 'Arbeitsamt'. Once in the office, by means of a combination of sign language, a degree of mime artistry that would shame a professional actor, and some hastily-drawn sketches, Goran and his fellow-travellers were all four interviewed and found jobs working for the Stadt Frankfurt - the City Council - on the massive programme of rebuilding the roads. As they turned to leave, the young civil servant who had helped them spoke to them for the last time. 'Sie müssen Deutsch lernen, meine Herren, und Sie müssen es schnell machen,' he said – 'you must learn German quickly, gentlemen'. Goran replied with one of his few words of his new language. 'Ja' he said.

With the small amount of money they had been given in Italy – and Charlie was moved to hear that the authorities there had been thoughtful enough to provide actual cash to these men – they found a single room to rent and there they set up what could just about be called 'home'. They had a kerosene heater which doubled as a stove, and a supply of water from the dingy communal bathroom on the floor below. It was certainly no palace but they could keep themselves and their few clothes clean and cook basic food. Like many of the other foreign workers they met, the hostility towards them was noticeable, simply because they were so different from the usual run of Germans. The older women disliked them because they had not fought and died in the war like their men, and the young men hated them because they saw them as competition both for jobs and girls. None of this was true, but it did not prevent groups of youths taunting the incomers and sometimes even attacking them physically. The old myth of racial superiority, put about for so long by Hitler and the Nazis, was still engrained in many people and they resented these swarthy foreigners with their funny food, their even stranger languages, and for the fact that they were prepared to live in un-German conditions and work for less pay than any self-respecting German would demand. Charlie looked on and wondered how it would be if at some point people from other lands started to arrive in numbers and form separate communities within German towns and cities. Then you could imagine that the barely concealed fascism of the gangs would come to the surface and real problems could ensue. For now, while there were relatively few foreign workers, and those that were there were not a united group likely to fight back, the situation could be contained. Goran and his kinsmen kept their heads down, did their work and did not court unwelcome attention. Every month they sent what money they could back to Serbia, in the hope that it would reach their own wives and children and the widows of the two men who had drowned trying to escape from the Communists. With every month that passed the likelihood that they would ever see their families again diminished. The Iron Curtain, as Churchill had so cleverly foretold at the end of the war, was indeed being pulled tighter and tighter around them. Goran's eyes filled with tears as he confided this fear to the kindly stranger from Switzerland. Herr Weiss seemed to understand suffering and the hardship of loss. For a Swiss, he was unusually perceptive and caring. He was also generous, for every time they met, he pressed a few precious American dollars into the hands of Goran and his companions, dollars that went a long way and with no questions asked, even in so-called anti-capitalist Zagreb.

After a few weeks of living in Frankfurt, one day in early May Charlie decided that the Schmidt youngsters could now be left to get on with their lives. They had work which brought in enough money to live on as long as they were careful, and they had places on training courses in local colleges. Their grasp of English had improved vastly thanks to Charlie, and they all now attended language night classes at the American base. It amused Charlie slightly that these young Germans would inevitably end up speaking like natives of New York or Chicago. Maybe they would even end up living there one day. General Green would be sure to give them all the help they needed to make the most of the opportunity they had been given by their mother. Charlie started to make plans for his departure. Lieutenant Jones, through the offices of the good General, wangled him onto a military flight as far as Rome where he could report to his paymasters and explain his lengthy absence. After that it would be up to him to cover the remaining kilometres to Matera whatever way he could. With luck and a following wind, he could be home within the week.

On his last day, he went to the site where Goran and his companions were working to bid his new friends goodbye and to wish them good luck. The men shook hands warmly and although they said 'Auf Wiedersehen', they all knew a reunion was highly improbable. Comings and goings were a normal part of life now that all the old certainties of the times before the war had been utterly swept away.

Charlie had already booked tickets for the opera for himself and the Schmidts by way of a farewell treat, and had arranged an after-show meal at a nearby restaurant. Later that day, all four got dressed up in their finest clothes – for the opera was not the place you went dressed for a stroll in the forest – and made their way into the centre of town. The opera house, the Alte Oper, had been severely damaged by the merciless Allied bombing, so for the time being performances were taking place in a variety of venues, usually churches, and tonight 'Die Zauberflöte' – Mozart's 'The Magic Flute' – was being put on in just such a space. The pews were a bit hard, and the view somewhat restricted, but the acoustics were, as expected, magnificent. The work was a little light for Charlie's taste, but it was one he thought the youngsters, who had never been to the opera before, might enjoy as an introduction to the genre. And so it proved to be. Mozart's music captivates people of all ages and backgrounds, and the Schmidts, farmers' children from the rural East, were soon drawn into its charm. When the opera finished and the performers took their bows, the Schmidts along with everyone else there got to their feet and clapped their hands enthusiastically, crying 'Bravo! bravo!' as they did so. All at once Rainer, forgetting where he was, let out a piercing whistle of approval, a whistle so loud a sheep dog could have heard it from a great distance. A ripple of laughter went around the cast and Rainer slumped into his seat, his face red with embarrassment. Charlie patted the young man's shoulder and assured him that actors and singers love it when people tell them they're good, however they do it. Rainer was grateful for Charlie's kindness, and stood up again to clap some more. Finally the ovation ended, and the group made their way out into the night air for the short walk to their restaurant. The meal was excellent, one which Charlie hoped to remember for a long time. German cooks do wonderful things with game, and this night they were not disappointed. After a substantial bowl of Leberknödelsuppe – broth with tiny liver dumplings floating in it - they were served tender slices from a roast saddle of hare, larded with smoky bacon and accompanied by a red wine and blueberry jelly sauce, with earthy boiled new potatoes liberally strewn with fresh parsley and a spicy casserole of finely shredded red cabbage with apples. After such a feast there was no need of, or room for, a dessert. Instead they all had a cup of rich dark creamy coffee and a delicious little white chocolate truffle. Physically and mentally replete, they made their way back to the apartment and their beds.

The next morning after an early breakfast with the young ones, Charlie stood up, shook hands with Rainer and Werner, and kissed Gisela fondly on both cheeks. 'Like the French!' she said. 'Wie die Franzosen' he agreed. Then he slipped on his coat, picked up his bag and left the apartment. From the street below it was only a short ride on the Strassenbahn to the American HQ and his jeep to Rhein-Main Airbase. As he waved back to the Schmidts leaning out from the balcony above, he thought to himself 'I'm coming home, Giovanna, at last I'm coming home.' Even though, thanks largely to Lieutenant Jones, he had been able to speak to her on the telephone occasionally , it was over a year since he had seen her and he could hardly wait another minute.

CHAPTER SIX

Family matters

Precisely a week later, Charlie walked back in through the door of his and Giovanna's house in Matera. He had not told her exactly when he was coming, for to be fair, he didn't know himself. Leaving Frankfurt, he had no idea how long his employers would want to grill him about what was going on in Germany, East and West, indeed whether they would want to employ him ever again. But far from being cross with him for the long time he had been out of communication, they were glad of the valuable insights he had picked up, not least his validation of their own view that Stalin was not an ally but someone to worry about, and his 'yes men' in the surrounding countries a justifiable source of concern. It also pleased them to hear how their own people were treating with humanity the lucky few who were managing to escape to Italy from oppressive Communist regimes in the Balkan states. They had had enough of Italian policemen being seen as jumped up bully boys. The legacy of Mussolini had died hard, and it was heartening to hear good news for once. With the promise of a full written report to follow, Charlie was congratulated, paid – at last – and sent on his way home for some well-deserved R and R, as his American friends would say. He was even furnished with a small car to make the journey back to his wife and family quicker and infinitely more comfortable. Before he left Rome, though, he took the time to write and send a cheery holiday postcard – ironically a sort of 'dear cousin Christina, having a wonderful time, wish you were here' message - to Frau Schmidt back behind the Iron Curtain in the German Ost-Zone, so that she would know her beloved children were safe and well. That done, he could put the immediate past behind him and look forward to the future. As a special treat, he also managed a quick coffee with Alessandro, who was still very much involved in the corridors of power and the rebuilding of the Italian nation. Then, and not a moment too soon, home.

There was so much to catch up on with Giovanna. First of all, there was the matter of all the missed kisses. Then there was a whole year's worth of love to be made, all the more passionate for them having been apart for so long. It was as if they were discovering each other for the first time. After that, laughter and tears as stories and experiences were exchanged, and then some more kisses, and so it went on. So much to do and so few hours in the day. It was a week before Charlie felt he had even begun to make up for the months away from his wife. At that point Giovanna suggested they should go and visit the family on the farm before they started being offended by their non-appearance. They understood that lost time had to made up for, but even so, they would certainly be thinking by now that enough was enough. Well Sophia would anyway and she might just pick up the telephone to say so!

It was a delicious spring day when the pair finally prised themselves out of their love nest and took to the road. Entering the del Piero's driveway, Charlie was pleased to note that the farm house looked exactly as he remembered it. Why it wouldn't he could not imagine, but so much had changed in the world of late, it was comforting to see that some things remained constant. The car rattled over the gravel of the drive, and the noise brought people and animals alike out into the open to see who might be approaching. First to reach the vehicle were two of the farm dogs, closely followed by what Charlie thought must be Albert and Caterina's youngest son, the clever talented Ricardo.

Although surely not yet much more than ten or eleven years old, the boy was well-built and strong-looking, several centimetres taller than when Charlie had last seen him. From his stature and athleticism he was showing all the signs of becoming the sportsman Charlie thought he would. As he had done those six years ago, when Charlie had first visited the farm in the latter stages of the war, the boy approached the man, extended his hand and said 'Welcome Uncle Carlo' in a tone of genuine pleasure. He then kissed his aunt, gravely, once on each cheek. Suddenly he remembered he was a child, and he turned sharply and raced towards the house screaming at the top of his lungs 'Mama! Papa! Come quick! It's Aunt Giovanna and Uncle Carlo!'

He was a deal too late though. His parents were already on their way, closely followed by his brothers Carlo and Giorgio. Bringing up the rear, making a rather more stately progress, Charlie would see the somewhat bent figures of Giovanni and Sophia. In no time Charlie and Giovanna were surrounded and were being showered with hugs, kisses, handshakes and firm slaps on the back. The two dogs took the mayhem as a cue to start barking and howling, jumping up and down, chasing their tails and generally contributing to the chaos as only dogs can.

Once order had been restored, and Charlie's thinness commented upon ad nauseam, it was time to go into the familiar kitchen for some of Sophia's scrumptious coffee and a slice of her rich dark pan forte crammed with sweet dried fruits and nuts. Sophia urged a second piece upon her son in law, commenting that it was obvious that 'those Germans' had not been looking after him properly. Despite Charlie assuring her that 'those Germans' had precious little themselves, she was not convinced. She had read that the Americans were showering their former enemies with all kinds of luxuries, which they were probably hoarding in secret, just like all the art they had stolen from Italy in the war! 'Some things never change', thought Charlie and he smiled wryly to himself. It was good to be back.

For the next hour or two, the family grilled Charlie about his experiences over the past few turbulent months. Albert and Giovanni were shocked to hear about conditions behind the Iron Curtain, and the extreme lengths people like Goran and his compatriots were prepared to go to escape from Communism. They realised how lucky Italy had been not to have been occupied by Stalin after the fall of Mussolini. The story of brave Frau Schmidt and her children moved Caterina to tears. She could scarcely imagine having to give up even one of her precious sons and daughters, let alone three of them. Which brought the conversation neatly around to Giuseppe. It seemed the baby he and the Contessa were expecting was due any day now. Giuseppe was in frequent contact by telephone and kept them fully up to date. The Contessa, now to be referred to by her given name of Francesca, was apparently in good health and there were no complications to report. Albert and Caterina were as pleased as dogs with two tails that they were at last to become grandparents, for none of their other offspring were showing any signs of obliging. The fact that their first grandchild would be born out of wedlock was something they had long since come to terms with. Let he who is without sin cast the first stone, after all. They planned to travel to Milano as soon after the birth as the work of the farm would allow. Even Sophia expressed her pleasure at the imminent new arrival, though for her and Giovanni the long trip was not really an option. They would have to wait for Giuseppe to being his child to them when he or she was old enough to travel.

The other young ones, it seemed, were doing well. The two older boys did most of the work of the farm, spent all their free time together walking or fishing, and apparently had little or no inclination to do anything else. To Caterina's evident chagrin this anything else included meeting girls, getting married and having babies like other people's sons. Where had she gone wrong? The girls were away at secretarial college, living in residential halls in Milano and being helped and guided for the time being by Francesca. Whether this would continue once the baby came would have to be decided, but this item was on the agenda for discussion as part of her older sister's Milano trip. Young Ricardo was at school still and was getting on reasonably, but despite his obvious intelligence, his heart did not lie in academic work. He was a very physical type of boy and, even at such an early age, had already decided he wanted to make his living as a professional sportsman. Mercifully, especially as far as his mother was concerned, he had tried and rejected boxing, and was now turning his attention to the altogether more civilised pursuit of football. The Italian football Liga was gradually returning to something like its pre-war status, and the big clubs were once again starting to look for skilled young men to take on and for promising lads to nurture and develop. Talent scouts were travelling the length and breadth of the land to seek out the players of the future to replace the many men killed or wounded in the war. Ricardo had been spotted by one such chap whilst playing in a match at his local club in Matera, and there had been some initial contacts made with the family. This fellow seemed to think Ricardo had real talent and wanted to take him into the club's academy where he would train as a footballer but still continue with his education until he was of an age to leave school. At that time, if he was good enough, he could join the men's team. The scout was from none other than famous - and very rich – Juventus club, whose home ground was in far away Torino. Albert and Caterina were flattered and pleased for their son, but he was only eleven, and too young to their minds to be going away from home, especially so far. With a maturity beyond his years, Ricardo had fluently argued his case for taking this once in a lifetime opportunity, pointing out that 'Juve' was one of the most successful football clubs in the world, but as yet no decision had been reached. As so often before, Albert wanted to hear what Charlie thought before making up his mind on a big issue. Charlie could be relied on to provide a clear analysis of the situation, without a load of emotional complications getting in the way. He and Caterina could hardly see beyond their love of their precious youngest boy and their desire to keep him close to themselves for as long as possible.

Gosh! This was a bit of a bombshell! Charlie hadn't reckoned on being plunged into a major family matter so soon after his return. This was important stuff, and it needed to be carefully considered. He would have to handle it with all the impartiality of one of his diplomatic missions. He pondered a while, as he nibbled on a third slice of Sophia's glorious cake, and then he spoke, slowly and precisely. First, he said, he must do his background research by talking to all the protagonists. Then he would weigh up the pros and cons, before delivering his opinion. Even then, and he was at pains to stress this to his brother, it would only be his opinion. The decision on what to actually do would have to be made by Ricardo and his parents. Because the football season would soon be at an end, he was sure that staff of the club would have time to talk to him, so he would start with them. He would also interview Ricardo, his parents, his siblings, and his grandparents. Albert was pleased, and his face showed it. Making these important decisions required brains, and Charlie had plenty of 'em. The way he could speak all those lingoes, and play the piano like a good'un were proof of that. A clear head was called for, and Albert was the first to admit that his own thinking was easily befuddled by silly things like love. Much relieved, he thanked Charlie fulsomely, and took him in yet another bone-crushing Donkin bear hug.

A new assignment

A few days later, Charlie set off from Matera again, but this time his darling Giovanna was with him in the car. He wasn't leaving her behind if he didn't have to. They would travel north, making a holiday of the journey, and planned to arrive in Milano with any luck at just about the time of the birth of Giuseppe and Francesca's baby. A few days there, then they would move on to Torino where Charlie would arrange meetings with the coaching team at Juventus, to get an idea of what kind of an experience Ricardo could expect if he decided to take up their offer. It was mid May and the weather in the south was already pleasantly warm. However, further north it might still be cold, so prudent Giovanna loaded the back seat of the car with thick woolly blankets and some stout rainwear. This was, it transpired, a good idea.

In Rome, after Charlie had handed in his report to his paymasters, he and Giovanna managed to arrange a splendid dinner with busy Alessandro, a pure delight for them all. Then the pair at last managed to grab a couple of free days and take in the famous sights of the city, just like tourists. It was the first time they had been in Rome just the two of them together with time to spare. The sky was blue, a gentle breeze played and the ancient sites looked at their best. At the Trevi Fountain, the white marble figures glistened in the warm spring sunshine. 'We did return, after all,' Charlie said to his wife. 'And we will again,' she said, taking a small coin from her purse and tossing it into the water, 'There, I've made sure of it.' With a long drive ahead of them, they crammed everything of Rome they could into two hectic days. Not last on their agenda was to attend Mass at St Peters as Charlie had in 1918, dragging poor old grumbling Albert along with him. How the chapel boy had changed! A veritable Catholic patriarch these days, back then the ostentation, the gilding, the incense, the, well, the everything had outraged his protestant sensibilities. As Charlie recalled the circumstances of his first visit he and Giovanna smiled fondly together. God had blessed them indeed, and beneath the exquisite ceiling they knelt to give thanks.

Over the next few days, they retraced Charlie's earlier solo journeys, but this time in considerably more comfort. Little family-run hotels welcomed them and provided pleasant sleeping quarters and delicious breakfasts. In tiny stone built villages, charming rural restaurants served them the best local produce, artfully and lovingly prepared by a succession of mammas. Charlie remembered why it was that he loved this country so much. They cared for everything they did, no matter how humble. Their adage seemed to be, if you are making a cup of coffee, make the best cup of coffee you can. Ditto the pasta, the roast meats, the tiny fresh spring vegetables. Not once were they offered anything less than perfect. Some evenings they ate a leisurely meal at the same table with mamma and her family, enjoying and commenting on the food with warmth and gusto. It was a long way from the austere greasy spoons of post war London and it made Charlie think of his family back in England, still living on such meagre food as the ration book would allow. For them food was not a pleasure but something you needed to sustain life, something to be prepared, consumed and cleaned up after as quickly as possible. Why would you linger over a watery plate of bland nearly meatless stew and stodgy dumplings? What on earth could you say about it? What was there to discuss? He could imagine his father silently putting away something Mary had taken most of the day to queue for and produce, not even thinking to comment that it had filled him up - 'well, that stuck to me ribs, lass' - because it probably hadn't. Hideous. There was better food and more of it even in Germany. Poor old Britain had won the war and lost the peace. Charlie sighed. Giovanna caught his eye across the laden table. She knew exactly where his mind had wandered. Her visit to London courtesy of the RAF had been a short one but she had seen enough to realise what the people, Charlie's people, were suffering. Under the table she reached for his hand and gave it a tender squeeze. 'I know', she whispered, 'I know.'

After a few such days, the pair arrived in Milano and made their way directly to the small house in the old town that Giuseppe and Francesca shared. The house was medieval, the windows tiny, and the floors, especially upstairs, well, interesting! The kitchen was basic, as were the washing facilities, but they were adequate for two, and would probably suffice for another small one. With impeccable taste, though little money, Francesca had made their dwelling extremely attractive. The colours were vibrant and brought the sunshine into what could otherwise have been rather a dark space. Heavy fabrics doubtless begged or borrowed from wealthy relatives adorned the windows and acted as coverings for chairs that had seen better days. Giuseppe's practical skills, inherited from his dad, were in clear evidence too. Using wood that had no doubt seen several incarnations, he had constructed a nursery for the new arrival in a corner of the sole upstairs bedroom, and this too had been painted in cheery yellows and blues, and adorned with images of flowers, fruits and baby animals. Francesca clearly had some artistic talent to complement Giuseppe's handiness with saw and hammer.

Giovanna, once the obligatory hugs and kisses were bestowed on and received from her niece and nephew, insisted on the guided tour, and gasped with delight at everything she saw. 'E bella, Francesca,' she said.' It's lovely.' 'Si, Giovanna,' came the reply, 'ma piccola.' Small it certainly was and it was obvious that there was no chance whatsoever that Charlie and Giovanna would be able to stay there. However, there were many hotels to be found in the neighbourhood, and the four could certainly dine together in one of the numerous excellent trattorie which lined the surrounding streets. In fact, as Giuseppe pointed out, it would soon not be possible for him and Francesca to go out to eat, at least for a few months, so it would be a good thing to take advantage of the arrival of his dearly beloved uncle and aunt, and extract as many decent meals cooked by someone else as possible, especially if they came free! With much laughter, this was agreed. An opera singer, even a good one, is not paid vast amounts of money, and with two mouths to feed and a third due any day, any contributions from the 'old folks' would be welcome indeed. Charlie and Giovanna knew their duty and were glad to perform it. Once they had found a place to sleep they would return to the little house and take 'the young'uns' out. In the meanwhile, Giuseppe should contact his sisters and get them to join the party as well.

Later that evening, all six – five Weisses and a da Mosto – sat for several hours around a scrubbed wooden table topped with a spotless red and white gingham cloth. They chatted animatedly, for they had not all been together for a long time, and ate course after course of excellent home cooking, washed down with some decent quaffing wine from a large earthenware jug. It was simple working man's food, the kind that Charlie had first enjoyed years before in Torino and still enjoyed today. Light home made pasta filled with spinach and ricotta was followed by a delicate dish of poached trout with lemon, a hearty beef stew redolent with rich red wine and a good slug of brandy, then creamy northern cheeses and fresh fruit. The conversation flowed as freely as the wine. The girls had lots to tell their aunt and uncle about their new lives in Milano, about the secretarial college they were attending and what they were learning there, as well as all the exciting things they were doing in their free time. It was a far cry from Matera with its single cinema and travelling shows. In Milano there was live theatre as well as a number of cinemas, and of course the opera, for which Giuseppe could get them tickets in the gods any time they liked. The restaurants were plentiful and cheap, and there was no shortage of young men wanting to wine and dine a pair of beautiful clever girls. This latter piece of information was, of course, delivered in the utmost confidence and should not – on pain of death! - find its way back to Caterina and Alberto, much less the formidable Sophia. She'd be just as likely to get on a train and come and haul them back to the country if she thought they were seeing young men! Francesca assured Giovanna that her nieces only ever went out together, never alone, and that she personally vetted those with whom they spent their time. Only young men of impeccable backgrounds and the highest standards of conduct were good enough for Teresa and Gina. Giovanna was relieved to hear it, and this brought the discussion neatly around to the subject of who would offer this support to the girls once the baby was born and Francesca was a busy young mum. This much they owed Caterina, to be certain and to able to promise her that her precious girls were safe and that their reputations would remain untarnished. Giuseppe, as ever, wise beyond his years, had pre-empted his mother's concerns and had already arranged a replacement chaperone and mentor in the form of the sister of his own patron, Signor Marco Bocelli. She was an unmarried lady of about thirty whose fiancé had sadly been killed in the bloody battle of El Alamein. She knew what it was to be a single girl in a big city and what protection was necessary. She liked a laugh as well, and Teresa and Gina found her great fun. Finally, he had arranged for Uncle Carlo and Aunt Giovanna to meet the lady the next day, so they could see for themselves how suitable she was. 'Well done, lad' Charlie said, very impressed by his nephew's maturity. If Ricardo turned out to be half as sensible as his brother, he would do well at Juventus.

This thought in turn moved the talk on to the subject of the youngest Weiss brother and the chance that had been offered to him. It came as no surprise to Charlie that Giuseppe was all in favour of Ricardo leaping at the opportunity. From his own experience in the cut-throat world of opera, Giuseppe knew how infrequently such chances came along. The country, he assured his family, was full of singers just as good as he was who never got to show it because they never met the person who could give them the leg up. The same would probably be true for football. The men from Juventus would not wait for Ricardo forever. If he seemed to be less than a hundred percent interested in their offer, they would move onto the next boy waiting on the sidelines of some provincial team. Charlie knew that his nephew was right. 'Carpe Diem' he thought. You had to seize the day in this life if you were to achieve anything. Charlie resolved to get himself over to Torino as quickly as possible. There were just the small matters of the birth of a baby and a meeting with a potential chaperone to take care of. Then it would be full speed ahead for himself and Giovanna to cover the hundred and thirty kilometres to the west where lay the great industrial city which was the home of the Italy's most famous football club.

The next day Charlie and Giovanna, along with Giuseppe and Francesca, went to La Scala where it had been arranged that they would meet up with Signor Marco Bocelli and his sister Marguerita. It was to be an informal meeting over an unhurried lunch which would give all parties the chance to get to know each other. Just walking into the magnificent opera house made the hairs on Charlie's neck stand up. He recalled his very first visit when he had unexpectedly stumbled upon a rehearsal of 'Un Bel Di' from Madama Butterfly. He also recollected the time he and 'I Trovatori' had belted out the Toreador song from Carmen. The memory made him smile to himself. God! those days had been full of fun. Marco Bocelli clearly remembered it too, for he came rushing up to Charlie, his right hand outstretched, calling out 'En Garde, Carlo Weiss! En Garde!' And the two men laughed out loud and fell into a warm hug. Marco then turned to the attractive blond-haired woman standing a few metres behind him, and said to her 'Marguerita, this is Signor Carlo Weiss, the man who restored my faith in myself, the man who saved my life and made me a singer!' And to Charlie, 'this is my dear sister Marguerita, and she promises to look after your nieces as well as you looked after me, and at least as well as I hope I have looked after Giuseppe.' 'Hear hear!' said Giuseppe and Francesca, applauding their benefactor. Charlie took the sister's hand, bowing slightly. His handshake was returned firmly and confidently. Nothing on the Donkin scale of things, mercifully, but enough to let him know that this was a woman of some spirit. Giovanna, another woman of spirit if ever there was one, stepped forward to her husband's side and formal introductions were made.

Business done, the group adjourned to a fine nearby restaurant, the C'a d'Oro, where Marco had booked a table for six. The maitre d' welcomed them effusively and guided them to their seats, the best in the house. There was a ripple of applause as they made their way through the busy lunchtime service, for Marco was a very famous man, much loved in Milano, and Giuseppe too had a following amongst those members of the opera-going elite who could afford to dine in this place. 'Bravo Signor Bocelli, Bravo Signor Weiss', people said and the two men bowed their heads modestly by way of acknowledgement. This was a first for Charlie. He could not recall ever being on the receiving end of such a welcome in his life. Marco and Giuseppe were clearly used to it though, they simply smiled and silently took their places at the table with the aim of blending into the background as quickly as possible.

What followed was a delightful three hours of food and wine and a conversation which ranged from the everyday and the immediate – like what names Francesca and Giuseppe had chosen for their baby, and how the nursery was coming along – to the theoretical and the political – Charlie's experience of getting out of East Germany and his views on Stalin, for instance. Somewhere in the midst of it all the sad tale of Marguerita's doomed fiancé was told, and Charlie was forced once again to confront the fact that he may have been in some way responsible for this woman's tragedy just as he could well have been for poor Frau Domke living her lonely life in Eschwege. It was extraordinary how the after-effects of those awful wars kept turning up in unexpected places. Of course, nothing could be said. Only Giovanna was fully privy to the secrets of Charlie's past. For the rest a discreet veil was drawn over the detail. It was better that way, for all concerned.

With lunch out of the way, and Marguerita well and truly accepted as a suitable chaperone and mentor for the girls, the Bocellis left for their afternoon appointments and the others wandered home through the busy city streets. Charlie and Giovanna decided that they would spend no more time in Milano, but would head to Torino to set up meetings with the Juventus people as soon as they could. Giuseppe's advice about seizing the day had galvanised them into action. In any case, the baby might not come for days. First babies were often late, weren't they? As none of the four of them had ever had a baby, first or any other kind, this was only pure conjecture, but they believed it to be true. They would easily be back in time for the birth. After a few pleasant hours chatting together in the little house, the older couple returned to their hotel. Bliss! Room to stretch the ageing legs at last! They fell onto their large comfortable bed and were soon intertwined in a companionable slumber. The next morning, pausing only in reception to pay and to telephone Caterina and give her the good news about her girls, they packed up the car and set off for the next stage of their mission.

Torino again

Giovanna's powerful car covered the hundred or so kilometres between Milano and Torino with ease. The terrain was hilly and the roads narrow, but there was little traffic, and the views were splendid. Tiny stone villages perched on the sides of steep slopes, rivers cascaded beneath ancient arched bridges, cows lazed in the upland meadows to which they had not long been returned after the winter snows. It was a very comforting landscape, and one which had remained virtually unchanged for centuries. With Giovanna at the wheel, Charlie was able to sit back and take a leisurely look at his adopted country. What he saw, he liked a lot. He recalled how he and Albert had both felt at home the moment they set foot this land. There was something about the place that suited them both. For Charlie it was the culture, the food, the wine and the pace of life. For Albert it was the opportunities presented by the unpolluted great outdoors, oh and the food, and later on, Caterina of course.
All too soon they arrived at the outskirts of Torino. Like any large industrial town, it was busy and noisy and the air less than fresh. It put Charlie in mind of the Lancashire towns he knew from his youth, except that here there was much more by way of road traffic, as was fitting for a place that made its living from car manufacture. Mill workers in Lancashire could not afford cars. Clearly Italian factory staff could, and they all seemed to be out and about in them at once, racing from A to B at breakneck speed, their hands permanently on the horn to warn off other drivers. It was nearly 3pm, and people were in a hurry to get back to work after the long lunch break. Giovanna pulled the car over to the side of the road and stopped the engine. 'That's it for driving for me' she told Charlie, 'I'll have to hand over to you. I never wanted to be a racing driver, and I'm not about to start now!' Charlie laughed softly, and the two swapped seats. To be fair he had never really wanted to be a Malcolm Campbell either, but it was his turn to enter the fray. The first job was to find a place to stay, and using his unerring instinct on arrival in new places, Charlie headed immediately for the central railway station. Luckily, the road was well signposted and the station easy to find in the chaotic Torino afternoon. Hotels near stations might not be the poshest in town, but they would be adequate, and would surely do for a night or two. And so it proved to be. By choosing the dearest one, they ensured

that they had a clean and comfortable room near 'the luxurious facilities'.
Once installed, Charlie availed himself of the assistance of the hotel's helpful and very talkative receptionist who found him the telephone number of the football stadium. Juventus, or 'Juve' to the locals, played their home matches at the ground now known once again as the Stadio Communale, though for a while it had been called the Stadio Mussolini. Obviously that had had to change, what with the way things had gone towards the end of the war and everything. You couldn't have 'the lads' - the best team in the world - playing somewhere named after a disgraced fascist dictator and a dead one at that, now could you? Without pausing for breath, the receptionist doubted, furthermore, that Bayern München's ground was known as the Hitler Stadium. Charlie agreed that it probably was not and quickly wrote down the club's number before extricating himself politely but firmly from the possibility of an even longer speech. Disappointed at losing his catch so quickly, the receptionist sighed audibly and returned to his post. Charlie fled gratefully in the direction of the lobby, the public telephone booth and a modicum of sanity. In no time at all he was speaking to the very man that had spotted Ricardo playing in Matera, and had arranged to meet him and his colleagues the next day at 10am. Oh the joy of northern Italian drive and efficiency! The same result would have taken days to achieve in sleepy Taranto, let alone Matera. The south was lovely, and Charlie wouldn't live anywhere else, but its wheels did grind awfully slow at times. Most times, to be fair.

Charlie returned to Giovanna with news of his success, and the story of the unfortunately-named stadium. Charlie was good at telling tales, and he took off the mannerisms and the accent of the receptionist to a tee. Giovanna was soon howling with laughter. She begged her husband to introduce her to the man so that she could see for herself what an odd character he was, but Charlie was obliged to refuse her. The idea of another diatribe on dead fascists was just too much. He suggested they try out 'the luxurious facilities' and get dressed for dinner. A nice meal would be just the ticket at the end of a busy and productive day. Charlie was reminded that he and Albert had had their first ever proper Italian meal in this town, and told Giovanna the story of the spaghetti and how much better at eating it Albert had been than himself. 'He's still better at eating than you are!' Giovanna retorted, giggling. 'He gets plenty of practice,' came the reply, 'his wife can cook!' Giovanna let out a shriek of mock horror. She wrestled her ungrateful man to the large soft bed and pinned him down there, threatening to kiss him to death. Charlie succumbed with almost indecent haste. The bath and the meal, it appeared, would have to wait. There were other, more pressing, items on the agenda.

It was an hour or two before the pair emerged, still slightly breathless but suitably groomed and perfumed, to find a place to eat. By this time the day clerk had clearly gone home only to be replaced by a huge woman whose hostile expression defied them to approach her. No point in asking her for any information. She looked the exact opposite of her obliging, if slightly mad, colleague. From her nothing would be forthcoming. They would just have to find a suitable trattoria on their own. Well, so be it. They headed off into the balmy Torino evening, positively starving. Once again, the city did not let them down and they soon found somewhere where the food was just as good as Charlie remembered, and the atmosphere equally convivial. They returned to their hotel as a nearby church clock was striking midnight, replete, relaxed and contented. The woman behind the desk looked even crosser than before, probably because she'd had to stay awake to let these damned visitors in. How dare they go out enjoying themselves when she had to sit here in this godforsaken dump? Both Charlie and Giovanna thanked her profusely for opening the door, and when Charlie pressed a large banknote into her hand, her face almost, but not quite, softened into an unaccustomed smile. 'Buona notte, Signora', they chorused cheerily as they climbed the stairs to their room. 'Hmm' was all the reply they got. 'Hmmmm'.

To the match

The next morning, after a pleasant breakfast of doughy white bread and jam, and several cups of scalding sweet espresso, Charlie and Giovanna made their way to the Stadio Communale and their meeting with the coaching team of one of the greatest football teams in Europe if not the world. The ground had been built for the World Cup of 1934, and it was a stadium of which the city fathers were very proud, as indeed they were of their team – 'I ragazzi' – the lads. It was an imposing place, huge, with rows of seats as far as the eye could see. It must have held many thousands of spectators. Charlie wondered if it was ever full, and put that question to the head coach almost as soon as the formal introductions were over. 'Yes' came the reply, 'regularly. Our boys are very popular, they are the best team in Italy and our supporters are numerous and extremely passionate. They travel from far and wide to see Juve play.' And this was where young Ricardo could make a career for himself. What an opportunity! Charlie looked at Giovanna and realised that she too was very impressed by what she had seen at first glance. It remained to find out what these people were like and what care they proposed to take of her nephew, but so far, so good.

The morning was occupied with a series of meetings and visits which enabled Charlie and Giovanna to form a very good opinion of their hosts and Ricardo's potential employers. The youth academy appeared to be very well-organised and professionally run. The boys received the best sports coaching available, but they also continued with their education in a private school in Torino known for its high standards of academic work, especially in modern languages and the arts. This was a great relief to Charlie, because Ricardo was gifted in both languages and music, and if for any reason the football career had to end, he would always have something he loved to fall back on. In terms of personal support, each boy had a designated player whose job it was to ensure their safety and happiness. No young person was ever expected to cope alone with the demands of a new life away from their families. On hearing this it was Aunt Giovanna's turn to be reassured.

The talk then turned to money, and the sums involved made Charlie's eyes water. Not even the great Manchester United paid their players the sort of figures these men were talking. Ricardo would receive a substantial annual payment for the period of his training. Of this, fifty percent would be placed in a savings account and would be untouchable until he was eighteen years old or left the club, whichever came first. Of the rest, thirty percent would go to his parents, being the sort of amount they could have expected to receive had he worked locally. The remaining twenty percent would be paid direct to the boy as a weekly allowance. As all his living expenses would be met by the club, his monetary needs would be small – just the odd treat here and there, perhaps a book or two if he liked to read. What did Ricardo's aunt and uncle think? More to the point, how did they think his parents would react? Without wishing to pre-empt anything Albert and Caterina might say, Charlie replied that he thought they would be happy with the proposed arrangements. Ricardo himself was, of course, as keen as mustard to take up the offer. He adored football and would play for free if he had to. Hearing this, the head coach expressed his pleasure. A bit of motivation went a long way in any sport and helped players to soldier on through the tough times as well as the good ones. This Weiss boy sounded like a good lad.

For the rest of the day, Charlie and Giovanna explored the impressive facilities which would be available to Ricardo, and watched the various teams practising. The youth teams were good, with boys as young as twelve training hard to master basic skills. The under 21s were clearly very skilful, kicking balls to one another over great distances with incredible accuracy. It was easy to see how come the club was the most successful one in Italy and had been for years. However it was when they saw the senior team that they really had their eyes opened. Charlie had only ever read about Manchester United, and had seen Blackburn Rovers play just the once. That was because his cousin Bobby Clayton was a player and he got a free ticket, otherwise he could not have gone. These Juventus lads were built like Greek gods by comparison with the pasty English boys. One in particular stood out. Tall, tanned and healthy, with dark curly hair, he flew up the left field at lightning speed, dribbling the ball between his toes, dancing around defenders, eventually to score a beautiful lofted goal from fully thirty metres out. The goalie had no chance. Charlie couldn't help himself. He burst into applause. 'Bravo!' he called. 'Grazie Signor!' called the player, well pleased with himself. 'Who's he?' Charlie asked the coach. 'That's Sergio,' came the reply, 'Sergio Parisse, our best striker.' 'Well I hope he becomes Ricardo's mentor,' Charlie said, rather cheekily given that the deal wasn't finalised yet, 'he's superb.' 'I'll see to it,' promised the coach, and with a laugh, he and Charlie exchanged knowing winks and a firm handshake. Agreeing to be in touch by telephone as soon as they could, Charlie and Giovanna left the Stadio and headed back to the hotel and the amusing but slightly dotty ramblings of the afternoon reception clerk. Giovanna was thrilled. The man was at least as loony as Charlie had promised. Just wait until she told Caterina!

A life begins, a life ends

Back in Milano the next day, they arrived at Giuseppe's little house only to find on the door a scribbled note which read 'Gone to hospital, baby imminent, come quickly!' They sped to the maternity ward to find that their great nephew had been born half an hour earlier. Giuseppe had only just been allowed in to the delivery suite where his beloved Francesca was in bed, exhausted but ecstatic, her new son wrapped in white linen snuggled up on her breast. Only when a stern-faced nurse had placed a loose green gown over his clothes was Giuseppe permitted to approach. When Charlie and Giovanna appeared at the door, the woman turned sharply and shooed them out. 'Fathers only!' she barked. Charlie was reminded of the midwife who had delivered Giuseppe and how fierce she had been. Nothing, it seemed, had changed much in the intervening couple of decades. Men were still kept out of the birth process as much as possible. Only women knew the rules apparently. So be it. Chastised, he and Giovanna retreated to the waiting area until such time as their nephew might appear.

Within a few minutes the new father emerged, his face wreathed in smiles, and embraced his aunt and uncle. 'It's a boy,' he said, and burst into tears of relief and joy. As he told it, the birth had been relatively straightforward, though, unable to be with her, he had been pacing up and down outside almost literally tearing at his hair as he heard Francesca's cries of pain. Luckily the labour had not gone on for too long and soon their friendly old midwife had come and given him a hug and the news that his son had arrived. The rest they knew. The hatchet-faced nurse, who ran the ward like a top security prison, had eventually said he could go in. Now Francesca was resting and the baby was in a little cot beside her bed. He was a dad! He was a dad! He had to tell his parents at once. Charlie had spotted a telephone booth in the hospital lobby and the three made their way down there as fast as their legs would carry them. Fortunately, Giovanna had a purse full of coins, for Giuseppe had left the house without thinking of such details, and soon the new dad was talking to his mother in faraway Matera. Once he had passed on his news and received Caterina's congratulations, Giovanna took the phone and spoke to the new grandmother. 'Well, well, grandmama,' she joked, 'do you feel very very old?' Caterina at once replied she did and that it was fantastic! Then Charlie took the handset for a short chat with Albert, taking pains to point out that this grandchild was probably only the first of many if his offspring were anything like him, and that he might as well get used to it. 'Bloody good too!' came Albert's reply, 'now bugger off you silly sod and look after my boy!' Albert clearly hadn't forgotten how to swear in English, despite all the years in Italy. Charlie was delighted to hear him do it, since it usually meant he was happy. Quite right too. Promising Francesca to return later in evening visiting hours – for hatchet-face wouldn't let anyone into her ward at any other time – the three set off again for Giuseppe's little house. There were so many people to telephone with the news. First Giuseppe would need to brave the wrath of Francesca's parents, the Duke and Duchess da Mosto, known to himself and Francesca as 'the dinosaur and the dragon.' They disapproved of him actively and totally, or at least had done so until now. Maybe being presented with a grandchild and a male one at that would soften their hearts? Who knew? Then the girls must be told, and after that Marco and Marguerita, and so on through family and friends. It could turn into quite a costly afternoon. Charlie and Giovanna exchanged knowing glances. It was donation time again!

For a few days, Charlie and Giovanna remained in the little house in Milano, mostly to keep Giuseppe company while Francesca and the baby were in the hospital but also to spend some time with Teresa and Gina. They were, however, keen to get back to the south for Charlie to complete his work on the Juventus proposal, so that a decision could be made. Fortunately, not long after the birth of her first grandson, formal written contact was made by Francesca's mother expressing her desire to see her daughter, something she had not done for many months. Was the ice melting? Giuseppe at once arranged to meet her at the hospital to reunite her with Francesca and to introduce her to the baby, as yet un-named. There was no question of Francesca's father being involved, for his stated disproval of the young ones' living situation was absolute. He was one of those old-fashioned Catholic aristocrats who saw things in black and white, and what his daughter had done was a mortal sin. The modern world might think differently, but the modern world was wrong. His wife was rather more liberal, weak and wishy-washy and typically female as he saw it, and if she wanted to be in touch with the harlot Francesca, that was fine, but he would not.

To deflect the anticipated maternal hostility Giuseppe asked his aunt Giovanna to be with him when he met the Duchess at the hospital and she was glad to oblige. At the agreed time, dressed to the nines, Giovanna and Giuseppe found themselves waiting rather nervously in the hospital lobby for 'the dragon' to arrive. This she did in a flurry of squealing brakes and slamming car doors. Brushing aside her chauffeur, she swept in through the main hospital doorway, scattering nurses, doctors and patients alike before her. She strode across the foyer towards Giuseppe who at once leapt to his feet. 'Duchesa', he said, bowing slightly 'buon' giorno.' The woman looked at the younger man with obvious disdain. 'Yes, yes,' she said, 'where is my daughter?' Then, looking directly at Giovanna, ' And who is this?.' Giovanna rose and drew herself up to her full height, a full five centimetres taller than the Duchess. 'And a lot slimmer and prettier too,' she was thinking. 'I am Signora Giovanna Weiss, Giuseppe's aunt. Pleased to meet you, Duchesa.' And she extended her hand towards the other woman. The Duchess was visibly surprised at this gesture of equality, and only by reflex action returned the handshake. Giovanna realised at once that this lady did not mix with the hoi polloi and was used to being treated as something special. Well, if that was what it took to build bridges between Francesca and her family, something special she would be. 'What an absolute delight to see you, Duchesa,' she purred, 'you must be dying to see your grandson. Why don't we go up right away?' Giuseppe's gratitude to his aunt was plain to see. He could not bring himself to lay on the unction like Giovanna, yet that was clearly what was required. Grrrr! how he hated the aristocracy. Pity there hadn't been a revolution in Italy, like the one they had in France. The dragon would be working for a living now instead of swanning around wreathed in furs and perfume, lunching and gossiping with her lady friends and shopping, shopping, shopping. The image of the dragon toiling over a hot stove in a steamy kitchen crossed his mind and almost made him snigger. He bounded up the stairs to catch up with the two women as they made their way purposefully towards the maternity ward. He could hear Giovanna and the Duchess talking and they seemed to be getting on famously. What a turn up! As far as he knew the dragon hated pretty much everybody that wasn't posh. Perhaps she'd realised that his aunt was rich. It was fairly obvious that she was from her smart clothing and expensive jewellery. Perhaps dear wise aunt Giovanna was ladling on the flattery. Whatever it was it seemed to be working. From a distance behind them, he thought he even heard the dragon laugh! Impossible, surely? Dragons don't laugh do they? They'd be a fire hazard! The three arrived at the door to the ward only to find hatchet-face, arms tightly folded, standing beneath the hospital clock. It was five minutes to two. Spotting Giuseppe, she began to growl at him that it was not yet visiting hours and he must wait until two. The Duchess was having none of it. She felled the nurse with one of her withering looks, and said in her most imperious tone, 'Nonsense, woman. Let us in at once! Do you know who I am?' It was clear that the nurse, like everyone else in Milano, did know who she was, and suddenly all the fight went out of her. 'Si, Duchesa,' she said, her tone obsequious, and she opened the door to her precious domain a whole three minutes early. The visitors brushed past her and went in. Hatchet-face looked shattered. God forbid that matron should get wind of this! Her life would not be worth living. Nothing, nothing, should ever upset hospital procedures. Without them anarchy would ensue. She could only pray that no-one would talk.
Giovanna led the way to Francesca's room. She was pleased to see that her

niece had really made an effort to look beautiful for her mother. Her hair was freshly coiffed, and her makeup immaculate. Giuseppe had even gone out and bought her a decent nightie, something she did not usually feel the need of let alone possess. It looked promising, but the interaction that followed left Giovanna uncharacteristically speechless. The Duchess approached the bed in which her daughter lay , and in a flat formal voice said 'Contessa, buon' giorno,' to which Francesca replied 'Duchesa.' Good Lord! these people addressed each other like royalty! Didn't they use names? Was the word 'mamma' foreign to them? She caught Giuseppe's eye. Out of sight of the Duchess, he gave a resigned shrug. These people were emotional cripples. They wouldn't know what love was if it came up and bit them on the backside.

Francesca reached into the little crib beside her bed and picked up her son. 'Your grandson, Duchesa,' she said. The older woman came forward to inspect the baby. Catching sight of his sweet little face, the bright eyes and the head of thick dark curls, she was visibly moved, and Giovanna heard a sharp intake of breath. Aha! maybe the old girl did have feelings after all! The Duchess's voice shook only slightly as she asked if she may hold him. 'Of course' said Francesca and proffered her precious bundle to her mother. Holding the boy carefully and supporting his head, the grandmother then asked what the child's name was. 'We haven't quite decided,' came the cleverly considered reply, 'what do you think?' Clearly smitten, the Duchess thought for a moment, and said in a serious tone, 'I think it would be helpful if you named him after his grandfather. Doors might open.' Giuseppe and Francesca's eyes opened wide. Was a truce being offered? Could the parents' hearts be softening? It certainly looked as if the mother's was, and in Francesca's experience where the Duchess went the Duke would surely follow. 'Very well then, mother,' she said, 'we'll call him after father. His name will be Francesco Weiss.' 'He'll need a few more names than that if he's to be anybody at all in society,' retorted the new grandmother. This time Giuseppe spoke. 'We don't go in for all those posh aristocratic names, Duchesa,' he said, 'but we will agree to one more, as long as we get to choose it.' The Duchess was taken aback by the forthright manner the young whippersnapper was adopting, but she could see from the look on his face that he was not about to back down. 'Very well', she said, 'what shall it be?' Francesca and Giuseppe spoke as one. After all they had actually decided on a name weeks earlier. 'Alberto', they said, 'a fine name which just happens to be that of his other grandfather.' So Francesco Alberto Weiss it was to be. This seemed to please the Duchesa, for she then did something completely out of character. She kissed the baby and handed him back to his mother, and as she did that she whispered, 'Francesca, you and Giuseppe have a beautiful son,' and embraced her daughter warmly. Giovanna could have sworn she heard the pack ice cracking. Wait 'til she told Charlie about this! Even better, just wait 'til she told Caterina, Alberto and the rest. This was a tale to go down in the family's history. Discreetly, her job done, Giovanna said her farewells and departed, leaving the others to plan the poor unsuspecting Duke's capitulation.

The next day, at last, she and Charlie were able to head back south. This time they travelled by the most direct route possible, resisting the urge to play the tourist. Even so, it was almost a week later that they got back to Matera. It was mid June and the weather was sunny and exceptionally hot every day. At the farm, once the tales of the arrival of little Francesco had been told, Charlie got down to the business of tidying up his work on Ricardo's offer from Juventus. The views of Giuseppe and the girls he already knew. They were for it, a hundred percent but then they were all three naturally adventurous. He spent time with the boy himself first, not so much to gauge his appetite for the move but to ensure that he fully understood what his obligations would be. He was reassured that the lad did recognise that alongside the chance to be paid to play the game he loved, he would have responsibilities to the club, to his family and to himself. He then talked with the older boys, both of whom were keen that Ricardo should take his chance, not least because of the possibility of free tickets to watch matches when Juve came south. His meeting with Sophia and Giovanni was a short one, because Giovanni was feeling very tired, something he blamed on the excessive heat. Having heard what was on offer, the elderly couple were satisfied that their dear boy would be in good hands and gave the project their blessing. All that remained was to tell Albert and Caterina everything he had seen and heard and let them make up their minds. With overwhelming evidence that their son would be safe and well looked-after, they too arrived at the conclusion that the move would be an opportunity too good to miss. The whoop of joy that emanated from their kitchen and echoed across the farm let the neighbourhood and the world know that Ricardo had been told their decision. In just under two months, he would leave Matera for Torino and a whole new chapter of his life would begin.

Before that there was the summer to get through, and summer on the farm was a busy time. There was plenty to occupy Carlo and Giorgio and they could always find something useful for Ricardo to do to take his mind off his impatience to get going. This year, for the first time ever, Giovanni seemed to have lost interest in spending time with his youngest grandson. Ricardo would call for him of a morning but the old man would just wave him away, saying 'domani Ricardo' – tomorrow. As the summer wore on, each day hotter than the one before, all the energy appeared to drain out of him, until in the end he took to his bed for most of the time. He gave the impression that he was just worn out. The doctor came but could find nothing specific to treat. 'He is old,' he told Caterina and Albert, 'he's getting ready to die.' Caterina protested loudly that her dad wasn't even eighty yet, how could he die? But the doctor's reply was chilling. 'The war in the mountains aged him, my dear,' he said, 'what he went through probably took ten years off him. I've seen it before, with men who haven't lasted nearly as long as your father. In the end war kills everyone who takes part.' Sophia was beside herself when Caterina sat her down and told her what the doctor had said. 'I lost him once before, now I must lose him again, she wailed, 'It's not fair!'

New of Giovanni's ill health was quickly passed around the family and arrangements were made to come and spend time with him before it was too late. Despite the very young age of their child, it was Giuseppe and Francesca who were the first to make the journey. The Duke, well and truly won over by now, furnished them with one of his extremely comfortable cars and a driver to make the journey from Milano as stress-free as possible. To avoid overwhelming the old man, it was agreed that the two girls would travel by train a week or so later accompanied by Marguerita Bocelli. Alessandro had arranged some leave and was on his way. Rooms would be provided for all these visitors by Caterina and by Giovanna and Charlie. July 1949 looked like being a hectic and sad month as well as a very hot one. And so it turned out to be for as the month slipped by, so did Giovanni gradually loosen his once tenacious grip on life. He had no more appetite for the daily struggle, he had seen and done everything he wanted to see and do, and a lot more besides. A lot more. On the last day of the month, in the presence of his adored Sophia and his treasured daughters, he closed his eyes for the last time and was gone. On that day Sophia donned the traditional black, a step she had long resisted, even though most Italian women of her age wore nothing else. Along with her darling Giovanni all the colour had left her life, and she would never adorn herself brightly again. On the day of Giovanni's funeral, a week or so later, the local church was packed with people who had come from all around the district to pay their last respects to a much-loved friend and neighbour. Bereft, the three del Piero women clung to each other and tried to stifle their sobs, at least until they were out of the public eye. Once back at the farm, they could let down their guard and just howl. The men, shocked by the intensity of the raw emotion they were witnessing, could only stand silently by and wait to see how they could be of use. That night Charlie and Giovanna stayed at the farmhouse so that Sophia would not be alone there overnight for the first time ever.

A couple of days after the funeral, the visiting members of the family took their leave and headed back to their busy lives faraway. The seven-strong Milano contingent fitted easily into the Duke's capacious motor, and were the first to go. Alessandro took a day or two more, spending some rare and precious time with his mother as well as with Charlie and Giovanna, before he too had to get back to his duties. A scant week later, Ricardo and Alberto boarded the train which would take the boy to Torino, to Juventus and his new life. In ordinary circumstances, Caterina would have gone too and they would have driven, combining Torino with a visit to Giuseppe in Milano and making a real holiday of it. As it was, there was no question of leaving Sophia with just the older boys. With the best will in the world they could not provide their grandmother with the kind of support she needed. Perhaps no-one would be able to, ever again. Through it all, the unrelenting summer heat went on and on and on.

CHAPTER SEVEN

Making a difference

At last, towards the end of September, the searing heat began to abate and life was more bearable at least physically. Charlie and Albert were deeply concerned for their wives, who seemed to have taken the death of their father very hard. Worse, though, was Sophia. Since the funeral she had clearly become severely depressed. Charlie recognised the signs from his own father's experience of bereavement, and discussed his concerns with Giovanna. Was there any point in involving the doctor?, he wondered. But Giovanna felt not. The family doctor in Matera was very old-fashioned and did not believe in new fangled 'American' concepts like 'depression'. He would not understand in the way the sympathetic doctor in Great Harwood had. This man was rich and insulated from the things that worried ordinary mortals. He was very unlikely to have read about the condition or to know what treatments there might be. Indeed he was just as likely to tell Sophia to 'pull herself together', advice she hardly needed at this point. The poor woman could just about bring herself to get out of bed and dress herself, and as for eating, well, she had to be practically forced by Caterina to take any nourishment at all. As a result, she had lost a great deal of weight and was rather weak and tired all the time. The heat had not helped. Soon after the funeral, given that Sophia would not under any circumstances leave her family home, they had all agreed that the older boys Carlo and Giorgio would move into the big farmhouse so that she was not there alone all day and all night. If she could hear others moving about she might feel less deserted. For Caterina and Albert, this meant that they had a whole house to themselves for the first time in almost a quarter of a century. It was a strange experience, one that was not altogether enjoyable. The empty nest felt very, well, empty. There was plenty to do on the farm to keep the men busy, but for Caterina, with the girls and Ricardo away, the days seemed very long. She spent as much time with Sophia as possible, but she found her mother's heavy heartedness very wearing. She needed a new focus for her life if she too were not to follow the older woman down the slippery slope into melancholia.

At exactly that unfortunate point in time, Charlie was summoned to Rome. There were exciting major political and economic developments in the offing which involved close co-operation with other European nations, and Charlie's linguistic and diplomatic skills were needed once again. Encouragingly, Italy had already been accepted into NATO, the new North Atlantic Treaty Organisation, which the western nations hoped would counter the growing military threat being posed by Stalin and his communist allies. Now on the mainland of Europe, countries that had once been enemies were looking for ways to work with each other to prevent a recurrence of the conflicts that had so damaged the continent over many decades. 'Never again' was an oft-repeated phrase, and it was one with which Charlie heartily concurred. If he could do anything to help the cause of peace, he was ready to stand up and be counted. Despite his reservations about leaving three vulnerable women in the care of Albert, not always the most sensitive of souls, he had to go. Promising to telephone regularly and to visit as often as possible, as autumn arrived with its crisp clear days and chilly nights, he left.

In Matera, Giovanna felt the loss of Charlie's support and company acutely. Of course it was not a loss on the scale of that experienced by her mother, but she missed him dreadfully. She could fill her days with a bit of this and that, lunch with women friends, shopping or a trip to the coast, but somehow her life seemed to have lost its purpose. She suspected that her sister felt the same but was too proud to say so. There is nothing so pitiable as a woman who lives only through her children and comes unstuck when they no longer need her. She and Caterina needed a project, something to absorb and fulfil them, something that could maybe offer a role for Sophia as well. She remembered meeting Giuseppe Maldini for the first time at the sanatorium in Tuscany. That was when he explained the important part that meaningful activity had played in the process of mental and physical recovery for Alessandro and the other damaged souls in the hospital. Well, she, her sister and her mother were damaged souls now so maybe some work could help them too. The question was, what work?

The answer presented itself quite quickly, once she had decided to open her eyes to new possibilities. On one of her boredom-induced visits to Taranto, she was shocked to see a family group begging on the street. There were three young children, poorly dressed but clean, standing around a man who was sitting awkwardly on the pavement, an upturned hat by his side. As Giovanna approached, the children tried their best to sing her a song, and the man called out to ask if she could spare a few lira. As she got closer she could see that the man had badly deformed legs, and she took pains not to pay them too much attention, deliberately keeping her facial expression neutral. She did not want him to feel that she was shocked by him or that she pitied him. Charlie had told her about Albert's cousin Fred and how he hated it when people treated him like a freak or an idiot just because his body was damaged. She squatted down by the group and placed a few coins in the hat, thanking the children for the lovely song as she did so.

She asked why they were begging for money, why weren't they in school? ' We have to help our dad,' the oldest child answered, 'our mum has gone away and our dad can't do lots of things.' The father was clearly mortified by his child's forthrightness. 'It's not that I don't want to!' he exclaimed, 'I was shot up badly in the war, and it's left my body in ruins and my mind nearly as bad. It was all right while my wife was around, but she got fed up with me and now she's gone off with some other fellow who can do things and isn't half mad. I do what work I can but it isn't enough and sometimes we have to beg. It's as simple as that.' What an awful story! Giovanna was very moved by the open way these people discussed their misfortune. She was also shocked that such deserving people were not getting more help. Then it occurred to her that there were probably many thousands of families in Italy where husbands and fathers had come back from the war terribly scarred physically and emotionally. Alessandro had been lucky in that his family could give him the love and support he needed. This man clearly had not. Her mind was racing. 'I'd like to help you if I can, if you would let me,' she said to the man, 'what do you need?' 'A decent place to live and a job that pays enough to keep myself and the kids, that's all,' came the reply, 'we're not posh, we don't want a lot. I was a carpenter before, but no-one will take me on now because of my useless legs. I have to do whatever unskilled work I can pick up, and that's not much. There's loads more men like me, you know, lady. When you lose a war you don't come back to a hero's welcome, especially when you come back in pieces.'

This was something Giovanna had not considered before. The Italian leadership had dragged the people through a very turbulent period of time in which loyalties were obliged to shift dramatically. One moment they were on the side of Mussolini, Hitler and his Nazis, the next opposed to the Fascists and all for the Americans and the British driving the Germans out. Men who had fought alongside the Germans were not regarded highly, even though they had been doing what they were told –'only obeying orders' in the now-famous phrase. It must have been hard to come back to a hostile reception, particularly when you had laid down your health in the service of your country, its disgraced leader and his dubious pals. In the Great War, Italy had been on the winning side and even then many people had returned seriously traumatised. How much worse to be a loser as well.

'Can I buy you all a meal?' she asked the man, and at once his face darkened. He hated to be patronised. He could feed his kids. 'We've eaten,' he replied, and, almost as an afterthought, 'thanks all the same.' Giovanna knew he was lying, and the children's reaction proved it. Too young to have learned the art of deceit, the little one, a girl aged about five, cried out 'I haven't eaten Papa, I'm hungry!' 'Me too! me too!' the others chorused. The man at first looked cross and then his expression softened. 'Kids eh?, he said and gave a resigned shrug, 'well, at least they're honest.' Then he went on, 'we're starving actually, so yes, we accept, thank you, whoever you are. But nothing fancy, mind. We're not posh, as I told you.' In a side street near the harbour, they found a simple trattoria much beloved of fishermen and sailors for its unsophisticated atmosphere and for the quality and quantity of its food. It was the sort of place where you got a big steaming bowl of excellent pasta and great chunks of bread for mopping up the sauce. Main courses were optional and desserts unheard of. Fresh fruit would end the meal, with cheese on offer in the unlikely event that customers still had any room left. She and Charlie had eaten there before so Giovanna knew that it would fit the bill perfectly. It was the kind of restaurant that Charlie loved. Not posh, not fancy, and no-one would even bat an eyelid at the shabbily dressed group coming in with the obviously rich lady. All kinds of people came in here, many of them with things to hide. A few scruffy kids only added to the interest. And the food was fabulous.

Before they ordered, while they settled themselves at a table, the formal introductions were made. For the children, this was a completely exotic environment, a place where someone else cooked for you and you could have what you liked. At home you had what there was and if you didn't learn how to cook from a young age you went without. The oldest child, a girl of not much more than twelve by Giovanna's reckoning, had probably been cooking for years. Anyway, names were exchanged and hands solemnly shaken. Signora Weiss insisted on being called by her first name of Giovanna, which was very unusual. Their father therefore gave his name, not as Signor Alessi, but as Martin. The children, Maria, Marco and little Carla of course expected to be addressed familiarly. That done, it was time to choose what they would eat. It was, despite what the children thought, a very basic trattoria and there were only three pasta dishes to choose from. One was served with a mixture of locally-caught seafood, one came with aubergines in a garlicky tomato sauce finished with a sprinkle of parmesan, and the other had a rich meaty sauce with mushrooms. The children all chose the meat option, Carla letting slip that they didn't get it much at home because it was a bit dear. Martin and Giovanna went for the fish, both knowing that whatever was in the sauce would have been landed at the quay that very morning and as fresh as a daisy. In no time they were being presented with large white bowls filled to the brim with pasta – in this case curly fusilli - and the sauce of their choice. A basket of fresh bread and a carafe of icy water completed the feast. For a time silence reigned as they did justice to the splendid food. Giovanna wondered if the children might find the portion too big, but it was not so. Maria and Marco had soon wolfed theirs and were looking across at Carla to see if she might have some they could snaffle, but their father gave them a stern look which told them to wait until she offered. Meanwhile he and Giovanna waxed lyrical about the delicious light mix of white fish, giant prawns and tender mussels in white wine and cream that they had been served. In due course little Carla conceded defeat and the other two finally got their second helpings. Amazingly, they also had room for fruit, while the adults settled for a simple espresso to round off their meal. Declaring it the best food they had ever ever ever eaten, the children thanked Giovanna profusely as she settled the bill. Thinking that the five of them had just eaten for less than the price of two coffees in the fashionable arcades in Milano, she placed an arm on their young shoulders and said it was her great pleasure. 'Now,' she said, 'let's get down to business and see what we can do to help your dad to find some decent work.'

They agreed to talk where strangers could not hear them, so they all piled into Giovanna's car and headed for the rundown part of town where the Alessi family lived. The children's eyes were like saucers. Signora Weiss, no – Giovanna - must be really rich. This car was amazing, big and powerful and Giovanna drove as well as any man. As instructed by Martin, she parked the car outside the big old stone-built house where the family had a fifth floor apartment. They poured out onto the pavement. where they were at once surrounded by a crush of neighbourhood children, all jabbering excitedly. How did the Alessis get to ride in such a flash car? Who was this older woman with the smart clothes and the jewellery? No relation of theirs, surely. Everyone knew they were poor because their dad was a cripple. Even their mum had taken off with another man because of him. Martin heard all this and for once did not shout at the neighbours' children to shut them up. He turned to the assembled crowd and said in a dignified tone, 'this is our friend Signora Weiss, who is paying us a visit. We would be grateful if one of you could keep an eye on her car to make sure no-one harms it. I will pay for the service of course. Who would like the job?' The response was deafening. 'Me me me!' came from nearly every child's lips. In the end Martin gave each child there a small sum of money, thus guaranteeing the complete safety of Giovanna's vehicle and the everlasting good will of the local ice cream vendor.

The apartment was reached by five flights of increasingly steep stairs. Exhausted as he was by the effort, Martin was apologetic. 'You get what you pay for I'm afraid,' he told Giovanna, 'and this is all we could afford.' Giovanna thanked God she was still reasonably fit so that the stairs did not knock her out too much. All the same, she was a bit out of breath when they got to the flat, and she needed a few moments to recover. While their father rested his poor aching legs, the children fussed around over her, bringing her water and fanning her with sheets of paper taken from their school books. 'Where do the children play?' she asked Martin. 'They don't,' he replied, 'not unless I'm with them. I can't let them go down onto the streets, not round here. There's too many shady types out there.' 'What happens if your legs are too sore to manage the stairs?' Giovanna went on. 'We all stay in.' It seemed to Giovanna that these children were being deprived of their childhood through no fault of their own or their father's. Forced to take on adult roles far too young, they were also denied the right to just be kids. She compared this family's life with young Ricardo's experience, and it came up seriously wanting. 'What would you like for them?' she asked. 'A safe place to live, a decent school where the teachers don't hit the kids, and some space to play in the fresh air,' was Martin's response. 'Oh, and some proper work for me so I can feed them good food with real meat.' Giovanna was impressed by Martin's honesty and dignity. He did not think the world owed him a living, indeed quite the opposite, he wanted to shoulder his responsibilities as a man. He just couldn't do it in this place. Promising to try her hardest to find a way to help, Giovanna made to leave. 'I know some people who may be useful,' she said, 'but I'll have to talk to them first. I obviously can't commit them to anything, but I am hopeful.'

On her way down the long staircase she was accompanied by the two older children. Arriving at her car she found it surrounded by a phalanx of protective little guards, all of them in the last stages of polishing off their tutti fruttis and their napolitanos. The cornets did look good. 'Here,' she said to Maria and Marco, pressing some coins into the older girl's hand, 'take this and get a nice big bowl of ice cream for yourselves as well. We can't have you lot missing out!' 'Grazie cara Giovanna!' they cried and then, to her immense surprise and pleasure, they both reached up and kissed her cheek before racing off excitedly in the direction of the ice-cream man. Their calls of 'arrivederci' wafted back to her on the late afternoon breeze.

Well pleased with her day's work, she headed back as fast as she could to Matera, and within seconds of arrival at her home, was on the telephone to Caterina. A family conference was called for as soon as possible. 'There's a plan I need to talk about,' she said. Caterina was intrigued and agreed to make the necessary arrangements. Two days later, at the appointed hour, Sophia, Caterina and Albert and the two older boys sat themselves down around the big farmhouse kitchen table to hear about Giovanna's 'plan'. What on earth could it be? They were about to find out.

Giovanna had prepared herself well for this important meeting. She had made notes and done her sums, so that nothing would be left to chance or decided by emotion. She planned to propose that the Alessi family be offered the rental of half of the big farmhouse with the boys in the other half. The children would attend the local school, and Martin could set up a carpentry workshop in one of the empty barns and run a small business from there, paying rent and overheads in the normal manner. She had made calculations about his likely income and outgoings and the figures added up. He may even in time be able to offer employment to another or other ex-soldiers who found themselves in need of a job. There were certainly plenty of farmers and other locals who needed the services of a good wood-worker, especially as the war had taken so many craftsmen. Sophia, she would suggest, should move in with Albert and Caterina and no longer try to manage such a big household now that housework had become so much harder for her. Before she made any such proposals, however, Giovanna made a short and carefully-considered speech on the state of the family as she saw it, emphasising her view that the women especially needed a role, to feel useful and valuable. She explained how she had met Martin Alessi and the children and described the parlous state they were living in. They needed to move and get a better life, and there was certainly room at the farm. Supporting Martin and his family would give the women a focus, and they could he helpful teaching skills to the children, especially the girls who had no mother on whom to model themselves. Giovanna planned that she would take a role in the conduct of Martin's business, for he had little formal education, especially in matters of finance. In this way all three would have something to fill the chasm left by the death of Giovanni and the departure of Ricardo. 'We have been lucky,' she told them. 'When we three were in trouble Charlie and Albert turned up and saved us. Well, now Martin and the children are in trouble and we can try and save them. What do you think?'

Albert was the first to speak. He turned to Giovanna and said, 'I'm proud of you lass. There's a tradition of helping people in this family, and it looks like you're giving us the chance to carry the job on. I'm all for it. I don't see why this chap should suffer because he served his country and got injured doing it, and his kids certainly shouldn't. We're well off. We can afford to be generous to another human being. I say yes.' Hearing this, his two sons voiced their agreement. It would be good to have some more people about the place. It had been getting horribly quiet of late with just the older ones around. Caterina said she too was in favour.

Giovanna then looked over at Sophia. She was looking rather anxious. Change of any kind upset her these days, and here she was being asked to make a really big move for some complete strangers. Prompted by her daughter, the old lady spoke. Her voice was surprisingly calm and strong. 'I am asking myself what Giovanni would say,' she said, 'and I am thinking that as a man he would agree with Alberto because he would never let his heart rule his head. But I am a woman and I must listen to my heart as well. Everything worth doing in my life has been done in this house. Before I came here I was no-one, a girl with nothing. Giovanni made me his wife and later on the mother to his children. I loved that. Now he is gone and I am no-one once again. Giovanni's widow, poor pathetic sad Sophia.' At this there were cries of protest from the others at the table. Sophia went on. 'The only things I have which mean anything to me are memories of things that have happened in this house. My wedding, and the births of my children took place here. Giovanni and Alessandro went off to the war from here. Charlie and Albert arriving and saving us from ruin, that happened here. Alessandro was found and we were reunited here. Here we have had parties and celebrations, welcomed new lives here and said farewell as young ones have moved away to seek their fortune. All in this house, mostly in this very kitchen. Everywhere I look in this house reminds me of the past. That is why I don't want to leave it, even just to move a few metres away.' The family sat silently. If Sophia felt this strongly, they could not expect her to go along with 'the plan', however noble it might be. Then she surprised them all by saying, 'but I will move and give my home to this young family who need it so much because Alberto is right. We do have a family tradition of helping others and we should not forget that. It is what Giovanni would want and what our God would expect of us. We have a chance to make better the lives of four people, maybe more, and selfishness or sentiment should not stop us. Therefore I accept Giovanna's proposals too.' After a few seconds' stunned silence, the younger ones burst into spontaneous applause. 'Brava Nonna!' 'Well said, mother,' with which Giovanna leant over to Sophia and embraced her fondly. Albert, in his position as the new head of the family posed the formal question, 'well, people, do we need to take a vote?' 'No,' said Sophia, 'this time we don't need to vote.'

New life at the farm

Within a fortnight, the Alessi family had gratefully left their tatty little flat in Taranto and had moved into the farmhouse, lock stock and barrel, not that they had much to bring with them. They had used the intervening time to get to know their new hosts and to reassure them that they were not only nice but trustworthy and hardworking. Sophia was instantly taken by little Carla, who reminded her of Caterina as a child, and soon found herself in grandmother mode, spending time reading to the child and helping her to make little things to play with. Carla was strong and independent for her age, and said it as she saw it. Her antics and her funny expressions quickly had Sophia laughing, something the old lady had not done a great deal in the months since Giovanni's death. Precisely what Giovanna had hoped for was actually happening. For Caterina as well, the presence of the children was a joy, and there was always something that needed doing with or for them. Caterina it was who went along to the school with the older ones and settled them in, since Martin was busy setting up his workshop. Caterina made the clothes they needed to replace the shabby items they had worn in the town so that the local children would have no cause to mock them. Caterina also spent some time each day with the older two children, helping them with their homework and their little domestic chores, generally playing the role of the mother who had abandoned them.

The men of the family took to Martin at once. They liked him and admired his courage and his complete lack of self-pity. Albert especially was only too pleased to have a new project as the work of the farm took less and less of his time these days. What with the two boys and the tractors, there was not much a grey haired old man of fifty-two was needed for really. His skills as a carpenter, however, he had not forgotten and he was glad to share his expertise and his tools with the younger man. His good legs meant that even an old boy like himself could be of use when Martin needed something fetching from town in the car. He also had his contacts in the locality which would be helpful in drumming up business. All in all, the new arrangements looked promising. Giovanna made herself fully available from the outset, helping Martin to set up the systems he needed for running a company. She went with him to the bank, and to the local government offices to make sure everything he did was above board and by the rules. She also worked with him to devise enticing advertisements for the Matera and Taranto newspapers, and leaflets which would be put up in local shops and delivered by hand to the more isolated farms in the district. These were produced by a skilled printer in Taranto, and looked very professional. When they were ready, Caterina and the older children set off on their bicycles to distribute them. It was a real team effort. With everyone pulling together, how could they fail? It was like 'I Trovatori' all over again, but without the music. It seemed no time at all that word about the new workshop got about and commissions started to trickle in. Martin soon had as much work as he could handle alone and sometimes had to engage the services of Albert to get a job finished on time.

Certainly it was to a very different family that Charlie returned when he came home for Christmas. Giovanna had kept him informed of all the latest developments but he had not anticipated how beneficial the new setup would be. The women's spirits had been lifted beyond all measure. Sophia had found a renewed purpose in life and was now seen to smile and even share a joke with little Carla. Caterina had a new role with the older children, and even Albert was markedly less grumpy than he had been, no longer feeling he was surplus to requirements. For Giovanna too, the chance to do something she was good at and at the same time to improve another person's life, had helped her to forget her sadness. Of course they all missed Giovanni and always would, but they could now see that life must go on. Charlie felt a great sense of relief. It had seemed to him that he was the only one of the older generation doing anything interesting and fulfilling, now they all were. Giovanna was a genius, inspired! Seeing the happy faces of his loved ones as they sat around the table, he realised that he adored her even more than ever.

For Charlie it was an exciting time too, for there were moves afoot which would restore Italy's badly-damaged standing in Europe. For the first time, the old enemies, France and Germany, were planning to co-operate on a major development, the European Coal and Steel Community. Along with them would be Italy and the three nations referred to as Benelux – Belgium, the Netherlands and Luxembourg. Initially, this was a move to ensure that the production of coal and steel was carried out sensibly, but Charlie could see more far-reaching benefits. If these nations, all of whom had suffered terribly from the wars they had fought against each other, could work together economically, might they not also work together at a political level? The way Charlie saw it, as did many of the people he was meeting on his diplomatic visits to Germany and France, this was the continent's only hope of achieving a lasting peace. History must not be repeated. Old enmities needed to be buried and new ways of living together found. Charlie was both proud and pleased to be part of something that looked like becoming so important. He wondered if Britain might be involved at any time, after all there were considerable resources of coal and steel in that country which could be of use to the whole of Western Europe. The promise of a lasting peace would also go a long way to ensuring stability and prosperity for the poor battered hungry land he and Albert used to call home.

Now, however, it was time to put political matters aside and concentrate on the serious business at hand, namely Christmas. The Alessi children had never known a really good family Christmas. Either their father had been away at the war or he and their mother were fighting about money. For them the festive season was not a time of goodwill. There was an opportunity to redress the balance, and the best, indeed the only, person to organise it was the family's acknowledged Christmas expert – Sophia. Despite her years, for she was by now seventy-three and slowing down a bit,   Sophia threw herself into the preparations with the energy of a much younger woman. It was something she loved to do, and as long as she had help with the practical bits, she could manage. This year, rather than have some of the food made in Matera and Taranto, she decided that she and the three children, with assistance from Caterina and Giovanna, would make everything from scratch. It would be a good chance for the young ones to learn new skills, and it would also ensure that they made a proper contribution, rather than just allowing it all to be paid for. In any case, their dad Martin needed not to squander his precious earnings, nor to feel patronised by the much wealthier del Pieros and Weisses because he couldn't pay his way. All children needed to learn the value of work and earned income. Charlie was impressed by the old lady. Still taking the adult role seriously after all these years and not about to spoil anyone, even though she easily could.

The couple of weeks before Christmas were a hive of activity. The food that was not home-produced was brought in from the local shops and neighbouring farms by Caterina and Giovanna in their cars. In the big farmhouse kitchen, drafted back into service, everything that could be made in advance of the day was cooked, pickled and preserved. Great tubs of ice were placed in one of the barns to keep the produce as fresh as possible. Baking was the order of the day and sweet smells filled the house. In particular it was the aroma of Sophia's pannetone wafting through that drew people in. Lemony and fruity and lightly dusted with icing sugar, it looked as good as it smelt and it was all Charlie could do not to steal a slice and run off with it. The older boys were sidling about, casting covetous glances as well, but their grandmother spotted them and drove them out. Nothing would be eaten before the day of the feast. She was determined that Christmas 1949 was to be perfect, one the Alessi children would never forget. Charlie was thrilled to see her so alert and interested. 'Bless these children and bless Christmas', he thought, 'they have brought Sophia back to life.' He bowed his head and thanked God for the gift of his son.

In addition to the food preparation, there was the matter of guest accommodation to be attended to, for Sophia was set on having the whole family together again, only this time for a happy occasion. With the farmhouse fully occupied, it was up to Caterina to provide lodgings for Giuseppe and his family as well as for her daughters and Ricardo. This she was thrilled to do, for the inevitable chaos would bring back memories of her happiest days as a wife and mother. Alessandro would stay with Giovanna and Charlie in the adult peace and quiet of Matera. The five-strong Milano contingent travelled together, thanks once more to the generosity of the Duke. This time they made the long trip by rail, the fares sponsored by the doting grandfather. The Duke, it seemed, was now completely won over and had even consented to allow his precious daughter to become Signora Weiss. A church wedding being out of the question, there would be a simple civil ceremony in January with no fuss and certainly no party. The old boy may have softened but he still pulled all the social strings! A day or two before Christmas, Alessandro arrived from Rome, by car, and installed himself in Charlie and Giovanna's best spare room. Ricardo was the last to arrive, as training commitments kept him in Torino until the latest possible minute. To compensate, the club paid for a chaperoned flight to Naples and a first class train ticket to Taranto. How the other half lived! By the afternoon of Christmas Eve, the assembly was complete. Later that night all of them, including baby Francesco, well-wrapped against the December cold, piled into several cars and went to midnight mass in the little village church where they sang the familiar carols with gusto. Sophia looked around at her own precious family and at the Alessis, all together and happy, and her heart soared.

On Christmas morning, after early mass and communion, permission was at last granted to cut and toast the precious pannetones and slice after delectable slice disappeared as thirteen adults and five children crowded around the table in the cosy coffee-scented warmth of the farmhouse kitchen. Even baby Francesco had a taste. What a start to the day! Breakfast done, it was all hands to the pump to help prepare the celebration meal. Clever Sophia had managed to get hold of the most enormous goose Charlie had ever seen, so big it needed a man to carry it, full of sweet chestnuts and dried apricots, to the range. Charlie was glad to oblige. He still liked to cook, although he had fewer opportunities these days. He was given goose-basting duties, but cunning Sophia had another task for him as well. He was to see to the pasta course. The home- made spaghetti was hanging by the side of the stove ready to go. All it needed was a great vat of sauce. The ingredients, she told him, were in the pantry waiting for him. As Charlie suspected, the old lady was testing his memory, for arrayed on the bench along with the dark green olive oil were fat cloves of garlic, onions, tomatoes preserved in jars, shiny black olives from the farm's trees, and salty little anchovies. A fine chunk of parmesan completed the line-up. The makings of spaghetti alla puttanesca! 'Well done, Sophia!' he called, 'let's hear it for the working girls of Napoli!' And he set to with a will to replicate the sauce he had first tasted in this very kitchen more than thirty years earlier.

Everyone had a task allotted to them in this masterpiece of organisation. For some it was to do with food, for others with decorations, firewood, table setting, whatever needed doing. By one o'clock, everything was ready and Sophia indicated to Charlie that he could now do the job he liked so much, namely opening the sparkling wine. Several bottles were fetched in from the chilly barn, and soon all the adults had a frothing glass in their hand. The Alessi children were allowed a small taste, much diluted with mineral water, so that they could join in the Christmas toast. 'Buon' Natale tutti' said Charlie, raising his glass in salute. 'Buon' Natale!' was the mass response, 'Buon' Natale!'

The day passed by in a pleasurable blur of sumptuous feasting, the giving and receiving of gifts and, later on, in keeping with Weiss family tradition, music around the piano. First Charlie, then Alessandro, sat at the keys and thumped out a few of the favourites from the 'I Trovatori' days and those who could, joined in. Sophia laughed to hear the old songs again. It reminded her of Christmases in the 1920s when they had all been together, not thinking that it would ever end. Suddenly a shadow passed across her face as she remembered her darling Giovanni, now gone forever. Carla saw this and went over to the old lady. Climbing onto her lap she kissed her cheek and whispered in her wise little way, 'don't be sad, nonna, you've got me now. I'll look after you, you'll see.'

The New Year was just a few days old when a letter arrived for Charlie. The envelope was edged in black ink and addressed in the distinctive copper plate handwriting of his sister Mary. The stamp bore a Blackburn postmark. There was almost no need to open it to find out what it was about, but Charlie did so, very carefully, sensing that this was a document that he would wish to keep for some time to come. Mary's letter was little more than a note but said all that was needed. Their father had followed their mother to heaven on Christmas Day. In early December, he had had a bad fall at home and his poor old body never got over the shock. He took to his bed and bit by bit relinquished his grip on life, finally passing away peacefully in the early hours of Christmas morning. He had not been in pain as the nice National Health doctor had given him some strong medicine after the fall. Mary concluded by saying she was sure he was now where he wanted to be, buried alongside his beloved wife in the little Catholic churchyard in Great Harwood. The letter ended with the words 'Joe and Annie send their love, as do I. Your sister, Mary'. Charlie sat for a while at the table, reading and re-reading the note. Coming so soon after the death of Giovanni, this was a blow. Not unexpected, for his father had achieved the great age of seventy-seven, unusual in the unhealthy climate of a Lancashire mill town. Not unwelcome, for he knew that his father had yearned to be re-united with his wife. But certainly sad, because there was now no chance whatsoever that Charlie would be able to tell him how much he loved and admired him. With Giovanna at his side, he laid his head on his hands and quietly wept.

CHAPTER EIGHT

Seeds of conflict, signs of hope

As the second half of the century began, in the east Stalin continued to strengthen his grip on the satellite nations surrounding the Soviet Union. He had been obliged to abandon the blockade of Berlin in the May of 1949, realising that he would never be able to starve the city into submission. However, he exerted a formidable control over all the communist nations of Europe, with the exception of Yugoslavia, and seemed able to appoint and dismiss leaders at will. At home and abroad, his methods were ruthless and brutal. Opponents silly enough to make their views known simply disappeared. A reign of terror was set up in all the Soviet Republics and the neighbouring lands. Millions lost their lives in forced labour camps and in front of the firing squad. The 'Man Of Steel' and his henchmen made Hitler look like a rank amateur. Winston Churchill's evaluation of him, made at the end of the war, was proving to be horribly accurate, and now that he was Prime Minister of Britain once again, people were starting to realise that.

In the west of Europe, events in the east were seen as threatening not only regional but global stability. Stalin's hostility to the USA and the capitalist nations, was explicit and total. His commitment to permanent revolution meant he would stop at nothing to destroy their way of life. The presence of a common enemy had the effect of drawing nations who had once been at war closer together. Finding themselves on the front line between the United States and the Soviet Union's sphere of influence, they began to seek ways to co-operate more fully to protect themselves and preserve their hard-won peace.

It was against this background of Cold War tension that Charlie carried out his work on behalf of the Italian Government. The European Coal and Steel Community came into being in 1951, but already in France and Germany voices were being heard putting forward the notion of a wider economic union which would abolish import and export duties between member nations and might even one day lead to some kind of political alliance. Men like Adenauer, now the leader of West Germany, and prominent figures in France seemed keen on the idea as a way of putting an end to war in Europe forever. In Italy, too Government figures were broadly in favour of closer ties, and commissioned Charlie to do some research work in the business and commercial sectors to see how the giants of industry and banking felt such a notion could be advanced. It was this work that took him once again to the major financial centre of Frankfurt. It was the spring of 1952, and in the sunshine on the Römerplatz, the trees were bursting into life. Once settled into his hotel, not a cheap one in the little streets by the Hauptbahnhof this time, Charlie got in touch with the American base, to see if perhaps General Green or Lieutenant Jones were still about. It was over two years since he had been there, and a lot can change in that time, but it was worth a try. He at least owed them a thank you for all the help they had given him. He thought maybe they would know where the Schmidt youngsters were, if they were still in contact with them. As one might predict, there had been a flood of correspondence for a few months after Charlie had left them, but this had become a trickle before drying up altogether in 1950. You couldn't expect anything other really. He must have seemed very old to them. He seemed it to himself too some days. He spoke on the telephone to a friendly receptionist. Lieutenant Jones, it seemed, had already moved on, having been promoted and posted to none other than the Pentagon where she held an important developmental brief linked to NATO. Charlie suspected as much. She was far too clever and talented to languish for long as a General's dogsbody. She reminded Charlie of Gayle whom he had loved all those years ago in New Zealand. He liked strong women he decided, and there was none stronger than Giovanna. Look how she had stepped in and found a solution to the family's woes after the death of Giovanni. Thinking of her, he felt reassured that things would be going well for the ones he loved that were so far away and beyond his ability to help. General Green, however, was still around, and was pleased to invite Charlie to his office. The Schmidt youngsters, it transpired, had done exceptionally well, being hard-working and determined to make the most of the chance their mother had given them. After two years in Frankfurt, with the General's help and a lot of US government sponsorship, they had all three moved to America to continue their studies. They were attending university in New York. Two of them, the boys Rainer and Werner, were studying business administration and law respectively at Columbia, while their sister Gisela had shown herself to be a gifted musician and was at the Juilliard. Impressed and grateful, Charlie wondered if Frau Schmidt knew about this, and decided to see if he could find a way to contact her that would not get her and Johann into trouble with the East German secret police, the dreaded Stasi. 'They have you to thank, Mr Weiss,' the General was generous enough to say, as he had his secretary give Charlie the youngsters' postal address. To Charlie's eye, it was very exotic. New York, New York, eh? Belt and braces? And why 'Zip Code'? Puzzling indeed. All the same, he sat down later that night and wrote a letter to them, vowing to do the same for their brave little mum if he could.

His chance came later in the same year when he was asked to go to Berlin to meet with some business men there. The 'Wirtschaftswunder' was underway, and all over the nation men and women were rebuilding their shattered country with zeal. Despite the difficulties caused by its location, surrounded by a hostile state, industry and business were re-establishing themselves in West Berlin, thanks to vast amounts of investment and the sheer hard work for which the Germans were so famous. In contrast with the last time, when he had crossed the Ost-Zone slowly in a battered farm truck, this time he flew direct from Rhein-Main in Frankfurt to Templehof. It was interesting looking down, to see how little progress had been made rebuilding the East after the war. In the West many places now bore few scars of the bombing and the shelling, but once the border had been crossed, there was still much evidence of destruction. Charlie was also quite shocked to see how reinforced the border had become. There was no chance of just sneaking out and crossing a river, as he had done with the Schmidts. The East Germans were now definitely prisoners in their own homeland. Arriving at Templehof, he was struck by how much less hectic it was than when he had seen Giovanna off to London at the height of the blockade. Some form of normality had clearly been restored, albeit under very problematic conditions. Despite, or maybe because of, the ever-present threat from the Communists, West Berliners went about their daily lives with gusto. In the city, bars and coffee houses were well-patronised, and the shops seemed full of everything the west had to offer. Like the French before them, in the Great War, the citizens of Berlin refused to be ground down by the enemy. There it had been flowers in window boxes and here it was conspicuous consumption and dedication to having fun.

However it was done, Charlie rather approved of people who stuck two fingers up to those who would oppress them.

Charlie's meetings with Berlin's leaders of commerce and industry went well. There was a lot of interest in the idea of a closer European economic union, and maybe even one day for a political one to emerge. People were keen to forget what had gone on during the war and make some progress toward restoring a civilised society in Germany, one that would have some standing on the international scene. The men Charlie met were too young to have been actively engaged in fighting the war or in the running of the concentration camps. They were a new breed, and they totally disparaged as spineless 'die alten Nazis' still living amongst them. Most of them had been forced to join the Hitler youth movement and told tales of the uniforms, the marching and the endless, incessant bloody Mahler. They knew how lucky they were that where they lived, one tyranny had not been replaced by another. Many of them had relatives in the Ost Zone whom they could no longer see. Some were only a short distance way, just the wrong side of the Zonengrenze – the inner German border. They might as well have been on the moon. It was a constant source of pain for them and their families, one which would not go away until the Communists were driven out. But Stalin's grip was tight and there were no signs that Germany or even Berlin would ever be reunited. Not in Charlie's lifetime anyway.

One of the men did have links behind the Iron Curtain and was able to come and go with relative ease. His name he gave as Norbert Onnen, but, as was the custom in Germany, first names were never used. He was a sugar importer, and most of his sugar was grown in the Ost-Zone or Poland. Even the Communists needed a market for their products, so he spent some time at various collective farms agreeing prices and arranging supplies. Of course, he was constantly searched and interrogated, made to wait in draughty border posts for hours and generally mucked about with, but he did get to visit the east, and was sometimes able to take messages or even small gifts to those trapped behind the border. Charlie saw him as the chance to get word to Frau Schmidt on the whereabouts of her children. He might also be able to gather some information as to her well-being and that of the children's father for Charlie to pass on to the youngsters in New York.

Over an excellent meal one lunchtime, he told Herr Onnen the story of the Schmidts and how they had escaped from the communists. The younger man was especially taken by Charlie's account of how the older son Johann had feigned madness to convince the border guards that he was trying to break into the Ost-Zone. As if anyone in their right mind would! Those border guards were even thicker than he thought. Having established that he did indeed buy from a sugar farm near the Schmidts' place, he agreed to try and make contact with the family. The head of the collective, he was sure, would readily accept a small financial consideration in return for arranging a meeting. They hated the government for its blind allegiance to Stalin and its reign of terror as much as people in the west did, maybe more. In any case, Herr Onnen was always looking for something on which to spend the ridiculous amount of East German currency they made you change at the border. There was nothing worth buying in the East, and the food in restaurants was as cheap as it was disgusting. You couldn't bring money back, because they made you donate any leftovers 'to charity' on your way out. A likely tale. As if a Communist state needed charities. The border guards' beer fund, more like! He often gave a handful of coins to the children on a farm, or took a couple of complete strangers out for a meal on his last night. Next time he went over the border, he would use the excess cash to facilitate a discreet get-together with Frau Schmidt and Johann, and hopefully with Herr Schmidt as well. Charlie was thrilled. It was far more than he could have hoped for. Herr Onnen was a charming and intelligent young man who would easily be able put Frau Schmidt's mind at rest. He also promised to write to Charlie in Italy and tell him how it had all gone. Pleased as Punch, Charlie returned to Rome, his paymasters and then, Giovanna and home.

A month later, as summer turned to autumn, a letter with a Berlin postmark arrived in Matera. Herr Onnen was as good as his word. He told how he had made contact with Frau Schmidt through the good offices of the chief of the sugar beet collective, always glad of a bit more money than the state was prepared to put his way. A meeting had been set up at the chief's office, since a stranger arriving at Frau Schmidt's little farm would draw unwanted attention and get her into trouble with the Stasi. They had watching eyes everywhere, and were especially interested in citizens suspected of being sympathetic to the West. Herr Onnen was sorry to advise Herr Weiss that Frau Schmidt's husband had not returned to the farm in 1949. He had simply disappeared the day he was picked up by the secret police, never to be seen again. In the unlikely event that he was still alive, he was assuredly doing hard labour in one of Stalin's infamous prison camps for daring to speak his mind about the Berlin blockade. Frau Schmidt and Johann were carrying on the work of the farm, and eking out a very meagre living. Because Herr Schmidt was seen as a traitor, his wife and son were tarred with the same brush and no-one would even dare give Johann a job of any kind, however menial. To describe their life as hand to mouth was to understate the case. This time, Herr Onnen had had no trouble deciding to whom he would give the rest of his cash.

He had passed on the good news about the three youngsters in America, and Frau Schmidt had cried from sheer happiness. It was all worthwhile, the poverty, the surveillance, the overt hostility from neighbours and villagers, all of it, to know that her precious kids were safe and well. She asked Herr Onnen to thank Herr Weiss most warmly for her once again for having rescued her beloved family. Charlie was moved to read Herr Onnen's account of this brave woman's life and that of her poor damaged son. It made him angry too, to see what was being done to people in the name of so-called socialism. This police state bore no relation whatsoever to the kind of socialism he supported. It was meant to make life better for people, not worse. Who was it that said 'power corrupts and absolute power corrupts absolutely'? If whoever it was was right, Stalin and his lickspittles in the surrounding lapdog states must be the most corrupt men on earth, for they had the power of life and death over people whose only 'crime' was to have been born with a mind of their own. Sad and sick to the heart, Charlie sat down to compose a letter to Rainer, Werner and Gisela. It was one of the most difficult letters he had ever had to write.

Autumn melded seamlessly into winter, another Christmas came, was celebrated quietly, and went, and 1952 became 1953. As the soil began to warm, and in the southern lands the green shoots of spring started to appear, there came the news the whole world had been waiting for. Stalin was dead. After nearly thirty one years in power, with millions of his compatriots murdered at his command, one of the most evil men ever to walk the earth was no more. Charlie read the news and wept at the waste of life. Maybe now with 'Uncle

Joe' gone, some kind of humanity might re-establish itself in Russia, maybe even some form of democratic socialism. He prayed it would. Surely whoever followed him could not possibly be as tyrannical. Could they?

Of course, Charlie was doomed to be disappointed. Stalin was followed by Malenkov, who was soon elbowed out of the limelight by the ebullient, and rather coarse, Khrushchev. On the face of it he was a better man than Stalin, but he showed no signs of relaxing the state's hold on every aspect of ordinary people's lives, and no inclination to let the satellite nations choose their own path. In 1955, as a direct challenge to NATO, the Warsaw Pact was set up, giving the communist states a military as well as a political and economic unity. Both sides now had a powerful nuclear arsenal. In the Cold War, like was facing like.

The world was suddenly a much more dangerous place and Europe was on the front line. Nowhere was this more acutely felt than in Germany. Having been devastated by war only ten years before, people started to fear that the Americans and the Soviets might just try out their new toys in the skies over Munich and Hamburg. They listened in disbelief as American hard-line anti-Communists, whipped into a frenzy by the Un-American Activities Committee, mooted the possibility of 'limited nuclear war' against Russia in Europe. As if the power of the bomb could be 'limited.' They knew from Japan that it could not. They also looked on in horror as the Soviet Union brutally crushed the Hungarian uprising of 1956 killing thousands of innocent men, women and children. If they behaved like that towards their allies, how would they treat their enemies? The view began to spread that Western Europe should form itself into a stronger entity to counterbalance the influence and the might of the two superpowers. In many of the founding nations a broad consensus was emerging and work began in earnest on strengthening the links formed by the Coal and Steel Community. In March 1957, years of negotiations finally came to fruition with the signing of the Treaty of Rome, and the establishment of the European Economic Community. The way was paved for Western Europe to unite. Charlie was delighted. Maybe now the possibility that there might be a third war was banished at last. Charlie's next task was to persuade the Community to admit other countries, starting with Britain and Ireland. This would make Europe a much more credible force in the face of the threat from the east. However, with very vocal opposition coming from Charles de Gaulle the highly influential former Free French leader and French President-in-waiting, this looked like being a much harder nut to crack.

The more things change...

Sometimes, no matter what he had on, Charlie just had to be back with the family, and there were several such times in 1957. The first was the occasion of Sophia's eightieth birthday, in the April of that year. This was to be a major family event. Everyone was expected. Since the last great do, the family had increased in numbers. Giuseppe and Francesca had two more children, boisterous brothers for Francesco, and their arrival was bound to up the noise level. Teresa and Gina, now in their late twenties, both had fiancés in tow, but were not looking like marrying or having children in the near future. They were too busy with their own highly successful careers in the fashion industry for all that. Ricardo was now playing and scoring regularly for the senior team at Juventus and was to be seen on the back pages of the newspapers most

Mondays, as well as on the covers of the women's magazines, frequently in the company of some glamorous young model or aspiring actress. At the tender age of eighteen he was certainly not planning to settle down. Indeed it was reported that two other great European clubs, Spain's Réal Madrid and Germany's Bayern München, were keen to persuade him to play for them, for a vast increase in pay of course. Alessandro had at last found someone with whom to share his life, she was called Rosa, a brave partisan's widow, and she and her children had brought him great happiness and fulfilment away from the constant demands of his work for the government. Only Albert's two middle sons remained unchanged. Carlo and Giorgio were content to run the farm, go fishing and shooting, and to sing in the church choir. Their lives were simple and they wanted for nothing. Sometimes Albert asked himself if he had done something wrong as a father. Should he have stimulated or inspired them more? In the end he decided that they were as they were – his lads – and he loved them wholeheartedly. He told Charlie he wished they'd give him some grandchildren to dote on, but it didn't look like happening. 'Just as well,' Charlie thought, 'there's enough Donkin offspring around here to be going on with!' He didn't say so, though. He'd at last learnt when to bite his lip.

The Alessi family had had their share of changes too. Martin's woodworking business was doing well and he had been able to take on a couple of other ex-soldiers to train up. His children were growing rapidly, and the older two, both extremely clever and hard-working, were being groomed for University, the first ever from the farm to do so. This was a great source of pride for all concerned, especially Caterina who had spent so much of her time with them. Little Carla, now thirteen, was a much less intellectual child, far more emotional and intuitive than her siblings. She loved caring for people and animals, in fact it was through her love that Sophia had been brought back from the brink of despair after Giovanni's death. She was always finding something or someone to help – an injured rabbit, or a schoolmate in distress. She looked like being the one that would follow the traditional womanly path into marriage and family well before any of the others did. Sophia adored her.

The scale of Sophia's party was such that the caterers had to be called in and a great marquee erected in the garden. April in southern Italy is a warm month, and there was no fear that the weather would spoil proceedings. It wouldn't dare! Once again, Sophia, ably assisted by her daughters, had designed the event from top to toe. Everything was colour co-ordinated, the flowers, the linen, the candles, the clothes, even the food. Only Sophia remained in black. Her continued mourning for Giovanni was not to be forgotten, even for one day. All morning there was frenzied activity as the food was brought in, and the marquee decorated. Towards noon the musicians arrived, and set up on a raised platform at one end of the great tent. If the food was not to be home-made, neither, for once, was the music. Sophia had ordered a chamber orchestra to play her favourite classical pieces throughout the serving of the meal. This was to be a classy affair. It wasn't every day a girl turned eighty! At one o'clock, the horde of guests started to arrive from all over the local area, and were greeted individually by Teresa and Gina. Each person was given a glass of ice-cold Asti with which to toast the health of their hostess. As her oldest offspring, it fell to Alessandro to make the birthday speech, and he did it with great skill and grace as well as with love. He made it abundantly clear just what a wonderful woman his mother was, what a tower of strength she had been and continued to be, and how much he and all the family owed her. A small girlish voice was heard to say 'Brava Nonna!' and a ripple of laughter went around the room. At Alessandro's bidding, a hundred glasses were raised and a hundred voices said in unison 'to Sophia, long life and happiness!' Sophia remained seated throughout, befitting a woman of her years, but she put her hands together in a gesture of humility, and, visibly moved, thanked the many well-wishers for their kindness. Then, dabbing away a single escaping tear, she bade the orchestra strike up, and in the time-honoured way, ordered the feast to begin. 'Mangiamo!'

A few weeks later, Charlie returned to the farm for another celebration, this time a much more modest one. On June 10th, 1957, his best friend and brother in all but blood, turned sixty. Forty years earlier Albert had been under enemy fire at Ypres and more than likely to be killed. Your luck could only hold out so long, and his nine lives had been used up on the Somme. Now he was a proud father of six, grandfather of three, a much-loved husband, a successful farmer and an erstwhile professional singer. He had brought joy to so many people in those years. How could what he and Charlie had done be held against them still? It was, of course. Contrary to Charlie and Albert's expectations, there had never been an amnesty or a pardon for Great War deserters in the United Kingdom. Canada, Australia and New Zealand, realising what hell their men had been put through by bungling and callous generals, had pardoned those who had walked away from the trenches, seeing it not as a sign of cowardice but as evidence that there is a limit to the amount of violence and horror a human being can take before they lose their grip on sanity. There had been plenty written about those poor sods who actually had lost their minds and had wandered off into No Man's Land, dazed and muttering, only to be arrested, summarily court-martialled and shot. It was a scandal, especially as it was now known that members of the officer class were given the chance to repent their behaviour and were spared the firing squad. Once again the toffs and generals took it out on ordinary blokes, and protected their own kind. It made Charlie's blood boil. He and Albert had got out only days before almost certain death in the mud at Paschendale, and while they still had brains that worked. As a result, neither of them could ever tell the truth about what they had seen and done in those terrible years, nor indeed about who they really were. On the positive side, had they not walked away, they would never have come to this wonderful farm and these gorgeous women who were now their wives. Brushing dark memories aside, Charlie rose to his feet, the ever present glass of Asti in his hand, and proposed a toast to his best pal. Since no-one other than immediate family was there, he did it in English. 'Happy Birthday, you old bugger!' he said fondly, 'Happy Birthday and many more!' Albert replied in kind. 'Well, thanks a lot old chum. Just wait till you get this side of sixty. I'll insult you then!' 'It's a deal,' came the reply. 'Cheers!'

The third family event of that year was indeed the celebration of Charlie's own sixtieth birthday, in October. Officially he was already sixty-one according to his papers, nevertheless, Giovanna felt that some kind of small scale event to mark the occasion would be appropriate. She decided that the older adults would go out for a slap-up meal in the best restaurant in Taranto as her treat. Money being no object, she booked a window table for seven at a plush waterside establishment famous for its fish, and arranged taxis to collect Albert, Caterina and Sophia at the farm, and herself, Charlie, Alessandro and Rosa from the house in Matera. No-one would have to drive so everyone could relax and just have a wonderful time together. Which is exactly what they did. The food was superb, the wine exquisite and the ambience perfect. As for the price – that was Giovanna's secret. As it was autumn, a hearty fish soup topped with rich aioli was on the menu, as were fat succulent oysters and juicy orange mussels. It was jolly hard to choose between them, so some ordered one starter, the rest the other and they all shared. It was very convivial and everything was delicious. If the fish had been any fresher, it would still have been swimming, or so the waiter said! A choice of mostly vegetarian pasta dishes followed, as good as any Charlie had ever eaten, then some delectably sweet local pork roasted with rosemary, garlic and fennel – the very same porchetta the family had eaten together at the fair in Matera they day they started 'I Trovatori.' Gosh! the smoky taste brought back some memories!

Someone recalled that that was the day they had first met Arturo Maldini, and what a difference he had made to all their lives. Giovanna confessed she rarely thought of him now, but when she did it was with gratitude and affection. Not excitement though. No, definitely not excitement. Charlie pressed her hand beneath the table. 'You've got me to put up with now, girl,' he said. 'Oh well, I suppose I'll manage,' she replied, 'seeing as you're so old and everything'. Charlie laughed. The serious moment passed and they moved on to the cheese then fruit. Finally a fiery Strega, and a thick sweet coffee completed the feast. Charlie looked at his watch. It was midnight. They had been at the table for five hours! God! he loved the Italian way of eating. He loved Italy. Full stop. He looked around the table at the people who meant most to him in the world and knew he was a very lucky man.

Teetering on the brink

The next year, 1959, saw a number of major developments on the international scene, some of which positively threatened the peace that had been won at such a high cost. In Cuba, the dictator Batista was overthrown by Fidel Castro and his freedom fighters, causing a real flutter of anxiety in the United States. If ever proof were needed that the Communists were trying to take over the world, this was it. Old Joe McCarthy may have been right all along, after all. The Americans had already lost thousands of men in the war in Korea, now they had a Commie state right on their doorstep. In the Soviet Union, Khrushchev, although he seemed less vicious than Stalin, was still very hostile to the west and he kept his people and the satellite states under firm control. The nuclear arms race continued with much posturing and sabre-rattling, greatly to the concern of the citizens of Western Europe. It was almost a light relief when Khrushchev visited the United States, and made it known that what he most wanted to do was visit Disneyland and meet John Wayne! It could have been quite endearing, except for the fact that it was a graphic demonstration of just how limited the man was. Especially as he effectively ruled over a quarter of the world's population and half its weapons.

In East Germany, officially the DDR – the Deutsche Demokratische Republik – the state's control over the populace became ever more tyrannical. Getting out of the country became harder and harder and people resorted to ever more desperate strategies to be free. Some lost their lives trying, their bodies left hanging on the vast barbed wire fence which now encircled the country, as a reminder to others to think again. Back in Italy for a time Charlie pondered the use of terminology to disguise the truth. There had been nothing socialistic about Nazionalsozialismus, or Nazism, and there was nothing democratic about the DDR. He often wondered how Frau Schmidt and Johann were coping as the pressure to conform mounted. From time to time he had a note from Herr Onnen saying that he had been in the East and had given the poor old lady some cash. 'Die arme alte Frau' eh? Charlie reflected on the fact that Frau Schmidt was only five or six years older than himself and therefore not yet seventy. Years of anxiety, poverty, hard work and poor diet must have taken its toll on her. He worried about what would happen to Johann if his mother died. He knew, though, that there was absolutely nothing he could do. By an accident of birth, mad, brave Johann was a prisoner in his own country, the land he had fought and as good as died for. War was so unfair. The more of its victims you met, the more convinced you were that it solved nothing. Yet here was the world once again staring conflict in the face as the two most powerful nations on earth squared up to each other like bare-knuckle thugs. In the United States, President Eisenhower, who, after all, knew a thing or two about the realities of war, was surrounded by hotheads in the Pentagon and in the Republican Party he represented who wanted to bomb the hated Russkis into oblivion. On the other side of the Iron Curtain, Nikita Khrushchev was heard to boast that the Soviet Union could turn out nuclear missiles as fast as other countries were making sausages. It was a scary time to be alive.

The events of the following year made the world hold its breath. In May of 1960, the Russians shot down an American U2 aeroplane which they accused of spying in their airspace, and tension between the two superpowers, which had eased somewhat after Khrushchev's visits to the US and France, rose once more. The pilot, Gary Powers, was captured and held in Soviet custody where he was extensively interrogated for months pending trial for espionage. The incident seriously damaged the progress of the peace talks between Khrushchev and Eisenhower. In the US, it was an election year, with the eventual candidates emerging as, for the Republicans, Eisenhower's Vice President, the long-serving but rather unappealing Richard Nixon, and for the Democrats, the extremely vibrant and youthful Senator from Massachusetts, John F Kennedy. Charlie, watching from Rome, was pleased, along with many of his Italian colleagues, to see a Catholic candidate for the first time in American history. He also liked what Kennedy was saying. He seemed to offer a chance to make a break with the thinking of the past and develop a new way of doing things that was fairer and more relevant to the twentieth century.

Mercifully, 1960 was also an Olympic year, and in that year the games were held in Rome. This provided a welcome diversion from the serious events taking place elsewhere. The trial in August of the American U2 pilot was a short affair, and no-one believed he would be found anything other than guilty of spying. The severity of his sentence – three years' imprisonment followed by seven years' hard labour – was a bit of a shock to western observers though. A few days later, the Stadio Olimpico saw the beginning of a highly successful summer games, which at least served to give hope that the world could get together for peaceful purposes at a time when hostility was so rampant. For Charlie it was a joy to be able to watch a lot of the action on TV – for television had at last come to Matera – and to see young people's bodies being used for sporting achievement rather than as weapons of war. Two athletes stood out for him. One was a young New Zealander called Peter Snell who collected a gold medal and at the same time broke the world record for the eight hundred metre race. Charlie could easily imagine how proud the folks back in distant New Zealand would be of their boy, for going so far away from home and beating the rest of the world. In his former home country the Kiwis loved their sport and sporting achievers became national heroes. This young man would be remembered forever in his homeland.

The other sportsman to catch Charlie's eye was an American boxer called Cassius Clay, who also took gold at his weight. Charlie was not overly fond of combat sports, but in this man he saw something very special. Not only was he a great fighter, being both strong and graceful, he had a sharp intellect and an engaging personality. Interviewed by Italian sports reporters, he made it clear that he understood exactly what his achievements would mean to other young Americans, especially other negros. He wanted them to know that they were as good as anyone else and could do as well, regardless of the colour of their skin, if they were prepared to work hard. It made Charlie feel hopeful that Clay and Kennedy together could do much to improve the lot of the downtrodden coloured people in the United States, as were many of the GIs he had met in Germany at the end of the war. It all depended on the voters of course, the overwhelming majority of whom were white. Charlie just hoped that they too were ready for a change when the time came to cast their ballot.

Before the election in November, there were a number of important international developments. Nuclear testing continued apace. Having spent years carrying out tests on land, the Americans now successfully launched Polaris missiles from their submarines. The massive Russian programme continued, and other countries started to build their own nuclear arsenals. France, especially, seemed happy to test its weapons in the far flung parts of its empire without regard for the safety of the inhabitants. The Algerian desert and the remote islands of the Pacific all saw tests, much to the disapproval of neighbouring countries like New Zealand. The British too were involved in the race to acquire a nuclear capability, and like the French did not test at home but in Australia. The arrogance of it was breathtaking as far as Charlie was concerned. The former colonies were once again being used and abused to suit the purposes of the 'mother country'. Surely this would come home to roost at some point? How long would people put up with being treated in this way? It wasn't long before Charlie got his answer. On a visit to Algeria, the French President de Gaulle was confronted by angry rioting mobs who wanted rid of the French state by any means including armed rebellion. France was being inexorably dragged into yet another war.

In the United States, election fever was rife. Kennedy seemed to be winning the hearts and minds of people who had long been disenfranchised or simply disinterested. The debates between himself and Richard Nixon were conducted in the full glare of television publicity, and Kennedy was ideally suited to the new medium. He was handsome, young and smart and he made Richard Nixon look old, dour and shifty. Meanwhile, in New York, the General Assembly of the United Nations was discussing delegates' concerns about repressive Soviet policies and practices towards the countries of Eastern Europe, a debate which Charlie followed closely as it impinged so directly on his own work. Incensed by the explicit criticism of his country, Khrushchev leapt to his feet, took off his shoe and pounded the desk in front of him with it, all the while shouting in Russian and drowning out the voices of those who were seeking to make a point. The pictures which flashed immediately around the world showed clearly just what an oaf he was. A few weeks later the Americans elected their youngest ever President, a man of manners, style and learning as well as of principles. The contrast between the leaders of the two superpowers could not have been greater. Like many in the western world, Charlie was delighted to see Kennedy elected, even if it was a bit of a surprise to find you were a full twenty years older than the President of the United States. He hoped that a fresh approach in the White House would blow away some of the tired old enmities between nations and races. When JFK was inaugurated the following January, his speech provided a rallying cry for optimists young an old. 'Ask not what your country can do for you, ask what you can do for your country.' Reading and re-reading it from the wire in his Rome office, Charlie felt a wave of relief. It looked like a new dawn.

Poor Charlie, he should have known the glass was half empty. In the following year events took place which served to drive the nations of the world further apart rather than closer together. Worsening relationships between America and Cuba led to the ill-fated Bay of Pigs fiasco, which seriously tarnished the new President's reputation, certainly in Charlie's eyes. The Franco-Algerian crisis drifted into bloody war, and threatened the stability of one of Italy's most important allies, much to the concern of Charlie's paymasters. In April, the trial of Adolf Eichmann, who had been found living in Argentina by the Israeli secret service Mossad, began in Israel, and Charlie followed its progress avidly. Eichmann, like a number of the senior Nazis Charlie had seen tried in Nuremberg, was charged with committing war crimes, and with the more serious offence of crimes against humanity. If found guilty, he would assuredly hang. The Israelis' desire for revenge was clear, and Charlie regretted it in the light of the dignified way the post war trials had been conducted, but he could understand the Jewish point of view too. He had seen the inside of some of those camps and could still not get the images out of his mind. How much worse to have lived through it. Sometimes, he thought, two wrongs just might make a right. Six million people had paid the price that was probably about to be asked of Eichmann. The war had been over for more than fifteen years, and some of the wounds were as raw as the day they were inflicted. Perhaps, he thought, some things can never be forgiven. They should certainly not be forgotten.

In East Germany the Stalinist puppet regime was making it harder and harder for people to get out. The huge perimeter fence with its manned watchtowers and broad scorched earth minefield stretched along the whole border with the West and made escape from the land practically impossible. However, the relatively relaxed border within the city of Berlin was a frequently-used route by which enterprising East Germans could seek refuge. With the help of the allied occupying powers many thousands of men and women, most of them young, clever and well-educated, had made their way to the West. The communist authorities were naturally incensed and determined to put a stop to this outward migration which was having a detrimental effect on their own country's economy. To the shock and amazement of the world, in August of 1961, construction began of a wall which would cut West Berlin off from the DDR completely. The building of the wall was the brainchild of the political leader of the Ost Zone, Walter Ullbricht, despite the fact that he had strenuously denied the notion only months earlier. 'Der Mauer' had Khrushchev's blessing and encircled the part of the city not occupied by the Soviets. Checkpoints for those with permits to enter the city for work were set up at intervals, and these were rigorously guarded by armed officers whose instructions were to shoot anyone they suspected of trying to defect to the West. The aim was clear – to keep the people of the DDR firmly in their place, which was behind the Iron Curtain, and to keep them there by terror if necessary. To Charlie, and to many others like him who saw themselves as socialists, this was a damning indictment of the Communist system. It was never intended to force people to comply, rather it was seen as an ideology which would so obviously improve people's lives they would willingly work together for the common good. The only ones benefiting in any way as far as Charlie could tell, were the officials and the politicians who all seemed to have comfortable houses, big cars and decent clothes. For the rest –the proletariat as communist theory would have it – hard work generated just enough income to get by, with nothing left for extras or luxuries, not that there was all that much in the shops anyway. Shortages of even basic foodstuffs were commonplace. Some of those who did get away before the wall went up told stories of official corruption on a vast scale. Pockets were most definitely being lined. In the meantime, poor Frau Schmidt and Johann and others like them scratched out a living from the earth or in the factories with no hope of bettering themselves no matter what they did. Marx would be spinning in his grave if he could see what was being done in his name. And it wasn't just in Germany that such blatant abuses were being perpetrated. In some of the other satellite states too the people were being politically oppressed and kept in dire poverty while the leaders feathered their nests and lived like royalty. It was like the British class system all over again, only these self-appointed toffs didn't even have a sense of 'noblesse oblige'. They were self-seeking, greedy and ruthless. It was a tragedy, and the greatest symbol of that tragedy was the wretched bloody wall.

Back home with Giovanna in the middle of December, and preparing to celebrate fifteen years of marriage the following week, Charlie saw on the television news that in Israel Adolf Eichmann had been found guilty and was sentenced to be hanged. His ashes would be scattered at sea so that no one country would have the shame of burying him. Europe was to be rid of one bloody tyrant, but there were, it seemed, any number waiting in the wings for their moment in the spotlight.

Over the water, Kennedy, whom Charlie had once so admired, seemed determined that the United States should again fight the Communists. Although his nation had just slogged through the mud and the heat of Korea, with great loss of American life, this time it was in the former French colony of Vietnam that he sought to flex his muscles. Choosing to interpret the political unrest in that country not as a civil conflict but as an invasion sponsored by the Chinese, he deemed it fitting that America should offer military support to the patently corrupt regime in Saigon, and to that end sent many thousands of so-called 'advisors' late in 1961. Charlie sighed. Yet another damned war looked inevitable. Charlie was right. By the middle of the next year, the Americans officially had troops in Vietnam fighting the Viet Cong for control of South Vietnam in the belief that they would be able to stop the spread of communism. It was a knee-jerk response to the simplistic 'domino theory' widely espoused in Congress, and it was bound to cost lives.

The most terrifying moment of all came later in 1962, when the Soviet Union was asked by their communist allies in Cuba to extend them protection from what they saw as an imminent US invasion. For Khrushchev, the way to do this was to install nuclear missiles on the Caribbean island and point them at the United States. That would deter the capitalist imperialists, for sure! What the Russian leader in his ignorance hadn't banked on was the level of anti-communist paranoia which persisted in the United States. Everything that was happening in the world convinced the Americans and their leaders that the Commies planned to take over their country, either by subversion from within or by aggression from without. The legacy of McCarthyism and the Korean war was potent. The effect was to imbue Americans from all classes and walks of life, the rich, the poor, the intelligent and the downright stupid, with a fierce hatred of all those countries which had embraced a Marxist political stance. Castro, Mao, Khrushchev, Ho Chi Minh – they were all the same, all evil and all needed to be brought down. John Kennedy, young, clever, educated and travelled as he was, to a large extent shared this analysis. Surrounded by hawks, he could not sit by and watch his neighbour become an arsenal for a hostile superpower. So he demanded that the missiles be dismantled, and the ships bringing military equipment to Cuba be sent back. Failure to comply, he said, would lead the United States directly into conflict with the Soviet Union. In Moscow, Khrushchev was not in the mood to back down to this American whippersnapper, in the full glare of international publicity. For long days he hummed and haahed, and the watching world held its breath. Never had all-out nuclear war seemed more likely. Finally, with a face-saving deal brokered by the United Nations, he gave in, and the ships were turned around. In Rome, Charlie sighed with relief. With world destruction at least temporarily off the agenda, he could turn his mind to the task at hand, and that task was getting the European Economic Community to become less exclusive and expand to include, amongst others, the nations of Britain and Ireland.

Non, merci

To Charlie's way of thinking, no country had paid a higher financial price for Europe's freedom from the Nazis than the land of his birth. Poor Britain was still paying the Americans back for their contribution during the last war, old man Churchill having doggedly refused to accept 'charity'. Meanwhile, in the European Community countries, most especially Germany, economic growth was proceeding at an almost miraculous rate. In Britain, the Prime Minister Harold MacMillan was expressing concern that his nation was being both left behind and left out of things. He put forward the notion that application should be made to join the Community. Around Western Europe other leaders were having the same thought. If the Community were to be genuinely European, it should include all the states of that continent, not just a self-chosen few. There wasn't a land that hadn't suffered from the war, either directly or indirectly. Many still had the scars of battle or occupation to prove it. Others were dealing with the effects of vast influxes of displaced persons. All supported the reason for the founding of the EEC – to put an end to war in Europe. Of course, the eastern bloc states could not be a part of it, at least not while they were under the thumb of the Communists, but the rest could.

However, one of the existing Community Heads of State had other views about who should be allowed to join their little club. This was the President of France, General Charles de Gaulle and he was vociferous in his opposition to the admission of Britain. His view was that Britain was too closely allied to both the United States and to the Commonwealth to be fully committed to Europe and made it clear that he would exercise his veto to prevent their application, and this he duly did in the icy January of 1963. On hearing this Charlie was incensed. What a bloody cheek the man had! British and Commonwealth soldiers had come to the aid of his country in two world wars, had fought with great courage and suffered considerable loss of life, and if it hadn't been for the Americans in the last lot, the chances were pretty darn high that they'd all be speaking German down the Champs Élysées right now! The man had spent most of the war in comfort in London while his countrymen and women risked everything fighting the Nazis in the Resistance, and this was how he showed his gratitude to his hosts and supporters! Charlie felt the admiration and respect he had once felt for the General evaporating. He was showing himself to be snobbish, arrogant and disdainful of others, qualities Charlie had spent years trying to convince people, especially the British and the Americans, that the French did not all share. Well bugger him then! Let him say NON! It would just take a bit longer to get the right result, but get it they would.

Italy hadn't forgotten how much the British had done to set them free from the Nazis, and Charlie's paymasters were prepared to invest both time and money on advancing the view that the Community should include Britain as well as more of the mainland European states. Charlie would spend some time cultivating pro-British opinions amongst the politicians and diplomats of the other five Community nations, confident that de Gaulle would someday be voted out of office when the people's love affair with him came to an end. It had, to the surprise of many, happened to Churchill and would surely happen to 'Charlot' as well. Before he could begin this work, Charlie would need to revisit Britain and make some contacts with credible politicians, people who could command respect and show the kind of leadership that would be required to take the project forward.

In the coldest winter known for years – probably since the one that had taken his mother in 1947 – Charlie arrived in London once more. It was sixteen years since his last visit. Then war damage was everywhere to be seen and a decent meal nowhere to be found. How different it was now! All over the city ruined terraced streets had been replaced with tower blocks of flats to provide cheap rented housing for the ordinary people, those at least who had chosen to stay in London rather than be shipped out to the New Towns in places like Essex and Hertfordshire. Charlie wasn't sure he liked the new buildings. They were grey and soulless, whereas the rows of terraces had had some character, some individuality. He wondered how people managed if the lifts broke down, and how mothers kept an eye on their children playing on the communal greens ten stories below. Unlike French and German city-dwellers, the British were not used to living up high. Most people liked to have a patch of earth, however small, where their kids could kick a ball about or where they could grow a few tomatoes in the summer. He doubted the social experiment would be a great success somehow. He certainly wouldn't fancy it again, not after Berlin. Too exhausting by far! Or maybe he was just showing his age.

Thinking about age led Charlie to the notion that it might be useful if he could make contact with Churchill once more. He had after all given him much very valuable information on his last visit. The old man had stepped down as Prime Minister eight years earlier, but he was still an MP at eighty-nine, and must have some influence if no real power. If he supported the closer integration of Europe, it would count for a lot in France. De Gaulle may have forgotten D-Day, but ordinary French people had not. He telephoned Churchill's office at the House of Commons in the hope of arranging an appointment, but the response he got came as a bombshell. Sir Winston, it seemed, was not well and rarely if ever took his seat in the house these days. Instead he remained at his home, Chartwell, where he spent his time resting and recuperating from the series of strokes he had had. He was also, his pleasant but rather indiscreet parliamentary secretary went on to say, suffering again from the dreaded depression – the illness he called 'the black dog'. It was not likely that he would want to meet with anyone to talk politics. His mind was on the past now and he had little interest in the future. The secretary was very sorry, but there you were, that was how it was. There was nothing to be done. If it was any consolation, the aide went on, he remembered Churchill telling him all those years ago about the Swiss fellow he had met in the lobby of the House of Commons, the one who had done so much to bring the Nazis to justice. He had been full of admiration for the young stranger. Those days were gone now, and Sir Winston now had another battle to fight, probably his last one. The secretary's voice, previously so chatty and bright, caught suddenly, and Charlie could hear that he was choking back a tear. Not wishing to prolong the man's distress, he murmured his sympathy and understanding and said goodbye. Hanging up the receiver, Charlie took a few moments to digest what he had just been told. The poor old devil! Beset by the black dog all his life, and now with his body failing him, it seemed he was just waiting to die. It was a sad way for a hero to go. He should have died a glorious death, not come to a slow painful end. Charlie too shed a few tears for the man to whom the world owed so much. The search for an ally had just become much harder.

While Charlie made contacts with Members of Parliament and dug about in the British Civil Service trying to find like-minded men and women, across 'the pond' racial matters were coming to a head. Earlier in the year, the racist George Wallace had been installed as Governor of Alabama, and his scurrilous refusal to allow schools and colleges to be integrated was highly publicised. All over the country, but especially in the southern states, there were demonstrations and even riots in which coloured people were demanding their civil rights. At last they were shaking off the yoke of servility that had been bred into them from the days of slavery. The response to their empowerment had been frightening, however, and racially-motivated murders had become almost commonplace. Charlie knew from talking to coloured GIs in the push from Normandy to Berlin, that there were many white people in the south who were members of secret societies dedicated to wiping the Negros out if they could and keeping them down if they could not. These people, most of them stupid, all of them dangerous, would stop at nothing to preserve their way of life which had been founded on oppression. Men, women and children, all were fair game if they had dark skin. In the middle of it all, and as a real fly in the ointment, the young boxer that Charlie had first seen in the Rome Olympics was going from strength to strength as a professional, beating all comers including whites. As he did so, he repeatedly and emphatically demonstrated not only his physical prowess, but also his intellectual gifts and his ready wit. So much for the superiority of the white race! If it hadn't been so serious, Charlie would have laughed. As it was, it was appalling to see the most powerful democracy on earth struggling to offer justice and fair play to all its citizens. To his credit, President Kennedy made it clear that new legislation would outlaw segregation and pave the way for a greater degree of equality between the different communities. In the meantime, alas, blood continued to flow.

In London Charlie's meetings with members of the Conservative regime were proving less than fruitful. Most of them fitted neatly into his category of 'toffs' and he was pre-disposed to dislike them. Not very professional, he knew, but old habits die hard. Some of these were the very men whose aristocratic families had managed to ensure that they did not see active service in the war, instead manned safe desks in the Ministry or some such, well away from the blood and the bullets. All public school educated, narrow-minded and very comfortable in their lives, they had no understanding of people who were different and no desire to find out more. Eventually he came to the conclusion that his best hope lay with the Opposition, specifically with the Labour Party. In this way he was returning to his political roots and he felt more comfortable there. He was particularly drawn to the party's new leader, Harold Wilson, a man with whom he broadly shared a philosophy. Wilson, it seemed to him, was a democratic socialist, with a sound grasp of economics, and a liberal view on social issues. He was markedly less xenophobic than the majority of the Tories he had met, and espoused the European project quite openly. The only problem was, he was not in Government, though the pundits were saying that this could soon change as the people wearied of years of rule by posh old Etonians. Wilson's accent was gratifyingly ordinary and northern, and people could relate to what he said and how he said it. Wilson was also open to meeting with people from beyond the tight little circles of Westminster, and was happy to spend time with Charlie discussing the possibilities for a European Economic Community that included Britain. Obviously, whilst in Opposition there was not a lot he could do, but when – not if, Charlie noted – he became PM, he would certainly be having another crack at de Gaulle.

Charlie was pleased. He felt he had made something of a breakthrough and, without even thinking of attempting a trip to Lancashire, he returned to Rome just as spring was returning to his adopted homeland. After the dreadful ice and snow of the worst English winter for over a decade, he was glad to see the sun and green buds on the trees. More than that he was delighted to be reunited with Giovanna. It did occur to him that he had broken his promise never to leave her behind again on numerous occasions, but the Berlin blockade fiasco had shown him that work and sentiment do not mix. Until he could finally quit his job and become an old retired gentleman, it looked like they were doomed to spend significant chunks of time apart. Still you know what they say – 'absence makes the heart grow fonder' – and they were certainly still very fond of each other, you could tell. 'You're not bad for a geriatric, Signor Weiss,' Giovanna whispered as she lay beside him. 'Well,' came the reply, 'as old bats go, you'll do!' A cuff around the head was his reward. Charlie was home again. Bliss!

A chapter of losses

In April that year there was a General Election in Italy, something Charlie always rather dreaded because the electorate was so fickle, and he never quite knew who was going to be employing him afterwards if indeed anyone was. He needn't have worried. Despite a strong showing by the Communist Party – something Charlie always found puzzling in a land that enjoyed such a high degree of personal freedom – sense prevailed and business went on much as usual. At the beginning of the summer the nation was rocked by an event far more profound than a mere change of politicians. On June 3rd, the Pope, John XXIII, died, and the people went into mourning. John was already an old man when he became Pope only five years earlier, but even so his death came as a shock, largely because the Vatican had kept news of his illness out of the press. In his short reign, the nation had taken him to their hearts, and there was an outpouring of genuine grief when he passed away. Known as 'Il Papa Buono' – the good Pope – John had the common touch that belied his aristocratic (if impoverished) background. He had seen active service in the Great War. As Pope, he had visited seriously ill children in hospitals and criminals in prison, something no head of the church had ever done before. In churches all across the land there were masses and vigils on a scale rarely seen. The television showed crowds of weeping mourners gathering in Saint Peters Square, first for the funeral, then later for news of the successor as the cardinals deliberated upon a replacement. For a couple of weeks life in Italy seemed to go into a state of limbo.

At the farm, Sophia was especially affected by the Pope's death and wept inconsolably. She had seen a few Pontiffs come and go throughout her long life, but this one she felt had been the best of them all and to have him snatched away so early in his reign when he promised so much, seemed cruel. Even her favourite Carla, by now eighteen and a lovely young woman, seemed unable to comfort her. At eighty six, Sophia had had enough of enforced change. She swore she would never get used to another Pope, no matter how good he might be. She was plunged into a state of deep gloom, and despite the lovely summer weather, retired to her bed, refusing company of any sort. Worse than that, she also completely rejected food, accepting only the occasional glass of water. Giovanna thought her mother's reaction was so strong because the death of the Pope she had focussed so much of her love upon reminded her of Giovanni's passing. It was almost as if the Pope had replaced Giovanni in her soul and her heart. She was of the opinion that after a few days Sophia would recover and emerge from her room. For once, this time Giovanna was wrong. When, a scant two weeks later, the cardinals at last announced whom they had chosen to succeed her beloved John, it felt to Sophia as if an act of betrayal had taken place, and if anything her mental state worsened. Despite the protestations of her daughters, and the coaxings of Carla, Sophia now began to refuse even water. Her mind started to wander and she lay in her darkened bedroom muttering to herself, sometimes crying out to her God 'Why have you taken him? You should have taken me!' Caterina was not sure if her mother was referring to the Pope or to her husband. In any event Sophia was in a state of deep distress and would assuredly die if she carried on in this way. The doctor was called repeatedly, but the old lady would not let him in. She seemed determined to follow her beloved Pope John to a better place. Unable to force her to eat or drink, the daughters stood helplessly by and watched their mother fade away. There was nothing they or their concerned husbands could do. Finally, as June merged into hot July, Sophia's tired heart gave out, and the old lady relinquished her fragile grip on life. In accordance with her wishes, there was a simple funeral to which only family were invited, and she was interred in the local churchyard next to her darling Giovanni, reunited and inseparable in death as they had once been in their lifetimes.

It looked like 1963 was going to be one of those years you never forgot. It had started off quietly enough, even on a positive note, but then things went downhill. Early in the year, to everyone's delight, Martin had announced that he had met someone with whom he planned to share his life. He could not marry the lady in question, as the law of the land meant he was unable to divorce his wife, but he hoped the family would understand that he wanted her to come and live with him at the farm. With the older children off at university and unlikely to return, he and Carla were rattling around in the big house like pills in a bottle. Charlie and Giovanna were hardly in a position to object, not that they wanted to, and even straight-laced old patriarch Albert could see that a little flexibility was called for. Circumstances sometimes dictated the taking of an unconventional path – like the one that had led him and Charlie here in the first place. Sophia, still well and still pulling strings at that time, was persuaded by Carla that it was something she wanted for her dad, that he certainly deserved another chance at happiness, and so it was agreed that Carolina would move in when the spring came. By the time Charlie got back from England she was well- ensconced, and Martin was going about his work with renewed vigour and a song on his lips.

When Charlie had returned in spring with his news about Churchill, everyone felt saddened. The man was their hero, and it seemed so unfair that he should be suffering now after a lifetime of service to his country and the world. The death of the Pope, followed so swiftly by the loss of Sophia was a body blow to them all, and Charlie wondered how much more the family could be expected to take. But it was not over. In August, Albert received a letter from his older brother George telling him the news that their mother had finally gone to be with their dad. After forty-five years of widowhood in which not a day had passed but she remembered him with affection, the old folks were together again at last. She hadn't suffered for too long it seemed. A fall on the ice was followed by a little stroke, and that stroke a couple of months later by a much more severe one. She had died peacefully in Scarborough Hospital without regaining consciousness. Albert took the news well, but voiced regret that he had never been able to know his mother as a grown man, never been able to help her out when she needed a strong pair of hands or make her laugh when she was down. Only Charlie could understand the depth of his feelings, for he had made the same choice and suffered the same loss. Now none of them had any parents left, and all at once Charlie and Albert, Giovanna and Caterina became the older generation. It was a sobering realisation and one that made the two men seriously consider their own mortality for the first time since 1917.

By way of light relief, news came from Ricardo towards the end of summer that after seven highly successful years playing for the senior team at Juventus, he had been approached by a talent scout from the famous German club, Bayern München. An amazing financial offer had been made and accepted, and he would be moving to Bavaria at the start of the new season. Now he would need to add German to his repertoire of languages. Any chance his old uncle would like a job as a tutor? The sums involved in the transfer made startling reading. Ricardo would earn as much in a year as the rest of his family put together, and they were doing all right. Albert was so proud of his son he felt his heart would burst. Bayern München eh? It was one of the oldest and richest clubs in the world, and knocked that Manchester United lot into a cocked hat. Not to mention Blackburn Rovers, that Charlie's cousin Bobby Clayton used to play for. Lancashire rubbish, all of them! His son only played for the best and it looked like making a rich man of him. Bloody good too! Now all he needed was to find a pretty young wife and to produce some grandchildren for Albert and Caterina to fuss over and everything would be hunky-dory. From Charlie's point of view, the offer of a move to southern Germany was one he did not even contemplate seriously for a moment. Writing to Ricardo, he advised him to get hold of a good tutor through the American forces if the club couldn't help and to make sure he was better advised than President Kennedy had been when he had made the famous 'Ich bin ein Berliner' speech at the Berlin Wall a few months earlier. It still made Charlie chuckle that the most powerful man in the world had unwittingly described himself as 'a doughnut'!

The amusement didn't last long, though. It seemed no time at all after Ricardo's move to Germany, that the world was shocked to the core by the President's assassination in Dallas. Whatever his faults, and he had a few, he did not deserve to be gunned down with no chance to defend himself, and in front of his lovely young wife too. The poor woman had only just buried their infant son a matter of weeks earlier, and now here she was cradling her dying husband in front of the blinding flashlights of the world's cameras. Charlie's heart went out to her. Politicians voluntarily place themselves in the public gaze, their wives and children do not. Coverage of events in Dallas was shown continuously on the television, and it seemed impossible not to watch and be appalled as things unfolded. The image of President Johnson being sworn in on the aeroplane standing next to Mrs Kennedy, her pale suit soaked with her husband's blood, had barely faded when it was replaced a mere two days later by the on-air shooting of the man the police had arrested for the assassination. The speed with which they had pinpointed and picked up Lee Harvey Oswald was suspicious to Charlie's mind, and the stories that were quickly circulated about him as a dangerous Communist just too convenient. He seemed too simple to have carried out such a clever act. Charlie smelled a rat, but before the rat could be investigated, the suspect was dead. Even those who disliked Kennedy – and there were many – could not fail to be moved by the sight of his wife and young children huddled so closely together at the funeral, and even hardened hearts broke as the coffin was lowered into the ground and the cameras captured young John offering a final respectful salute to his murdered dad. Later it would be said that you never forgot where you were when you heard the news of Kennedy's death. For Charlie, while he would certainly remember November 22nd 1963 as one of the world's dark hours, there was no comparison with what he had seen in the trenches or heard at Nuremberg. It was a tragedy, but one the world would get over. The scars of the two world wars would take far longer to heal.

Christmas that year would be one of the most difficult the family had gone through. The loss of Sophia meant there was a major link missing in the usual chain of command. Try as they might, Caterina and Giovanna could not rustle up the enthusiasm for the task that their mother always showed, even when things were so tight in the Great War. Ricardo couldn't be there because of matches scheduled in Christmas week, Giuseppe and his family were stuck in Milano due to performing commitments, the two girls had made their own arrangements, and Alessandro was working in the United States, so it looked like being a pretty small affair by Weiss family standards. It was Martin's lady friend Carolina who came up with the solution. By way of thanking the family for all that they had done to help, she would personally cater her first Christmas on the farm and invite them all to dinner in the old farmhouse. It would not be as magnificent as the Christmases she had heard of that Sophia had orchestrated, but it would be festive, and it would involve the older Weisses in no work at all. She, Carla and Martin would do everything, with help from Giorgio and Carlo if needed. Martin's two other children were expected back from University for a few days at least, so they too could lend their hands to the task. The proposal was greeted with sighs of relief by Caterina and Giovanna. Thank goodness, at least for this year, they were spared the extra work that Christmas always generated. Maybe by the end of next year, they might feel up to it once more. Or maybe Christmas would never be the same again.

Which is indeed how things turned out. The final loss of 1963 was the loss of the family Christmas. Thereafter, the birth of Christ would be celebrated in a much more muted way with just the older Weiss family members sharing a meal with whichever of the younger generation fancied it. With the family grown up and scattered all over Italy and further afield, the logistics and the effort required to revive Sophia's dream were just too much. After all, Caterina and Giovanna were hardly in the first flush of youth either, both being, in Charlie's words 'on the wrong side of sixty'. Without little ones running about, it seemed pointless to be spending vast sums of money on food, drink and gifts. Better to return to the religious roots of the festival and leave the feasting and the over-indulgence to others.

Scaling down

1964 came and went and, to his relief, and perhaps in recognition of his seniority, Charlie had fewer trips to make. He spent some time in the summer in Berlin, where the existence of the Wall was continuing to cause anguish to the ordinary people of East Germany. Numbers of people, mostly young, gifted and well-educated, were being killed in their attempts to escape to freedom from the oppressive communist regime. The lucky ones who already lived in West Berlin just moved away if they could afford to, sensing that there was no hope that the country would ever be reunited under a democratically-elected government, and seeing no future for themselves in a city surrounded by a hostile presence. Young Norbert Onnen, it seemed, had gone on to run a much better business based in the beautiful University city of Heidelberg. No more flogging around muddy farm tracks in search of sugar beet for him! His entrepreneurial gifts had taken him into new areas. He was in classical music now and had offices in all six countries of the Economic Community. It did mean that contact with Frau Schmidt and Johann was lost, but there was nothing that Charlie could do about that. The Iron Curtain was as firmly closed to him from the outside as it was to so many from within.

Towards the end of the year there were some remarkable developments on the world political stage, and one of them involved Charlie in a return to Great Britain. Firstly, in October, as he had hoped, Harold Wilson's Labour Party replaced the Tory toffs as the government in Westminster. Charlie's work on getting Britain involved in the European project could begin again, this time with more hopes of success. A few days after Wilson's election, in an extraordinarily Russian coup, Khrushchev was deposed whilst on holiday, to be replaced by men who took a much harder line on internal and international affairs than he did. Chief among them was the sinister Leonid Brezhnev, a dyed-in-the-wool old Commie if ever Charlie had seen one. Khrushchev had mellowed over his years in power. He had denounced Stalinism and made overtures to the west, especially during the time of Kennedy's Presidency. The men who replaced him were hardliners, and Kennedy's successor could expect a tougher time. The Cold War looked like getting a lot colder.

In November the people of the United States re-elected Lyndon Johnson, who had come into office in such tragic circumstances less than a year earlier. Johnson lacked Kennedy's charm, intelligence and wit. It was like comparing a bar room brawler with Cassius Clay. Charlie feared that the hawkish Johnson would soon escalate the Americans' military involvement in Vietnam – as indeed he had already begun to do in his first few months in office – and that an all-out war would erupt in Indochina. It seemed the United States just could not get enough enemies. He hoped and prayed that this time they didn't drag Britain into the fray with them, as they had in Korea. In Europe, America's combative behaviour was largely viewed with disapproval. Tired of conflict, people wanted peaceful solutions to the world's problems. Especially in France, whose enforced departure from south east Asia had left the power vacuum that was now being fought over, they knew to their cost about the staunch determination and grit possessed by the Vietnamese. They realised that any war would be protracted, bloody and probably unwinnable. Even the mighty army of the United States was not fitted for jungle warfare. There would be no easy victory here.

As a diplomat, Charlie despaired. He spent his life trying to get people to agree, to compromise and to get along in peace, but the world's leaders seemed determined to have none of it. All over the planet there were savage little conflicts taking place resulting in human suffering and misery on a scale to rival the two world wars. The ending of the colonial era had led to all sorts of power struggles in Africa, the Middle East was on the boil as Jews and Arabs laid claim to the homeland they had both been promised, on the Indian subcontinent people were being killed for their religious beliefs, and in China for their political views. It was a mess.

Still, one thing was looking good from a work point of view – and a political one as far as Charlie was concerned - and that was the expansion of the European Economic Community to include Britain and the other democratic nations of the continent. Charlie was sure that de Gaulle would be impressed with Harold Wilson just as he had been, and he made plans to return to Britain to assist with the application process. All Charlie's linguistic and negotiating skills would be needed. This time it must not fail. In mid-January 1965, Charlie flew into London's impressive Heathrow Airport and got aboard the coach bound for Victoria. He would take a room in a comfortable hotel not far from the station, from which he could easily walk to the House of Commons, to the Foreign Office, to Downing Street or even Buckingham Palace if the call should come. For things further afield there was the fast and efficient Underground system. He was starting to love London, the more he got to know it. There was something interesting and different to see at every turn. He was sure to be kept amused and invigorated at the very least. Hopefully his professional endeavours would be rewarded as well.

It was incredible how London had changed over the years Charlie had been coming there. Just after the war, it was desperate. Almost in ruins with scarcely anything working and austerity measures in full operation, it had been a difficult place even to visit because there wasn't anything to do or buy even for those who had money. How much worse for the inhabitants trying to scrape a living out of the rubble. It was a matter of survival. Fun definitely took a back seat. Now, twenty years later, London was at the very heart of a cultural revolution based on popular music and youthful fashion, and it seemed that everything was achievable. People had jobs, they went out to restaurants, night clubs and cinemas, and increasingly, they took holidays abroad. It was a London very far removed from the one the previous generation had known. People had smiles on their faces, they wore colourful clothing and they laughed as they went about their business. It was a joy to see. Charlie wondered if other towns and cities had also changed so dramatically, or was it just the 'swinging' capital? He planned to find out at some point, once he had established the contacts he needed here. For now he loved what he saw as he walked about the famous streets – the Kings Road and Kensington High Street, Leicester Square and Piccadilly Circus – the names were evocative and the pavements buzzing. Everyone wanted to be in London. It was the place to be if you were young, and not bad if you were a bit senior, as long as you had an open mind. At last the shackles of the class system seemed to be loosening, and people from all sorts of backgrounds could rise to the top if they were good at something. The Eton and Oxbridge stranglehold was being unceremoniously broken, and regional accents were starting to be heard even in the corridors of power. It was those Merseybeat bands from Liverpool that had started it all, and a good thing too as far as Charlie was concerned. He couldn't imagine some toff singing 'She loves you, yeah yeah yeah!' He looked around and felt optimistic for his homeland for the first time in ages.

A few days after Charlie's arrival in London, on the 24th of January, the nation awoke to the news that Winston Churchill had died. He had slipped away peacefully, in the presence of his beloved wife and family, after a long struggle with both physical and mental ill health. A link with history had been broken. In his hotel room near Victoria, Charlie sat listening to the radio announcer's sombre tone, and wept unashamedly. A voice of wisdom and reason had been lost and the world was a poorer place for it. A period of national mourning was declared, something that was quite extraordinary for a political figure, and thousands of ordinary people came to London to pay their respects to the old man who had delivered them from the Nazis. Charlie too went to Westminster Hall and filed past with all the others. Somehow, he just had to be there to share in the intense wave of emotion. Only when the funeral was over would life return to some semblance of normality. It was like the death of a Pope, only this time there was to be no successor, no puff of white smoke. The shoes of the great man could never be filled. Charlie remembered Churchill's chatty secretary to whom he had spoken on his last visit, and imagined how devastated he must be after so many years of loyal service. Difficult as the old man assuredly was at times, to be serving him was to be taking part in the making of history and an honour, and his death would leave a real gap.

This time Charlie resolved that he would visit at least his family in Lancashire. There was not much point in going to Scarborough, for there was no-one there he really knew any more. Albert's siblings he hadn't seen in decades, and Jeannie Donkin had long since married, had her family and emigrated to New Zealand. His own brother and sister, predictably, were still exactly where they always had been, within a couple of streets of each other in Great Harwood. Not an adventurous lot, the Claytons. Never too far from a warm pint and a pie with mushy peas, our Joe! Still, Charlie loved them all and would be pleased to spend a little discreet time there. The chances that they would make their way to Italy were negligible so it was Great Harwood or nothing.

On a cold February morning, Charlie made his way to Euston for the train to the northwest. He was intrigued that the once-fractured railway system had been nationalised and seemed to run far better as a co-ordinated effort than it had as a series of competing private companies, most of which did not speak to let alone co-operate with each other. The long delays and missed connections seemed to be a thing of the past, and soon Charlie was in Blackburn, after which a short bus ride took him to his one time family home in Great Harwood. There his sister Mary was waiting to greet him with a warm embrace, and shortly they were joined by Joe and Annie for a 'nice cuppa tea and an Eccles cake'.

Over the humble fare, the chat flowed. Charlie was surprised at how old his siblings looked, until he remembered that he was sixty-six himself, so they were scarcely spring chickens. Even so, their lined faces and stooped bearing told their own stories of hard work and poverty. The two women had retired at sixty, and were now drawing their pensions. Joe, much to his chagrin, had to work on until he was sixty-five, a couple of years away, and he hated every blasted minute of it. He couldn't wait to be able to leave the damned mill for the last time and put his feet up. The stink of that bloody Oxo was in every pore of his body, he said, and once he was out of there he planned to scrub and scrub until it was all gone, every last whiff. His work clothes would be ceremoniously burnt on a bonfire at the allotment. It was all planned, down to the day. After that he would spend his time between the allotment and the working men's club, and on the weekends, as they did now, he and Annie would go out on the bus for a walk in the dales, if the weather was nice. Sometimes Mary would join them. Joe and Annie had never had children, to their regret really, but at least it meant they were free agents now, not spending their lives baby-sitting while their kids went out to work and raked in a blimmin' fortune. Other people of their age that they knew seemed to be on grandparent duty all week and never got so much as a thank you.

Their lives seemed very parochial and narrow – pretty much as they had always been. Holidays were not spent in Spain, but, as ever, at Blackpool. Anywhere else was unthinkable, even alien. Their idea of 'pop' music was a nice tune sung properly, not something by one of these noisy bunches of long-haired lads where you couldn't even tell what the words were supposed to be! Skirts stopped well below the knee and a haircut for Joe meant a short back and sides. The 'swinging sixties' did not seem to have made much of an impact up here! On the occasional weekend trip made on the bus to 'the smoke' – Blackburn to the rest of the world – Joe and Annie had seen groups of young people in colourful clothing hanging about in the streets listening to radios you didn't even need to plug in, talking animatedly about the merits of the so-called music they were hearing. It certainly wasn't the BBC they were picking up, they would never play such a racket even on the Light Programme. Someone said it was a foreign station, based in some place on the continent. 'Luxembourg?' Charlie ventured – for he had noticed the same phenomenon in London. 'That's it!' said Joe, and went on 'where IS that exactly? Have you been there?' Charlie had indeed visited the Principality often, as it had such a central role in the European Community. Now it seemed to be important in the world of young people's music as well. Well, well, well, staid old Luxembourg, eh? More orderly and traditional even than Switzerland! Who'd have thought it? Charlie smiled to himself. As that gravelly-voiced American folk singer chappie said, the times they were indeed a-changing, just not very quickly and not in Great Harwood. The next day Charlie returned to London. His parting from Mary was unusually warm. He felt that he would probably never see his brother and sister again. Lancashire mill town dwellers rarely make old bones, and he expected that before he had reason to revisit Britain, one or both of them would succumb to some illness that wouldn't kill a fly in Italy. Their resistance was very low just like the Samoans in the great flu epidemic of 1918. Like, indeed, Charlie's own mother in the winter of 1947, people who had breathed in cotton dust and smelly factory smoke all their lives were more vulnerable when the weather went bad or a new virus turned up. As were people whose idea of a healthy meal was a plate of fish and chips fried in lard. Thinking of the life he could have led, had he survived and returned to Lancashire after the first war, Charlie realised just how lucky he had been, and what a jolly good decision he and Albert had taken that hot night in July 1917.

For the rest of the month, Charlie carried on his advisory work with the new Wilson administration, helping them to prepare their bid to join the EEC. Once he had done as much as he could behind the scenes with the civil servants, it would be up to the politicians to sell the idea to the other member nations, especially to the ageing and apparently still hostile General de Gaulle. This process could take years, and involve interminable rounds of discussions and hard negotiations. But for Charlie, for now at least, the job was done, and on St David's Day, March 1st, he boarded a plane at a windswept and rainy Heathrow for Rome, and some early spring sun.

His workload much reduced, Charlie was content to spend time in Matera with Giovanna or on the farm with Albert, and watch the events of the world go by. He was glad to be less involved, as the planet seemed to be going mad. 1966 saw the conflict in Vietnam escalate into a full-scale war, with the Americans taking on the Communist world on its front line, as they saw it. They even managed to drag the Australians along with them. The Aussie boys, like the GIs, were drafted into the army, and this caused a lot of anger and resentment in that country, especially when they started being flown back in body bags. Even little New Zealand, swept along on a tide of US-inspired paranoia, sent a small force of regular troops to try and stem the Commie tide. Under the leadership of the Soviet Union, despite their disagreements with China, the Warsaw Pact nations pledged to support North Vietnam, and to Charlie it looked like all the ingredients for World War III were falling nicely into place. It was ghastly. One after another, Western leaders headed to Moscow to try and broker some kind of peace in Vietnam. Wilson went, even old de Gaulle made the journey, but to no avail. Hostility between the west and the communists mounted, fuelled by the war and by the ludicrously expensive space race. It was one-upmanship on a grand scale, well worthy of the school playground. 'My rocket's bigger than yours, so there!' The leaders on both sides taunted each other and to their discredit, these adult, even elderly men, rose to the bait. Watching the television news started to become a source of real frustration, even anger.

The only light relief for Charlie was the football World Cup, which was held that summer in England. To Albert's joy, Ricardo had been selected to play for Italy and he and Charlie planned to watch every match of the contest up to and including the final when they confidently expected to see their boy triumphantly hoist the Jules Rimet trophy. The two men sat cosily together in the comfortable living room of Albert's house avidly watching the group stages of the tournament unfold. Their wives had sensibly gone off to visit the Milano family and left them to get on with it, knowing there would be no talking to them for the best part of three weeks. The fridge was stocked with ice cold beers and the makings of sandwiches and simple meals. The old boys were in heaven! There hadn't been time for this kind of brotherly relaxation for years. It was a chance to renew their relationship and shout their bloody heads off! 'Italia! Italia!' they bellowed at the screen as the first week's games were played. Then it all went horribly wrong, when, in a famous victory, the North Koreans beat the Azurri one-nil, and deprived the Italian boys of a place in the later stages of the competition. 'Put out by a bunch of bloody Commies!' was all Albert could say, which made Charlie smile. The Cold War was being played out on a football pitch in England. The benefit of Italy's early exit was that Ricardo, his summer plans in tatters, came back to the farm for the first time in ages and hunkered down in front of the TV with the old chaps, adding his own deep notes to the decibel level. Out of loyalty to his club and his adopted country, he was vociferously supporting West Germany. His father and uncle threw their weight firmly behind England. A friendly rivalry developed over the plates of bread and cheese produced by Albert, and the bowls of pasta more cleverly concocted by Charlie. By the third week, however, it looked ominously like the two teams were heading for a showdown in the final and things started to get a little more heated. The quarterfinals were dramatic affairs, with the police having to be called to escort an Argentine player off the pitch in that country's match with England, in a controversial dismissal. In their semi final against Russia it was only Ricardo's Munich team mate Franz Beckenbauer's brilliant goal that kept the West Germans in the running. For England, victory over Portugal was more easily achieved, despite the blatant handball incident which conceded a penalty to the opposition. Ricardo was livid. 'Cheat!' he screamed at Charlton. 'Good lad!' was his father's riposte, and in a Mister Punch voice, 'that's the way to do it!' Charlie sensed that his diplomatic skills may well be needed to avoid all out war between the two especially if it panned out as Charlie thought it might – with the final was being played between England and West Germany.

Which, of course, is exactly what did happen. On July 30th the three men sat themselves down in front of the flickering black and white screen to watch the drama unfold. To begin with the teams seemed evenly matched, and full time arrived with two goals scored apiece, although the German Weber's ninetieth-minute equaliser was a bit of a shocker to the older men. Extra time, however, was something quite different. There was an urgency about the English players, they ran harder and tackled more fiercely. Inside the huge Wembley Arena, the predominately English crowd was shouting itself hoarse. 'England! England!' Albert and Charlie joined in. 'Deutschland! Deutschland!' was Ricardo's bellowed reply. With eight minutes gone, Geoff Hurst scored his second goal. Three-two. Now all the English lads had to do was to keep the opposition away from the goal mouth and the precious trophy was as good as theirs. The tension mounted as the minutes ticked away. Ricardo could hardly bear to look. Scoring opportunities came and went and still his team could not dent the home side's defence. The stadium clock showed that 119 minutes had been played. With only sixty seconds to go some English fans started to run onto the pitch. In the confusion, the German goalkeeper lost concentration, Geoff Hurst's sweet right foot struck the ball and once more found the back of the net. At the exact same moment, the referee's whistle blew in three shrill bursts. Time was up. It was over. England had won the World Cup four goals to two!

Charlie and Albert danced around the room, hugging each other and whooping for joy. Ricardo sat, head in hands, thinking how disappointed his team mates would be when he went back to Munich for pre-season training in August. Franz especially would be devastated. He hated to lose anything. Ricardo could hardly tell him he'd watched the match with two old England fans, now could he? Especially when his father and uncle were Swiss and therefore meant to be neutral. It looked like white lie time. Sensing his son's mood, Albert broke away from Charlie and went over to Ricardo. 'Cheer up son,' he said, 'it's only a game, not a bloody war. Nobody died.' Charlie watched his brother and best friend consoling the young man, and decided the time had come for him to do what he did best – get in the kitchen and knock up something delicious, which they could wash down with a few glasses of a decent red and forget all about the football. Food and wine as comforter and peacemaker! Charlie was pretty sure it would work. It usually did the trick. The rest of the year saw the world lurch from one crisis to another. In Vietnam there was all out bloody war, in China the murderous 'cultural revolution' started and in South Africa the architect of apartheid was assassinated only to be replaced by another rabid proponent of the same evil doctrine. If governments weren't killing people, they were oppressing them. The Soviet Union, not content with being in conflict with the free world, now turned its attention to China, and in East Germany the Berlin Wall continued to claim lives as desperate people tried to escape the clutches of the Stasi. Charlie began to feel that his work of the past twenty years had been all but in vain. His crumb of comfort was that at least there was no fighting on the European mainland, which was why the European Economic Community had been set up in the first place. If only it could be made more inclusive, Charlie would be able to consider his job done. He had high hopes for Harold Wilson's application which would take Britain into the Community and place that country at the centre of European decision-making. A decision would come towards the end of the next year, 1967. Surely to goodness that old curmudgeon de Gaulle wouldn't say 'non' this time? In the meanwhile, as Charlie had at last been allowed to retire from active service, on his 'official' seventieth birthday, there was nothing to do but wait and watch as events unfolded. Oh yes, and to celebrate twenty years of marriage to his adored Giovanna in the December. How had he ever lived without her?

CHAPTER NINE

The summer of love and remembrance

It was March and therefore spring in southern Italy. On the farm, the 'boys' were busying themselves with preparations for planting. They were still called 'I ragazzi' although they were both close to forty now. Mind you, Teresa and Gina were still referred to as 'the girls' but they were in their thirties and both long since married. Oddly for such a fecund family, none of the four had produced grandchildren for Albert and Caterina. The girls had their high-powered careers in the Milano fashion industry, and the boys, well, they were just as ever – no interest in anything but the work of the farm and exploring the countryside around it. They did not even show any curiosity about the rest of Italy north of Naples, and even a visit to Naples was only an occasional affair. Giuseppe had done his father proud and had sired a minor dynasty in Milano – Francesco now had two brothers and two sisters to keep him company. Albert sometimes thought to himself that his first-born, Giuseppe, was a 'real Donkin' in the original mould. His career was going from strength to strength. He had always had a deep and powerful bass-baritone voice, but now, as he approached his mid-forties, it seemed to have gained something extra, a richer tone, a weightier quality. He had released a couple of long-playing records, and his parents took great delight in listening to them over and over again, almost to the point of wearing them out.

At the other end of the family, Ricardo was also doing brilliantly. Last year's World Cup disappointment was fading, and the 'azurri' were already looking forward to Mexico 1970. They'd show the world what Italian footballers were really capable of! Ricardo was still playing for Bayern München, but the Réal Madrid scouts had shown up again, and were talking sums of money that mere mortals could only dream of. The likelihood that Ricardo would settle down with some young woman and start having babies was remote. Now long-haired and very handsome, he was often on the covers of the glossy magazines, and every time he had a different girl on his arm, each more beautiful, and (if Albert was being honest), more vacuous than the last. Perhaps it was a good thing that none of these women would be producing the Weiss grandchildren. A decent, honest hardworking daughter in law with some brains was what was required, not some dull-eyed 'dolly bird' whose stated aim in life was to have an acting career in CineCittà or Hollywood and to bring about world peace....

Because they now had more time, Albert and Charlie were able to put their heads together as to how they should mark their seventieth birthdays, which were to occur on June 10th and October 19th of that year respectively. Albert had long since given over the work of the farm to Carlo and Giorgio and was only involved with Martin's carpentry workshop on an occasional basis, so he too had effectively retired. There was nothing to stop them planning something fantastic, yet a great party was not what either of them wanted. There had been enough of those over the years, especially when Sophia was alive. They both felt the need to do something more meaningful, more significant, to mark the fact that they had lived so long and were still so well. Thousands of men who had started life at the same time as they had, with the same hopes and dreams they had, were either dead and buried in France and Belgium, or were living shattered emotional lives, carrying with them the baggage of everything they had seen and done in the Great War. Charlie and Albert had their memories too, after all, they had both been at Etaples and in the Somme before pitching up at Ypres. Somehow or other though, the way that they had turned around their lives afterwards had made the images easier to live with. They were not surrounded by scores of damaged men and fractured families as they would have been had they returned to Great Harwood and Scarborough. Of course they knew people who had endured terrible suffering, not least their precious brother in law Alessandro, but in rural Italy there were not the numbers and the constant reminders of just how devastating that war had been. Having a totally different kind of life to get on with had succeeded in distracting them and in so doing in diluting the pain. Both men knew exactly how lucky they were. Charlie had told Albert about the sad memorials that stood in the centre of every city, town and village in England, where the lists of names from the Great War were so long by comparison with those from 1939-45, and where wreaths of the little blood-red poppies made by crippled ex-soldiers, sailors and airmen sat wilting in the English rain. As one, they realised what they had to do. They had to make a pilgrimage in remembrance for the fallen and in thanksgiving for their own lives. The destination would, unquestionably, have to be Ypres. After all these years, it was time to return.

The first thing was to discuss it with their wives. Both men were clear that they wanted Giovanna and Caterina to share the experience with them, so that they could fully understand why they had taken that enormous and dangerous step fifty years before. Then they had to decide whether they wanted to retrace their original 1917 journey, or to take a more direct, more comfortable, route. In the interests of keeping the wives on board, it was decided that the latter course would be more appropriate. Tents and mountain paths had lost their appeal, and the advent of the autostrade and the autoroutes in France made driving it and staying in little country pensiones a real option. No need to rough it this time. It would still be an adventure, just a less painful one! In any case there would be no-one left from those days to visit – the café in posh little Portofino must have changed hands a dozen times, and the farm in Switzerland would no doubt be in the care of Wolfgang's great grandchildren by now, if it hadn't been sold off. No, they would find a new route, maybe catching up on some of the places they had pledged to visit before. However they did it, they would still end up where it had all begun, in Belgium, in the height of summer.

The first few weeks of spring were spent planning the trip. Neither Caterina nor Giovanna had been to Switzerland or France, let alone Belgium. Germany was pretty much a closed book to them as well, except for the one time Giovanna had overflown the country not long after the war. Neither had seen the West Zone. Once they left Northern Italy, it would be uncharted territory for them. Albert hadn't been outside of his adopted homeland in fifty years and his memories were a bit hazy. He and Charlie spent hours poring over the atlas, rediscovering the towns they had passed through at speed, towns where they had seen buildings they had sworn to revisit, the stunningly-located cathedral of Laôn for instance. Most had been glimpsed at night and deserved a better look. It began to seem like the first part of the journey would be a pleasant holiday as much as anything with extra memories for Charlie of some of the solo trip he had taken in 1925. It would probably only be when they got into northern France that they would encounter the aftermath of the war, if the evidence hadn't all been cleared away by now. They had no way of knowing what they would find. By leaving Matera in early May, they figured they could be in

Belgium by mid-July, in time for the fiftieth anniversary of the Battle of Paschendale. If there were other people there for that reason, two old couples would hardly draw attention to themselves. History buffs come in all shapes and sizes, even in the form of ageing Swiss men with smart Italian wives.

The local library provided a wealth of guidebooks, and it was fun for all four to sit down at the table in Caterina's kitchen and choose places to visit. Albert and Charlie had some destinations which were fixed and immutable – mostly towards the end of the trip. Charlie had read that there was an enormous monument to the missing of the Somme, at a place called Thiepval. Designed by Edwin Lutyens, it apparently was engraved with over seventy thousand names of men who had simply disappeared in that awful battle. It was a must. Before that, though, there would be less sombre ports of call. Milano, obviously, would give them the chance to catch up with Giuseppe, Francesca and their burgeoning young family, not to mention the girls and their husbands, as well as Marco and Marguerita Bocelli. Thereafter it would be strictly tourism.

Planning their route through Switzerland, it was agreed that they would stop at Bern, officially Albert and Charlie's birthplace, to see what the town was like these days, just in case they needed to know that. It was bound to have changed in the forty years since Charlie had last dropped by. 'That's where you bought those books off that girl whose brother had been killed, wasn't it Charlie?' Albert said. 'No, you old duffer, that was Torino. Bern is where we found out what was happening in the war after we'd been stuck on the farm for half a year without a newspaper!' 'Oh yes, how could I forget that?' was Albert's slightly hurt reply. 'I could still speak German in them days. No more though. We'll have to rely on you to tell us what's what this time.' 'Ah yes, but can you trust me Albert? I might lead you up the garden path!' said Charlie, a mischievous twinkle in his eye. 'Well if you do, you can take a bloody shovel and get digging!' was the retort, 'but you'll be going without me!' Oh dear, Charlie had over-stepped the mark again. He kept forgetting how sensitive his old pal could be. Making soothing noises, and promising to translate everything word for word, he suggested they look for somewhere to move onto after they had seen all they wanted to see in Switzerland.

'The Black Forest!' cried Caterina, and Giovanna chorused her approval. 'We want to try those great big schnitzels you told us about, Charlie,' she said, 'and that chocolate cake with the cherries !' Agreed. The Black Forest it would be. Next? 'I fancy driving up alongside the Rhine for a bit,' Albert proposed. 'I like big rivers, and from the map that looks like the daddy of them all.' Charlie was reminded of the vast Rhein barges he had seen, and agreed with Albert that as rivers went, this was indeed a good one. He could see his hopes of revisiting Dijon with its splendid rooves fading as the route veered further and further north and east, but he said nothing. Maybe on the way back from Ypres the opportunity might present itself. For now he was quite happy to go along with the others' plans. Alsace-Lorraine would do him just as well as the Burgundy hills. From Metz it would be a matter of heading west across the northern part of France following much the same way that he and Albert had walked all those years earlier but in reverse. The events of 1914-18 and their own memories would dictate where they went.

On May 8th, VE Day to those who still remembered the end of the second war, the two couples piled into Giovanna's luxurious big black saloon, stowing their suitcases in the capacious boot and placing their hats and coats along the back of the sofa-like rear seat. They had agreed that they would take it in turns to drive, and first at the wheel was Giovanna herself. She wanted to do her bit while they were in country she knew, so that she could get a good look at the scenery later on. Fair enough was the consensus. The women would drive to Milano, then Albert would get them through the Alpes to Bern, a stretch he had already walked anyway. The Black Forest leg would fall to Charlie as he had seen it before, as would the drive along the Rhein for the same reason. Then it would be up to the women to share the part of the trip from Metz to Ypres, to allow the men the maximum opportunity to rekindle their memories. This section of the trip would certainly involve a great deal of stopping and looking, and in any case since it followed a pretty direct Route Nationale over almost flat ground – if the atlas could be trusted – the drive should not be too arduous. Done! All that remained was to fill the car with petrol, check the oil, the water and the tyres, and turn the nose towards the north. Let the adventure begin!

The Italian section was accomplished as speedily as possible, with only one cultural detour, to which even Albert readily agreed as Caterina had never been there, and that was to Firenze. The autostrada made a drive which had previously been long, slow and arduous seem easy. With typical Italian brilliance the engineers had made the Apennines 'disappear' by means of a series of breathtakingly audacious bridges and tunnels, and soon after leaving Roma, it seemed, they were looking down on the terracotta roofscape of that fine old city, the great dome of the Cathedral in the foreground, and the glistening thread of the Arno bisected by the Ponte Vecchio behind. They spent a few days there, drinking in the art and culture by day and soaking up the superb Florentine cuisine – la cucina fiorentina – by night. The galleries, the squares, the architecture, the old market – everywhere they looked there was something of beauty to see, and in every ristorante and humble trattoria, there was something delicious to try. The artworks that they rated most highly were, predictably perhaps, the wonderful Botticellis at the Uffizi, and the food? A splendid tender well-aged beef steak rich with garlic, served with tender young asparagus and a sauce made from the dark local Chianti got the vote. Divine! The road from Firenze to Milano was similarly improved since Charlie's last effort, and the kilometres were quickly eaten up, this time with Caterina behind the wheel, and a calm and sensible driver she was too.

Until hitting the outskirts of Milano, that is, when the sudden rush of traffic put her off her stride and she had to do the unthinkable, and ask a man to take over! Giovanna comforted her, after all the same had happened to her the first time she and Charlie had gone to Torino. It was a huge city around which people seemed to need to drive at breakneck speed, leaning on their hooters and zipping in and out of such lanes as were marked on the roads. Whoever drove needed a navigator, and Caterina was a brilliant map-reader. Gratefully shuffling over to allow Charlie to take charge of the driving, she busied herself finding the shortest route to Giuseppe and Francesca's house. No longer camped in a tiny town house, the Weiss family now lived in some splendour on the northern outskirts, in an old villa set in huge grounds surrounded by trees and an impeccably manicured lawn. The indicators of success or the signs of a large allowance well spent? Bit of both, Charlie decided. Francesca's father had certainly been more than generous once his daughter had done the decent thing and given him five grandchildren to dote on. There was no way he would allow them to live in circumstances inappropriate to their station. They may have a humble Swiss surname, but they were the offspring of Italian nobility, of old money, which must never be forgotten!

They arrived as the hot sun was setting and found their hosts already sitting on the terrace, bottles of Asti on ice and six sparkling glasses to hand. The children, it seemed, had already bidden their parents goodnight and were in the care of nanny for homework, baths and bed, depending on their age. The grandparents were permitted a swift visit to say hello, but not to disrupt the young ones' regime, and Francesca led them off in the right direction. Giuseppe was not on stage this night – a rare treat - so there would be plenty of time for the adults to have a leisurely meal and a jolly good chat. After the Asti, of course! To accompany the Asti, a large silver tray of delicious-looking canapés was produced by the cook. These were taken to the long scrubbed wooden dining table which sat in the shade of a massive chestnut tree. There were clear signs that outdoor entertaining was very familiar territory indeed. Or perhaps, thought Charlie, when there are seven of you, a few of whom are bound to make a mess, eating outside makes perfect sense. Especially if you have cats and dogs to act as tame vacuum cleaners! Once Francesca, Albert and Caterina returned, the group made short work of the snacks and the ice cold wine, with much smacking of lips and appreciative noises. As the light was fading, the gardener, who turned out to be the cook's husband, came out with some flickering oil lights which he set about the place so that they could see to eat. Charlie began to wonder if there were any other servants stashed away – scrawny chambermaids perhaps or soot-blackened chimney boys? He dismissed the thought as unworthy as soon as it had crossed his mind. Giuseppe and Francesca were just rich, that was all, not cruel. They could afford to pay someone to do their routine work, so they did. Money, as someone once said, makes the world go round. It occurred to Charlie that the world inhabited by Albert's son was revolving at a fair old lick. Suppressing his anti-toff feelings, he decided to settle back, relax and enjoy the evening. You didn't get to dine with – and off - the aristocracy every day.

Luckily, Francesca was a very unusual aristocrat. She had absolutely no airs and graces, and the meal was served in a most convivial and informal manner. It occurred to Charlie that the Italian nobility was nothing like its British equivalent. In Britain, despite the apparent breaking down of the class system, the toffs still had a lot to say about what went on in society. Somehow they still wielded power behind the scenes. Here they had lost all their old status and influence when the state became a republic, and now only had their wealth and property to fall back on. What a shame! Ah well, they kept a few people in work, which had to be a good thing. Charlie resolved to stop analysing and just, as the Americans were wont to say, 'go with the flow.' It was nearly midnight when the last scrap of cheese and fruit was cleared away and the empty bottles consigned to the bin. It had been a delight. The conversation had ranged from the mundane to the elevated, and sometimes both at once! Albert and Caterina were obviously thrilled to see how well their oldest son was doing, and how happy he was. The next day they would spend some time with the grandchildren, then meet up with 'the girls' and their husbands for an evening meal. A trip to the opera was a must, as Giuseppe was currently playing the role of the bull-fighter Escamillo in a daring new production of Bizet's 'Carmen'. It was considered daring because it was set in Franco's modern fascist Spain, and the dress of the soldiers had obvious echoes of Italy under Mussolini and the infamous blackshirts. This was a time which many of the opera-goers had lived through and not forgotten. Giovanna especially adored this opera, possibly because the heroine's songs were so well suited to her own mezzo soprano range or maybe because the tragic ending touched a strain of romantic melancholy in her heart. Whatever the reason, she was keen to go and Marco Bocelli was once more prevailed upon to come up with some seats. He did them proud this time – the presidential box no less! How grand. And champagne to boot. Charlie began to suspect he could get used to this life style. He felt its seductive pull. Just as well there was no equivalent in Matera, or he might succumb and become a class traitor.

The few days in Milano sped by. There was so much to do, so many people to see. There seemed to be barely enough hours to cram it all in. But cram it in they did, and on May 20th, with promises to call in again on their way home ringing in the air, they set off once more on their great pilgrimage. Albert took over the driving duties to get them safely through the Alps and into Switzerland. It was a breathtaking journey. At every turn there were magnificent views of mountains and lakes, which Albert could remember comparing in 1918 with the Peak District, hitherto his only experience of high places. The Peak District had come off worse then and it came off worse now. This was gorgeous. It was interesting too, he thought, that en route they had had to pass through a border control where their documents were rigorously scrutinised. In 1918, paperless and on the run, he and Charlie had simply found a quiet place and stepped into Italy. Going the other way was an eye-opener, especially once they had passed into the German-speaking part of the country. Switzerland was so tidy, so orderly, so efficient after the gentle chaos that is Italy. Even the cows were pristine with their polished bells, and as for the alpine chalets festooned with bright red and white geraniums, well, they positively sparkled with housewifely pride. 'Hardly a flower out of place, eh Albert?' Charlie said. 'They wouldn't dare!' came the reply, 'they'd have the Schmutzpolizei after them!' Schmutzpolizei eh? – best translated as the 'dirt police'. It looked like Albert had retained more German than he was letting on. And more of a sense of humour. Maybe the trip would bring him out of himself a bit. He had become far too serious of late. Age probably, Charlie concluded, after all the old boy was perilously close to seventy.

In fact it was only a week or so later, having left Switzerland and driven into the Black Forest, that Albert did celebrate the beginning of his eighth decade. It was June 10th, and a glorious summer's day. The foursome went for a good long walk in the woods in an attempt to shake down the enormous German breakfast they had just taken at their Gasthaus near Tübingen. Charlie had been to this beautiful old University town at the end of the second war in an attempt to forge links with the French occupying forces, and had received a fairly icy reception. This time the welcome was warmer, the beds soft and comfortable and the breakfast, frankly, wunderbar. Full of rich strong coffee, several kinds of dark bread, assorted wursts, smoked ham, three or four cheeses, and a hard boiled egg each, not to mention the yoghurts, fruits and jams that came after, they decided some strenuous exercise was called for. Besides they needed to make room for Kaffee und Kuchen later! The women were getting impatient to try the Sauerkirschtorte for which the region was famous, and were even willing to forego lunch so that they could enjoy it. How the Germans managed to eat five times a day was beyond them, but they did it. They were a generously sized folk, it must be admitted. The schnitzels last night had well and truly lived up to Charlie's description, and they anticipated that the cake would too. Quick march! For Charlie it was interesting to note the obvious wealth that West Germany now enjoyed, especially by comparison with how things had been in the 1920s, and especially just after the second war, when people were almost starving. He could understand why they relished their food so – they had not forgotten the hungry years before the Americans came to their rescue. The Black Forest cake, when they were finally served it – at precisely 4pm of course! - was a perfect assemblage of everything the Germans had missed in those times – moist chocolate sponge, layers of rich cream and tart cherries stewed in Kirsch, the whole generously topped with thick curls of dark chocolate and cut in what could only be described as 'man-sized' portions. Individual pots of aromatic coffee completed the feast. Caterina, her eyes like saucers, passed the opinion that on this stylish white plate sat enough calories for a human being for a whole day, and it was supposed to be a snack – a little something to keep you going until dinner time! Albert groaned. 'Oh God! I suppose that means we'll have to have another great long walk does it? I'm an old man now you know!' The hoots of derision that greeted this remark may have temporarily silenced him, but they didn't stop him tucking in, with gusto. 'Happy Birthday, Albert,' said Charlie, 'you'll never get a better cake than this no matter how long you live. Just enjoy it. Then we'll walk!'

The few days spent in the Black Forest did not disappoint. The huge dark trees – which turned the winding roads into cathedrals, as Charlie had said – the exquisite old towns and villages, the splendid rustic food and the local Badische wine, which was dry, fresh and young and quite unlike the syrupy concoctions which sometimes found their way into Italy. Everything was delightful, and worked so well. Castles and museums were open when they should be, shops were spotless and had just what you wanted, and service was delivered with a smile and a polite word often sadly missing elsewhere. People seemed to be proud of the job they did, no matter what that was. Charlie did notice though that a lot of the routine or menial work was being done by people who were clearly not German. Cleaners, street sweepers and building site labourers, for instance, all seemed to be either Yugoslavian or Turkish men. They looked positively Mediterranean, being short of stature, brown eyed, olive-skinned and very dark haired. He could hear that they talked together either in foreign tongues unknown to him, or in a very naïve form of German which he was told was 'Gastarbeiterdeutsch' – or 'foreign workers' German'. It seemed that the handful of men from the Balkans that he had met in Frankfurt in 1949 may just have been the first wave of a much larger influx of workers whose sweat and muscle were needed to make the post-war Wirtschaftswunder the 'economic miracle' that it assuredly was. He thought about Goran, and wondered if he had ever got his family out of Serbia to join him. He hoped he had been successful and found happiness. By being prepared to work hard, as well as by the risks he had taken, he had certainly earned it. He hoped too that these foreign workers were being treated well by the hosts who needed them so much. In England he had been told how coloured migrants from the former Empire, lured to Britain to rebuild the nation after the war, had found themselves on the receiving end of shocking attacks by racialists, both verbal and physical. He prayed that this was not also the case in West Germany, but he feared it might be.

Crossing over the Rhein into France at the stylish spa town of Baden Baden, the party headed north alongside the great river. They were now in that part of France that had changed hands in war so often the inhabitants hardly knew what language to speak. There was an intriguing mix of French and a dialect of German on offer and Charlie had no way of telling which he should use. Should he go for the language of the oppressor or the liberator? And which was which exactly? Could he assume that German was hated and French adored? It was a conundrum. The river certainly lived up to Albert's expectations – wide and busy with barges carrying heavy cargo of every kind – coal, steel, stone for building and gravel for road making. The massive locks were examples of engineering on a scale that British navvies could only dream about. 'Makes our narrow boats look like toys, eh Charlie?' was his comment. 'That's the way to move stuff all right,' came the reply, 'long as you're not in a hurry. Shame they stopped using the canals in England for freight really, there'd be a lot less traffic on the roads.' 'Especially since they closed down half the ruddy train lines' said Albert showing that he did still keep something of an interest in the land of his birth. 'Let's just hope the oil never runs out eh Charlie?'

Oil it was that kept them going northwards through the charming countryside of Alsace, where the vines grew in impeccably tidy rows up the hillsides, producing French wines with German names like Gewürztraminer and Riesling. The place was very much to their liking. Charlie loved the mixture of the two influences in the lifestyle, and he felt he knew them both so well. The food was hearty and Germanic yet prepared with French elegance and flair. He had not expected to be offered a huge plate of sauerkraut and dumplings, topped with an array of cooked meats and sausages, yet served with a sophisticated dry white wine instead of the beer that would have been usual, even obligatory, with such a dish in Germany. As he had observed in other parts of the world where two cultures collide – French Canada for instance – the lucky folk who live there often reap the benefits of both. The draught beer in Alsace was far better than the usual French 'pression', having been brewed to German quality standards and valued for its own sake, not as a poor substitute for wine. The ambience, however, was more relaxed and French than in Germany – there was a lot more kissing going on for a start! – and people seemed to be in less of a hurry. Best of both worlds, no doubt about it.

With their Alsace holiday behind them, and having passed fairly quickly through less picturesque Lorraine, they arrived at the ancient city of Metz, a fortress town if ever there was one. Its bloody past was there for all to see. Romans, Franks, crusaders, old Uncle Tom Cobley and all – they'd all had a go at occupying and controlling Metz at some time or another, and the French were just the last in a long line who had succeeded.

From the city they would head fairly directly west along the top of France, with the aim of visiting as many Great War sites as might still be standing, and planning to arrive in Ypres in mid July. They had nearly three weeks to accomplish this, so they could take their time and have a really good poke about. Charlie and Albert felt fairly sure that much of the evidence of both wars would have been swept away, made good, maybe even forgotten. After all, in West Germany most of the bomb-damaged buildings had been restored and in some places Charlie had been, like Frankfurt, you wouldn't know there had been a war. They expected the French to have done the same, to put the past to bed, especially as the Great War was now such ancient history. How wrong they were! The French may have been in a mood to forgive, but they were not about to forget, and they didn't plan to let the rest of the world forget what had gone on here either. The first most obvious reminder was the cemeteries. Everywhere you went, in fields, in forests, up country lanes, on the edges of villages and in the middle of towns, there were the war graves. In their sodding thousands. The British and Commonwealth graves, with their squat little headstones in cream coloured sandstone, told the story of young lives squandered for King and Country, sometimes hundreds of them bearing the same few dates, testament to the ferocity of the fighting that had taken place in this largely rural landscape. Every one of the impeccably-kept cemeteries had its ornate memorial, and inside that a written record of who was buried there, kept safe in a cupboard. Beside the names there was space for messages, and some were heart-rending. 'Found you at last, Granddad', frequently accompanied by a very recent date, indicated a search that had lasted decades. Often, the single word 'Why?' was inscribed next to the names of men as young as seventeen, mown down as they were ordered out of the safety of their trenches and 'over the top'.

Then there were the French cemeteries, staggering in their vastness. Row upon row of white crosses, and above them the tricouleur fluttering in the breeze, showed the scale of the sacrifice that this nation had made.

The most upsetting in their pointlessness were the memorials to the men who had been killed in the last few days of the war, between the German surrender and the final ceasefire. Charlie and Albert could imagine that mother in rainy rural England or the Australian outback celebrating the end of hostilities along with the rest of the world, only to get the news, far too late, that her precious son had been killed in action at half past ten on the eleventh of November in some far-off place with a name she couldn't pronounce. Fighting for what, exactly? So that the toffs and generals could 'play on' until the ref blew the final whistle? Why wasn't the match just abandoned? The score was in, there would be no last minute equaliser, yet the slaughter was allowed to continue until 'Full Time' was officially called. Charlie could not keep his rage in. 'Bastards!' he shouted, 'you bloody bloody bastards!' Albert's reaction to this was simply to go pale and become silent, then they both wept.

They went to the town of Albert, which had been the assembly point for troops heading to the carnage of the Somme, and there they saw the remains of trenches, just the right depth for a short chap who could keep his head down. Anyone well-fed enough to be tall or silly enough to stand up could expect to be shot. Intended for shelter and not for living in, these places had become vermin-infested stinking holes as the battles went on and on, the rain fell and the mud rose. They remembered the church with the statue of 'the leaning virgin' – the golden sculpture of the Madonna which had been hit by a shell and left hanging at right angles to the spire. This had been a landmark for those on their way up to the front a scant three miles away. For many it was a sight they would never see again. Now restored and upright once more, she sparkled in the hot summer sun, a reminder that for some at least, life goes on. Charlie and Albert had been among the lucky ones, and had quite literally lived to fight another day.

Just how lucky was brought home to them forcibly when they stood before the vast Lutyens memorial at nearby Thiepval. This great brick structure had been built to honour the men who had simply disappeared without trace in the hell that became known as the battle of the Somme. Without graves to visit, families could only search for their loved one's name carved on one of the monument's high walls and place a paper cross adorned with a little red poppy beside it. There were over seventy-three thousand there, all chaps who had felt they were doing their bit for the Empire, hoping to return to England or Australia, Canada or Wales and pick up the lives they had left when they boarded the troop ships. All vanished as if they had never been. Reduced to an inscription on a wall in a foreign land. 'It's a bloody miracle we're not up there,' Albert whispered, 'we could have been, easily. There's blokes I knew in Étaples up there.' 'Me too,' replied Charlie, 'too bloody many.' Just as they were leaving this all too tangible reminder of man's inhumanity to man, the two men came across a party of school children from England, whose teacher was explaining to them just what it was that had happened here. In his bluff northern voice, he bade the pupils recite the lines from 'For the Fallen' that sum up that war so accurately. In hushed tones and in perfect unison, heads bowed and visibly moved, the young ones repeated the promise 'they shall not grow old as we that are left grow old, age shall not weary them nor the years condemn, at the going down of the sun and in the morning, we <u>will</u> remember them.' Wiping away a tear, Charlie turned to Albert and said 'thank God for teachers eh? They won't forget this, these young'uns.' 'It'll be a while before I do and all,' was Albert's immediate response, then, more prosaically, 'let's bugger off out of here eh, Charlie? It's too bloody spooky by far.'

For a day or two they gave the big cemeteries and the memorials a miss. The effect of the visit to the Somme had been profound. Every now and again they would come across a little graveyard in the middle of nowhere and they would always stop and pay their respects, but they felt instinctively that they would need to save themselves, gird their loins, so to speak, for Ypres. One thing that did impress was how well the cemeteries were kept. Every grave had a plant of some kind, often a rose in flower, and the lawns were immaculate. The sacrifice made by these men was certainly not being allowed to be forgotten. One thing they did do was to return to Laôn, with its great cathedral perched high above the town, visible for miles. In 1917 they had seen it by night but a return visit by day was something Charlie had promised himself. As he recalled it, it was his plan to come back and offer up a prayer of thanks if he and Albert made a successful getaway. Well, they had, and the time had come to thank God for taking such good care of them. Better late then never. The town of Laôn is a charming one, a maze of narrow medieval streets radiating out from the hub formed by the cathedral on the top of the hill. Houses and shops of all kinds rub shoulders, cafés spill out onto the pavements. The merchants display their wares outside their shops, confident that nothing will be stolen, and the result is a very appealing and colourful scene with vibrant flowers and fruits prettily offsetting the dull sheen of hardware and leather goods. It reminded Charlie of Naples in the old days when people still walked around places and took the time to look. Now they sped by, leaning on their hooters, racing from one 'essential' appointment to another. Here in Laôn, there was hardly room for a car to make its way through and the old streets were the domain of the people. Grandmothers in cardigans and headscarves, little girls in lacy summer frocks, teenagers with long hair dressed in their version of the latest 'hippy' style – all mingled and went about their business in an atmosphere of friendliness and mutual respect.

The smell of freshly-roasted coffee emanating from one of the cafés was too much for Charlie, and the four sat themselves down at a scrubbed wooden table in the shade of a dark blue awning to await service. First to greet them was the ever-present French cat. These little creatures live wild in most French towns and manage to eke out some kind of existence either through their own hunting prowess or by worming their way into the affections of complete strangers. This one probably came into the latter category, Charlie decided, because she was so pretty with her long grey coat, eyes of the brightest green imaginable, and a purr as loud as a traction engine. In no time at all, having schmoozed around his legs, she was on Charlie's knee, looking inquisitively to see what the table might have to offer. Needless to say, when the café au lait was ordered, an extra saucer of milk was requested, and soon the little moggy was installed on a chair of her own, lapping contentedly. When they left to walk up the hill to the church, the cat followed a few paces behind them, her tail erect, miaowing occasionally as if to remind them of her presence. Entering the cathedral, the four fell silent. The cool air, the atmosphere of age and the glorious light reflected through the magnificent windows all combined to overawe them. This place had borne witness to a lot of worship over the years. It had also, as Charlie noticed very quickly and pointed out to Albert in a whisper, seen some very unspiritual activity, for every one of the great stone columns was pockmarked with bullet holes, some almost large enough to have been made by shells. Clearly some very intense fighting had taken place here either in the Great War or the second one, maybe both. You'd think a church would be sacrosanct. Obviously not. When the enemy retreats, you follow, even if it is the Lord's house in which he takes shelter. Crossing themselves with holy water, the four proceeded up the main aisle to a pew just in front of the magnificent altar. As one, they genuflected then took their seats. The little cat was still close, and slid under the wooden bench so as to end up once again next to Charlie. This time she remained quiet, as if aware that this was a special place, not rowdy and raucous like the street where a girl could miaow to her heart's content. She settled down close to Charlie and allowed herself to be stroked, purring gently, almost asleep. Charlie found the cat's presence curiously comforting. The repetitive soothing action of stroking her soft fur acted like a mantra to him, and allowed him to concentrate on the reason for the visit. Fifty years before, he and Albert had passed this place stealthily and had vowed to return and give thanks if they were spared. Not only had they been spared, they had been blessed. They had each led very fulfilling lives, he through his work and Albert through his marvellously talented family. They could so easily have bled to death at Paschendale in the mud and the filth. So much was now known and had been written about that vile place and what had happened there, and they had missed it by a whisker. Regrets? None, except perhaps the pain he had caused his parents. Guilt? Not any more. He had paid his dues the second time around and paid them handsomely. He felt that he no longer owed anyone an apology or an explanation for what he had done. So, eyes closed, he spoke silently to his God and thanked him for allowing him to have the life that so many had been denied. 'They shall not grow old...'. A wave of emotion ran through him like a cloud passing over the sun. He opened his eyes slowly and blinked in the bright light filtering through the stained glass. Next to him, the seat was still warm but empty. The little cat had disappeared as stealthily and as suddenly as she had arrived.

The final few steps

Albert, it seemed, had been going through a similar process in the Cathedral at Laôn, but his thinking had been helped by the gentle touch of Caterina's hand on his leg. The warmth she transmitted reminded him of life itself, the life he had decided not to squander, and the life he had created with her. Seeing now how many young men had been slaughtered in this place, only to have war break out with the same enemy less than twenty years later, he knew that he and

Charlie had done the right thing. Faced with the absolute certainty of being killed – for having survived Etaples and the Somme, how could they expect to come out of Paschendale alive? – why stick around? His mother hadn't given birth to him just to have him disappear in some Belgian bog at the age of twenty. She wanted more for him, and by walking away from Ypres, he had made her wishes a possibility. She would have been happy to see how well his children were doing, as he was. Giuseppe was an international opera star, and Ricardo one of the most celebrated footballers in Europe. The boys ran a highly successful and profitable farm, and the girls had brilliant careers in the fashion industry. They were all clever, educated, kind and humane. None of them had become criminals or done anything to hurt other people. They were all contributing to society in their own way. He felt proud of them and of how he and Caterina had brought them up. It was a loss that they had never got to meet their grandmother or any of the other members of their Yorkshire family, but his part of the Donkin clan didn't like to travel, and Scarborough was not exactly on the circuit for either the opera or top flight football. Unlike Charlie, he could not return to England. He'd be recognised as a Donkin the minute he set foot in his old home town. 'Peas in a pod', they said, and it was true. Even at seventy someone would be bound to say 'eeh, is that thee Albert lad? - we heard tha wert dead', and the game would be up. No, the price he had to pay was to be excluded from his homeland forever, unless by some miracle the vindictive bastards in government declared an amnesty. As they hadn't and weren't showing any signs of even thinking about it, Swiss and living in Italy he must remain. It could've been worse, it could've been a bloody sight worse. So he closed his eyes in prayer and said his thanks to God as well – the lenient one the Catholics believed in, as well as the rather more forbidding one he had once worshipped as a chapel boy. He picked up Caterina's hand and placed it to his lips. 'We did all right didn't we?' he asked. 'We did my love,' she said.

At dinner that night, having been given God's permission in the Cathedral, the men at last felt able to talk freely about their feelings. Ever cautious, they did so quietly in Italian to ensure that no one would overhear anything they shouldn't. Having freed themselves intellectually from their guilt many years ago, they had still needed to feel spiritually vindicated by the Lord. Without recourse to a confessor, both Charlie and Albert sensed that they had been absolved for leaving the trenches, since to stay would have been tantamount to suicide. God's presence in that holy place on the hill had been palpable to them, and they were sure their prayers had been heard.

Over a substantial and homely Picardian meal lasting several hours, Charlie and Albert could say things to Giovanna and Caterina they had never dared say before for fear of upsetting their wives. They told them, without going into too much detail, how ghastly trench life had been, especially in the Somme. They were able to give true examples of the stupidity of the field officers and the callousness of the Generals. Both wives remarked how much lighter their husbands seemed, relieved even. It had taken fifty years to reach this point, but at last they had. With the evidence all around them, the women could see just how vast had been the scale of the killing. They were able to understand how Charlie and Albert had arrived at the conclusion that they had no alternative but to leave. They had done their bit. Two more dead English boys would not have won the war for the Allies, it was the eventual arrival of the Americans that did that. Others may well disapprove, but both Giovanna and Caterina could see the unfairness of expecting their husbands to continue to do the bidding of their so-called superiors in the situation of Ypres in 1917. The best they could have hoped for would be to be killed outright. At worst they would have been returned to Britain with their bodies and minds in tatters. No wonder they chose to risk execution and just walk away. No doubt others had done the same, and good luck to them whoever and wherever they were.

The last of the sweet cherry tarte having gone the way of the poached trout, the roast duck and the hearty cheese platter, the four took a leisurely coffee with a more than decent cognac, before retiring for the night. It had been a mentally and emotionally draining day for them all. The next phase would involve them following exactly in Albert and Charlie's footsteps the whole way to Ypres. This was bound to stir up some memories, not all of them bad. One of them would assuredly include the very smelly Fromage Fort de Béthune, and should raise a laugh with the girls. Just thinking of it made Charlie smile, and he fell asleep next to his beloved Giovanna almost giggling with anticipation.

Over breakfast the next morning, they consulted the trusty Michelin atlas of northern France that they had bought in the town. Of course, many of the roads on the map had not existed in 1917. In those days you passed right through the middle of towns, these days there were things called 'périphériques', known in English as 'ring roads', which were designed to keep the traffic out of town centres. And no doubt having the effect of denying local business people the benefits of any passing trade, they all agreed. The trouble was that all these 'périphériques' looked the same. You could not see local landmarks, so you had no real sense of where you were anymore. Albert and Charlie started to feel a tad grumpy, and just a little bit old. Why did everything have to change? Why was the damned car paramount? What was wrong with the ancient roads and paths – people had travelled on them for centuries, and now suddenly, you couldn't. It was all 'one way' and 'no entry', which meant you could not go directly to your destination but ended up taking some blasted 'Déviation obligatoire' or another. The traffic went so fast that if you weren't careful you had passed the town you wanted before you realised it. It had been bad enough in Alsace and Lorraine, but in this more populated part of the country everyone seemed to have a car or a van and most of them were on the road at once. They would have to plan their travel to avoid busy times or they wouldn't find anything.

In the end the solution was obvious, and it was Albert who spotted it. The French all take a two hour lunch break every day and adjourn to their houses or to restaurants and cafés for a leisurely scoff. As a result the roads are deserted between noon and two o'clock. That was the time to do the bulk of the driving. Get to where you were going just as they started to wake up from their little after-dinner nap! Play them at their own game! Brilliant! It worked perfectly of course. Each day they took their time over breakfast and explored the local area on foot. Then, having decided where they wanted to be later that day, they would set off just before twelve and drive for two hours. By the time they got to their intended location, the shops would be open again and they could buy the makings of a splendid picnic, the like of which only exists in France. Most towns have a river or a canal running through them and they would head down to the bank to eat in the shade by the water. After the crusty bread and the range of cheeses, charcuterie and salad, they would then work out what they wanted to see that afternoon and the next morning. In this way they were able to revisit all the places Charlie and Albert had passed through at the start of their epic journey and relive their memories. They went to Arras, by now a large town, and were impressed at how beautifully it had been restored. The two great squares, flattened in the first war bombardment, looked just as they must have in the seventeenth century. They explored the subterranean world which had kept the ever-resilient population alive through both wars. Being nearby, they could not miss Vimy Ridge where the Canadians had fought so valiantly, and where signs still warned people of the danger from unexploded bombs and shells all these years later! They came to the once-important and prosperous coal-mining town of Béthune, now much run down, and tried to find the little shed they had used as shelter for a few days, but either it was gone or they could not remember the place well enough to locate it. For old times' sake, for that day's picnic, Charlie bought a piece of the famous cheese which had so disgusted Albert – the Fromage Fort de Béthune - and was surprised and pleased to discover that his old pal quite liked it now. All those years of aged Parmiggiano had toughened up his taste buds! Charlie told the story of how crossly Albert had reacted to his first whiff of it, and the women howled with laughter, although they did confess to having some sympathy with him. It was obviously an acquired taste. The men recalled hiding out by day and walking by moonlight, and regretted the vegetables they had stolen from innocent people's gardens. In Béthune especially Charlie remembered his solo trips scavenging amongst the market traders' discarded produce, the crude cooking arrangements and their first taste of garlic. Progress was only made possible by Albert's superb skills as navigator and builder. It had been magic, innocent and bloody dangerous. Maybe they had not fully appreciated just how much danger they were in, being so young, only twenty, but they got had away with it.

Slowly and surely the four made their way towards Belgium. The men wanted to take their time to get a true feel of how it had been to be walking through this country. They needed to relive their experience as far as possible, to understand just what it was they had achieved. Of course they could not replicate wartime conditions, and had no need to travel by night anymore. All the same, it felt important to be there on that very patch of ground. Charlie was sure he had never thanked Albert properly for his part in their escape, and Albert felt the same – if Charlie hadn't spoken all them lingoes and been able to cook, God knows how they would have got on. They were astounded to find towns, villages and farmsteads virtually unchanged in their layout, maybe as they had been for centuries. Only the ubiquitous bullet holes served to remind them that two punishing wars had been fought here. There was hardly a building that remained unscarred, and it seemed to Charlie that the failure to repair them was deliberate. Lest we forget, eh?

Turning north, they quickly found themselves at a manned border crossing where signs in several languages indicated that they were leaving France and entering Belgium. Just beyond the check-point, at which their papers had been once again scrutinised and accepted, a local notice told them that they were now in the province of 'Vlaanderen' – Flanders fields, no less. Charlie whispered the translation to Albert. Both men shuddered. The landscape in which they stood was now the stuff of poetry. True to form, and because it was high summer, there were deep red poppies at the edges of the farmers' orderly potato fields, the flowers scattered like drops of blood amongst the greenery. The image was potent, almost overpowering. They crossed the too-rich flat earth, so perfect for growing crops, and made their way to Poperinge. Here they had spent their first night on the run. Here it was they had found clothes to give themselves anonymity, and tools to help them on their way, thanks to the disappeared business man and the Dutch carpenter. They wanted to try and locate the house again and see if they could find out anything about their unwitting benefactors. Of course they could not. Everything had been so ravaged by the two wars that few of the houses remained recognisable. Some of the civic buildings were still there, restored, and Charlie could remember going to them with various officers, as a translator. Ordinary houses were not worth saving and they had been replaced with simple brick and stone structures without much architectural or indeed aesthetic merit. They had seen such towns in northern France where the devastation had been almost total and a lot of dull grey concrete had been used to replace the destroyed housing stock. At least in Poperinge the church and some of the houses flanking the market square remained and everywhere you looked there were pots, troughs and hanging baskets filled with brightly coloured flowers, as an attempt to beautify what war had made ugly. Coming from a place that had not been invaded, except by the odd Roman or Viking, it was hard to imagine being overrun by hostile forces, not once but twice in just over twenty years. Yet these people had picked themselves up, rebuilt their town out of the rubble and even liked it enough to adorn it with great jumbles of fragrant blooms. You had to admire them for their resilience.

In the middle of the market place there was a simple kiosk surrounded by half a dozen wrought iron garden tables and chairs. The kiosk bore the legend 'Frituur'. It was just what Charlie had been hoping for – a Belgian chippie. 'Come and have a look at this Albert', he said. 'They serve the best chips in the world and you can get an icy cold beer to go with them.' 'At eleven in the morning?' was Albert's reply. 'I can't think of a better time,' said Charlie, 'let's see what the girls think.' Of course, the girls were always ready to try something new, and soon the four were tucking into hot smoky sausages and slender crisp freshly-fried chips topped with a generous dollop of mayonnaise. An icy glass of flavoursome local wheat beer completed the feast. Was it breakfast or lunch? Or something in between? It was simply a treat, a novelty for the women, chip shops being rather thin on the ground in Italy, and for Charlie a reminder of his last day in Ypres before he had headed back to England over forty years earlier. The fritten had been lovely then and they still were. 'Blimmin' sight better than any of the chippies in Scarborough, even if they do put mayonnaise on them,' Albert conceded. 'Thank God some things don't change eh?' replied Charlie. 'Just about everything else does. At least we've still got decent fritten in Belgium!' 'Aye, that we do, and a bloody good beer to boot.' For once, it was Albert who had the final word.

The two men seemed reluctant to move on, and wanted to hang around the area of Poperinge for a few days, spending much of the time together without the women. Artefacts and items of interest from the war were being collected there and museums were being set up. In particular, there was a lot of information about TocH House which had been located in the town throughout most of the war and was a place where soldiers could have a break from the trenches and a social get together. The man who had founded it, the quaintly-named Reverend Tubby Clayton – no relation as far as Charlie knew – had gone on to become a famous philanthropist after the war and had been very highly respected. Oddly, neither Charlie nor Albert had ever been to the house. 'Too bloody busy being shot at,' was Albert's explanation. A cosy place, which even housed a piano, they had no doubt that the club must have made the present more bearable for many men, although the future no less inevitable. Knowing what they knew now, it seemed like the equivalent of putting a plaster on a gaping wound. Given the opportunity, Charlie could imagine that he may well have led a sing song there while the bombs fell and the shells exploded all around the poor sods on the front line. 'Talk about fiddling while Rome burnt', he muttered, 'I'd rather be taking my chances on the road.' Albert agreed. 'They didn't know though Charlie,' he said, 'they thought they were doing something noble back then.' 'Dulce et decorum est?' said Charlie. Albert finished the line. 'Pro patria mori?' And with one voice , both men supplied the answer to the question - 'Balls!'

For some reason, they felt the need to try and find the approximate location of the trench they had been in when they had made their momentous decision to walk away. Albert could roughly remember the distance, but not with any accuracy. The landscape had been so cut up that it had taken an age to cover what could today be walked in minutes, so it was a bit hit and miss.   Also there had been no moon that night, which made calculating the exact direction they had taken even harder. Albert felt instinctively that they had covered about four miles, most probably heading due west since that was where Poperinge lay in relation to Ypres. But how close was their trench to the fighting, and how close the fighting to the town? Things had been so chaotic back then, it was likely that not even the officers knew the answer. No, come to think of it, it was highly unlikely that the officers knew, and even less likely that the Generals did, the dopy buggers. The Hun bloody well did though. Their fire was deadly accurate, as the front line boys found to their cost. Charlie was shocked by Albert's vehemence. The fifty years he had spent in Italy becoming a catholic patriarch had not served to erase his memories or soften his anger, and now, seeing again the place they had been sent to defend, the reasons for leaving came flooding back. They had been outnumbered, outgunned, filthy, underfed and led to their certain deaths by idiots who had no respect for them at all. No, no, to leave was not a crime, to stay would have been sure evidence of insanity. 'You don't have to justify yourself to me, Albert,' Charlie said, 'I half suspect it was my big idea in the first place.' 'It may well have been, but I went along with you, and it turned out you were right. Anyroad, we can't undo it, we can't tell anyone and we can't confess. We just have to live with it. What we don't have to do is forget it.'

Predictably, they could only get a vague idea of where they had been that hot July night, though Charlie was especially driven to persevere. In the intervening years the land had been ploughed and planted repeatedly with potatoes, cabbages, leeks and onions. The remnants of ordnance had been removed, and the bits and pieces of men taken away for burial at the Tyne Cot cemetery near Paschendale. So many British and Empire soldiers had been killed in the fighting in and around Ypres that the authorities had decided to make one vast graveyard in addition to the smaller ones located where men fell. They had heard a bit about Tyne Cot, and were dreading seeing it, although they knew they had to at some point. They also recognised, because Albert made it abundantly clear in his blunt Yorkshire way, that they would soon have to stop 'faffing about' in the fields near Poperinge, and get on. Their wives were starting to worry about them, fearing for their mental health as day after day they went over and over old ground searching for clues they would never find. It was, he said, time to call a halt to that part of the journey. There was nothing more they could achieve here and they would be drawing attention to themselves if they persisted. Reluctantly, Charlie agreed. He had hoped to see hell for himself, but it was not to be. It was all gone. Except in his mind.

They drove the few kilometres into Ypres, all the while remarking on the signs pointing them to the site of some famous battle or another. The place names were so familiar, both in the Flemish and in the anglicised corruptions. As Ypres had become Wipers, so Ploegsteert had become Plug Street, and so on. The Tommies were not noted for their command of other languages! The last time Charlie had been here, he had spoken to an excellent chap in the Town Hall in Ypres who had told him of the plan to erect a huge monument to the thousands of men who had simply disappeared, who had no known grave, a bit like the Lutyens one at Thiepval. He had heard that it had been finished not long after his visit, and that it was very impressive, if impressive is the right word. They needed to acclimatise themselves though, so started off their visit by parking the car on the old market square, near the Cloth Hall. The whole town had been razed to the ground in the Great War, and when he had visited less than ten years later, Charlie had been astonished by how much of the rebuilding work had been completed. Now, fifty years on, you would never have known what devastation had been wreaked. All the old buildings had been completely replaced exactly as they were. Ypres was to all intents and purposes once more the medieval city which in its thirteenth century heyday had had twice the population of London. 'Looks a bit different,' was Albert's rather obvious remark.' It was nothing but blimmin' great craters and piles of rubble last time I was here.' A number of museums had exhibitions of wartime artefacts and there were also big grainy blow-ups of photographs of what had happened in and around the town. Luckily, the faces of the men were not all that clear, what with the basic nature of the cameras available at the time, and the distortion caused by the enlargement process. You could just about tell if a chap was British, an Anzac or a Canadian by the cut of their uniform or the cap they wore. In one or two of the photos fellows were seen to be wearing turbans rather than military headgear, and Charlie did recall hearing from one of the officers he worked with that a Sikh regiment from India had been deployed here. Poor blighters! Fancy coming all that way to die in the rain and the mud of Belgium, defending the very Empire that for hundreds of years had taken every last asset their country had to offer in return for the honour of being British! It was a bit like the Maori regiments from New Zealand, who fought heroically and laid down their lives for the government that had robbed them of their land. 'Ah!' thought Charlie, 'hindsight is a wonderful thing.' 'If they'd known then what we know now, eh Albert?' he said. 'They'd have stayed at home in the sunshine and told the King where to stick his shilling!' was the reply, in English of course, to avoid offending the women.

It was late afternoon before they finally made their way to the east of the town, to the Menin Road, where the monument to the missing was to be found. They walked past attractive little shops selling all things Belgian – an infinite variety of chocolates of the highest quality, dozens of kinds of bottled beer, not to mention all sorts of smokers' wares. Caterina and Giovanna could not resist the call of the chocolate, so into a chocolatier they all went to be greeted by a pleasant woman wearing a spotless white apron over a dark green uniform on which was neatly embroidered the company's name. Very professional and not at all like the dusty corner sweetshops in England. Although Charlie could understand her, since Flemish and German sound very alike, it somehow didn't seem right to reply in German, given where they were, and he knew French would be an unpopular choice in these parts. He therefore did something he hated doing usually and asked if she spoke English. 'Of course, sir' came the reply, easily switching over, 'we speak English more than Flemish here in the summertime.' Wonderful. The attendant pulled on a pair of white silk gloves, and, with a knowing smile, asked, 'and what can I get you ladies?' Clever too. Of course men don't buy chocolate unless they have to, and even then nearly always for women. The sisters pored over the display of what was on offer through the shop's glass cabinet. There was almost too much to choose from. Dark rum truffles? a must! Cherries in kirsch wrapped in a crisp white chocolate crust? Yes please! Smooth pistachio cream, or a light champagne mousse? Argh! Where to start? In the end Giovanna bade the assistant to make up a good selection which would surprise and delight them later on – enough for four please, since the men would doubtless want their share, no matter what they said. The chocolates were individually wrapped, then placed in a gold box around which was tied a lacy white ribbon. Albert reached out for the bill. 'This is on me.' he said, 'since I have no doubt my darling Caterina will get the lion's share.' He read the handwritten invoice and gasped audibly. Their posh chocs had cost the best part of a hundred francs! 'Blimey Charlie,' he whispered, 'we could all eat out handsomely for that!' 'Not in Belgium, matey,' came the reply, 'these are Belgian francs, not French ones, they're only worth a fifth of the value.' Albert first sighed with relief and then looked embarrassed and just a bit annoyed. He handed over the cash and the foursome left the shop, after thanking the woman profusely. Outside on the pavement, Albert went into a bit of a rant. 'Bugger it!', he said. 'Why don't these blimmin' countries call their money by different names, or, better still, all have the same currency? That way you wouldn't get confused every time you had to change from one to another.' 'There there, old boy,' Charlie's tone was soothing, 'it's an easy mistake to make.' But Albert, still mortified, would not be soothed. 'Humph!' he said, 'Humph!'

He was still humphing when they suddenly came upon the Menin Gate, and then he fell silent, as did they all. It was an object of strange beauty, on a huge scale and with an overwhelming presence. Modelled on a classical arch and made largely of red brick, it was faced in pure white stone, and so constructed with numerous arcades, recesses and staircases as to have as many sides as possible. On every flat surface were inscribed the names of men who had passed through this gate, fought and died here but whose bodies had never been found – the missing of the Ypres Salient. In all, so the guide book told them, there were the names of nearly fifty-five thousand British and Empire service men carved here, with a further thirty-five thousand at the memorial at Tyne Cot. As at Thiepval, beside some of the names, there were little balsa wood crosses topped with a British Legion red poppy, indicating that someone had recently had a visitor. Even so long after the end of the war, families and friends were still making the pilgrimage from all over the world to pay their respects. Unprepared for the scale of the thing, and quite taken aback by their feelings, after a few minutes both Albert and Charlie were breathless and had to leave. They would return later once they had girded their loins, but for now they needed to sit in the sun on the market square with their wives, have a cup of coffee, try and relax and indulge in the great Belgian pastime of people-watching. All age groups were represented in the passing throng. Some were clearly old enough to have fought there or to have brothers or cousins who did. Others were much younger – candidates for 'found you at last, granddad' perhaps? Listening in to people's conversations, Charlie could tell from their accents that there were Australians, New Zealanders and Canadians there, as well as the more obvious foreigners like the Indians and the Pacific Islanders. All were united by their loss. The need to be here was still strong.

Later that same day, in a sombre mood but better prepared mentally or so they thought, they drove the short distance to Tyne Cot. What they saw there, however, came as a major blow. Nothing they had come across on their travels could match this. The neat little gravestones seemed to stretch for miles, all twelve thousand of them. Then there was the memorial wall. It encircled the cemetery and all over it there were yet more bloody names, the names of the British blokes who had died there after July 1917, and the names of all the Kiwis and the boys from Newfoundland who had just disappeared in the Paschendale slime. All around them people were looking on in horror at what lay before them. It was known that there had been a bloodbath here, but the magnitude of it quite took the breath away. How close had Albert and Charlie come to being a part of this? It was a matter of a few days, even hours, that's all. They had got away just in the nick of time. Their names could be on the wall here, or they could be on the Menin Gate. They could even be in one of the smaller cemeteries somewhere nearby, for who could say where their military identification had ended up? With any luck other chaps had done what they had done – 'gone missing' on purpose - and the death count was a few lower than it seemed. There was no way of knowing the truth. Suddenly Charlie had a staggering thought, and it was something that had not occurred to him over all the years of thinking about this place. Quite against his expectations, he realised that he didn't want to be a part of this, for the fellows commemorated here were an object of admiration and pilgrimage. He hadn't done what these men had done and paid the ultimate price, even if they had died needlessly. His name may well be here, but he wasn't even going to look for it, because it should not be. He communicated as much to Albert, who seemed to be shocked. 'I thought that's one of the reasons we were coming here, Charlie,' he said. 'So did I, mate, but I've changed my mind. I don't deserve to be up there and I don't want to know if I am. My family would never have come here anyway, so there isn't even that consolation. Anyway, that's what I am doing. You must do what you think best.' Albert was quiet for a while, then he said, his voice hushed, 'We got into this together, and we stay in it together. What's right for you, Charlie, is right for me. What you do, so will I. I don't really want to see my name next to these poor sods any more than you do.' They turned to their waiting wives and Albert said 'Come on lasses, let's go, we've seen all we need to see. There's no more for us to do here.' Giovanna took the wheel and in thoughtful silence, they returned to Ypres.

Later that night, they all stood close together in the shadow of the Gate and wept openly while the Last Post was played. This tradition had been repeated at eight o'clock every night since the Gate was finished in 1927 – except during the second war, when the occupying Germans had banned it. Apparently, Charlie reported almost gleefully, the very day the Germans were kicked out in May 1945, the local band assembled and played it again. Once more they were surrounded by visitors from the far corners the earth, many also in tears. It was always busy in July, they were told, but there were even more than usual as this year of 1967 marked the fiftieth anniversary of the so-called 'battle' of Paschendale. Those who had survived knew it for what it was - the slaughter of the many in the service of the few.

What an impact that conflict had had! All these engraved names here and at Tyne Cot, nearly ninety thousand of them, every one of them someone's son or brother, nephew or father. There can hardly have been a town or village in the Empire that had not lost someone. If you added the British and Empire chaps who had been killed in other battles, and were buried all over France and Belgium, there could easily be a million. Then there were the French who, as they had seen by the graveyards, had died in their droves to protect their own country, as well as the half million Italians, the Belgians – the list went on and on. For what? So they could do it all again twenty years later. Instead of treating the Germans fair and square whilst still making sure they could never again try and take over Europe, they crushed them so hard, that they had no choice but to rise up and fight back. Hitler may have been a madman, but he was a man for all that, and he and his defeated countrymen had their pride. By humiliating the German people as they had in Versailles, thereby demonstrating how arrogant and stupid they really were, the toffs and the generals had betrayed and belittled the deaths of the thousands whose names were recorded on these walls. It was a travesty and an affront to their memory.

Both Albert and Charlie knew that, having come back to the starting point, to the place that had irrevocably changed their lives, they now had to cast off their anger, for anger breeds bitterness, and bitterness is a cancer that eats away at a person from within. They could not forget what had happened here, and they certainly could not forgive it, but nothing they could do would change it. They had made their choice back then and walked away. Their lives had been saved and their destinies re-written. Charlie Clayton and Albert Donkin they were no more, but the lives they had now easily made up for the loss of a name or a nationality. Governments may not understand or condone their actions, but each of them knew that when the final reckoning came, their God most certainly would. On a hot night in July 1967, in a town in Belgium, two old men finally cried their last tear and found peace in their hearts.

The next morning, Charlie and Giovanna, and Albert and Caterina drove away from Ypres knowing they would never return. They would take the most direct route they could through France and Switzerland, this time stopping off to allow Charlie and Albert together to take that long-promised look at the spectacular roof tiles of Dijon. With any luck and a following wind, as Charlie liked to say, they would be through the mountains and in Milano in a few days. A welcome bit of fun with the young ones, a trip to the opera perhaps, a decent meal or two, then home, for a life of peace and quiet. Their war was over, at last.

CHAPTER TEN

A postscript

Although Charlie was no longer actively involved in politics, he continued to follow world events with interest. He was surprised and annoyed, given the work he had put in, that the old ingrate de Gaulle did veto Britain's second application to join the European Economic Community, late in 1967, just about the time of his own 'real' seventieth birthday. His last major assignment had come to nought, for the time being at least. Still, he thought philosophically, you couldn't win 'em all. Someone else would have to make it happen, probably after de Gaulle finally popped his clogs.

He watched, increasingly disheartened, as the leaders of the Soviet Union and its satellites, especially the Russian hard-liner Brezhnev, systematically oppressed their people, fostered hostility towards the United States and the West and generally made the world a far less safe place to be. In all of the Communist bloc, the ordinary people were being held down. The Prague spring came and was ruthlessly suppressed, in China the Cultural Revolution had made farm labourers out of doctors and torture victims out of dissidents and the Gang of Four's successors were only marginally less cruel. All over the world there were conflicts – in Vietnam, the Americans had, predictably, become bogged down in a guerrilla war they could not win, in the Middle East Israelis and Arabs clashed repeatedly with significant loss of life and showed few real signs of interest in the path of peace, and in Africa wicked dictatorships arose to fill the vacuum left by departing colonial powers. The 'winds of change' were indeed blowing across that continent, and some of them were ill winds. On a more positive note, Britain and Ireland were at last admitted to a European Community that looked like becoming less of an exclusive old pals' club, and this gave Charlie some hope for the future at least for the continent on which he lived. On the negative side, a new and more frightening form of warfare began to emerge, and that was terrorism. Planes were hijacked or blown out of the sky, innocent civilians were taken hostage, imprisoned and sometimes killed just for belonging to the wrong nationality. In Britain, in the interests of 'freedom', through their bombing campaigns, the Irish brought murder and mayhem to the streets of that nation's towns and cities for two decades and they did it in the name of God. Underlying it all, as the seventies and the eighties rolled by, was the threat of nuclear war and the complete destruction of the planet at some elected or unelected lunatic's push of a button. Frankly there was little to choose between the successive leaders of either superpower and Charlie distrusted and feared them both equally. The purchase of a daily paper became a thing of the past – you could get the gist of what was happening in the world from the television, and if it was abbreviated or over-simplified, so what? There was such a thing as being in possession of too much information, especially if there was not a thing you could do about it. He and Giovanna spent their time enjoying culture, history and nature in equal measure. It was pretty good, this retirement malarkey, all things considered.

For Albert and Caterina the year of 1978 brought unexpected happiness, for their middle son Giorgio – a complete misogynist for all they knew – suddenly at the age of just over fifty, brought home a lovely local girl, some twenty years his junior and announced that they were to be married. The union produced two boys – Giovanni and Alberto - and a girl – Sophia, of course - in fairly quick succession, and life at the farm was once more filled with the sound of young children playing. To have the little ones at all, and to have them close at hand was a joy, and they gave the doting grandparents a whole new lease of life. For them the eighties were a time of extreme contentment. They were in good health and were more than comfortably off. Their world centred on the farm and Matera, with the occasional trip by train to Milano to see the rest of the family. Ricardo's brilliant playing career had come to an end after the 1970 World Cup, in which Italy made it to the final only to be defeated four-nil by a rampant Brazilian team. Albert never did get to see his boy raise the Jules Rimet trophy, but he was fiercely proud of his many achievements on the pitch even without that. Ricardo's extreme good looks and his flair for languages had made him a target for the film studio talent scouts, and, now in his late thirties, he made a good living as a screen actor. It was a profession he had not considered early in life, but one for which he found he had a real aptitude. The Donkin talent for entertainment was embedded in him, and his intelligence, along with the sportsman's application and discipline allowed him to make the most of the gifts he had. All in all, he was doing rather well, though showing no signs of settling down. Maybe he would come to marriage and fatherhood later in life, like his brother. In the meanwhile, he hobnobbed with the rich and famous and kept smart apartments in Rome and London and a palatial ranch-style house overlooking the Pacific in southern California.

As the 1980s drew towards a close, developments on the world stage gave Charlie hope that there might be peace on earth after all and that he might see it before he died. After all, his whole life had been bound up with war of one kind or another. In the Soviet Union, there were positive signs that things might change, in the form of a remarkable young man called Mikhail Gorbachev who seemed keen to abandon the repressive ways of the past and lead his country into the modern age. As a result, people in the satellite nations began to believe that they too could experience the freedom that had been denied them for nearly half a century. In Poland's dockyards anti communist voices were heard. In East Germany, people started to find a way to leave their country via their accommodating neighbour, Hungary, and rejoin their families in the West. They streamed over the border in their smoky little Trabant cars and chugged their way to democracy. Even in brutally oppressed Rumania, the people were at last questioning the disgraceful Ceausescu regime and demanding their human rights. Old as he was, watching events unfold daily, Charlie felt reborn. Knowing only too well how hated the East German leadership was, and how despised were their henchmen, the Stasi, he was especially pleased to see that country begin to fall apart. He wondered if Johann were still alive and well enough to enjoy it and what his brothers and sisters in America would be making of it all. His mind wandered to brave Goran as well, who had risked so much to escape communism, and was now hopefully watching it disintegrate and rubbing his hands with glee.

On November the ninth, 1989, a few days after Charlie's ninety-second birthday, days which had witnessed increasing turmoil and mounting excitement, the Berlin Wall finally fell. Transfixed, silent, Charlie and Giovanna sat side by side at home, holding hands, and watched as, in full colour and lit by a thousand photographers' flashbulbs, young people from both sides of the divided city climbed onto the hated structure and started to tear it down. The last remnant of Stalinism was being dismantled, and the all too visible legacy of one of the